112 ELM STREET

112 ELM STREET

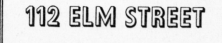

BY

HENRIETTA RIPPERGER

G·P·PUTNAM'S SONS · NEW YORK

This novel is based on a series published
in *Redbook* under the title "U. S. Today."

Third Impression

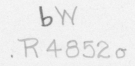

PJ

To

WALTER RIPPERGER

112 ELM STREET

Chapter 1

ONE DAY IN NOVEMBER 1940, OUR SON'S NUMBER WAS drawn in the draft, and my heart doubled up like a fist. He called us up long distance to tell us, in case we didn't know. This was the beginning of something different—for him, for all of us.

I had come home that afternoon past the Square and seen the laying of a cornerstone. In it was a time capsule with a copy of the daily newspaper and an address by the mayor. I wondered who'd find it and when. Suddenly I wished *I* had a time capsule filled by my grandmother, not with speeches and printed matter but with a record of the way she lived day by day. Did my grandfather unbend with the children? How did he manage his business? What did they have for dinner? What kind of problems in their children's lives kept them from sleeping at night? When she got hold of a little money all her own, what did she buy? Times have changed, and I shall never know.

They're changing now and much, much faster. We've always meant to leave our children and grandchildren a fortune, but the days of amassing one are perhaps over. So I am leaving them a story. It is a story of the American way of life, beginning in November 1940. It is about a happy home in a small city. It is about Ed, who, when the story opens, was forty-four and is my husband, about Freddie and Barbara and Dick, our eldest, who was twenty-one. I suppose it is about me, too. I am small and dark, three years younger than Ed, and my name is Elizabeth. It is about Norah, who has worked for us since Freddie was a baby, and about Rags, the wire-haired terrier who completed our household. It is about our schools, our church, our club, our business, and our home. It is about a way of life that I love with all my heart and that may never be the same again.

That day had started as usual. The children got off to school with their books and rubbers and lunches, Ed left for the factory, and the house settled down. I spent the morning putting up new curtains, organdy ones with ruffles, in all the bedrooms, with Norah handing me the rods and picking up screw caps I dropped from my perch on the stepladder. Ed and I are fond of our place, and every time we get a little extra money that's where it goes. Like most of the people around us, we own our home, Number 112 Elm Street. It's a yellow house set back a little from the street. The yard seemed big to the boys when they had to cut the grass or dig paths through the snow, but it isn't really. I can look across it through the bare trees right into my neighbor's sun porch.

I got my own lunch, a plate of salad and a glass of milk— helping with the curtains had put Norah behind—and turned on the radio. They were drawing draft numbers in Washington and reading them over the air. I listened a while. They were all big numbers. I turned the radio off. You never think what's happening to other people will happen to you. I went down to the store to do my ordering for the next day. The grocer charged me sixty-nine cents for a pint of olive oil. He said we'd be lucky, soon, to get any at all. "No shipments coming over," he told me. I finished my marketing, bought a bag of cookies, and took them with me for Freddie and the gang he brings in after school. Freddie is our youngest. He was nine, and in the fifth grade. He didn't put it that way, though. He would say, "I'll be in the sixth grade next year." As I came up the porch I could hear them all inside like stampeding cattle. They were playing Stukas, sliding down the banister, with the front hall as a landing field. That was what I opened the door on. When Freddie went away from home in the summer, as he sometimes did, Norah always said, "It's lonesome without the noise," but I could get along with less. I gave them the cookies on condition they'd go somewhere else. They went, in a body, with Rags barking and pushing around their feet.

I saw Barbara was home from school, too, so I got some chocolate squares from the pantry and went into the living room. She was curled up on the couch reading the ads in the afternoon paper. "Brownies? Oh, how yummy!" she said. "Look, Mom." She made room for me beside her and showed me a picture of a gold emblem for the sleeve. It cost two dollars. I promised to give it to her for her birthday; she would be sixteen soon. It was hard not to give Babs things, she was so eager and they made her so happy. Ed said I spoiled her and that the boys spoiled her, too. Somehow, though, I never worried about Barbara. Underneath, she was sound, I knew. She had a sturdy heart. She'd come out all right. Suddenly she flipped the edge of the page. "Oh, the draft numbers," she said. We bumped our heads, bending over the list: 6840, 120, 8060 ... "One twenty is Dick's number!" She sat up and stared at me. "Oh, Mother! Do you suppose he's seen it? Why, he'll have to go to camp. Maybe he'll drive a tank. Oh, Moms!" Dick got out of college that June and had just landed a job in New York.

"He'll have seen it," I said. Babs ran to the phone to call up her father.

I was putting supper on—it was Norah's night out—when Ed came home. He was unusually quiet and a little late. Although he merely said, "Hello," and went his way, I was glad that he was in the house. Barbara scrunched in on the edge of his chair to show him the living room-with-furniture she had drawn for art at school. Ed had his arm across her shoulder—Babs can always get his attention—and he was smiling down at her. I glanced at them. It came to me that he had looked just like that when I first saw him. I was a freshman at Blake. It was down at the football field and he was on the bench. Ed never made the team, he was too slow, but he was manager. A man was taken out of the game. He looked whipped. Ed got up and put his arm across the boy's shoulder and walked off the field with him, smiling down in a concerned yet comforting way. Half an hour later somebody was introducing us and I was looking into the kindest and deepest blue eyes I ever saw. In spite of his stoop, I had to look up. Ed is still the nicest person I have ever known. I am always happier when he is in the room, more at peace. That first glimpse I had was a true one; Ed is strong. Now I felt something was worrying him. Not Dick, I told myself; he would think it was too bad about Dick's job, of course, but he'd feel that going to camp was Dick's duty and good for the boy, too, that he'd come back better for a few months of camp life. No, something was wrong at the factory, I felt sure. I went into the kitchen wishing I knew what it was, wishing, too, as I always did just before a meal, that Dick was home with the rest of us. Then, as usual, I wondered where Freddie had gone to. I went to the phone and called up people's houses until I found him and told him to come right along.

We had supper: steak, baked potatoes, salad, and ice cream from the drugstore, a tradition on the night I get dinner, from the days when steak was the only thing I knew how to cook. Of course, nothing important came out; it was years since Ed and I had been able to put a word in edgewise at the table. But Thursday nights Babs and Freddie always did the dishes. Ed turned on the radio and then we sat and talked. It was the one moment in the week when he would say something about his own affairs. So it came out at last, the thing that was troubling him.

Before I can go into that I must tell you about Ed's business. Ed owned a little factory which turned out metal toys, teddy bears that rolled on their backs and monkeys that jerked their arms and legs. He even designed some of them. He began years ago with only two men, but our city had grown from ten to thirty thousand and the business grew with it; and now there were forty workmen.

With the war breaking out in Europe, there was a lot of talk about preparedness. The government had found that Ed's presses would be good for making shells, and that is what they wanted him to do. "I don't know," he said, "I don't like making shells to kill people with. I like the idea that my plant turns out things that will make kids happy. But maybe shells will be needed to defend something we've got over here. It could be. Maybe there'll still be a place in the world where children can play when we get through, if we do it right. Eh, Freddie?" he said. He gave Freddie, just sauntering into the room, a gentle poke, then grunted. A return poke from Freddie had an unexpected amount of power behind it.

After that, the children did their homework with their favorite band turned on. They always worked to jazz. I went to see that clean clothes were laid out ready for the morning rush. The phone rang. I heard Ed say, "Yes, right here, speaking." I ran down. "Yes, son," he went on. "We saw it. Too bad about the job, of course. Here's your mother." "Hello, dear." I heard Dick say, "I wanted to be sure you knew. Well, it's just the way things broke. A year isn't so long." Then, "Good-by." His voice withdrew suddenly, two hundred miles into the night, and there was no bringing it back.

I went out to open the garage doors while Ed backed the car in. As we walked toward the house the mail plane flew overhead, its green and red lights receding fast into the sky. By the open window the radio, left on, was repeating the drawing of the draft numbers. "6887, 4220, 8395 . . ." Ed put his hand on my shoulder and lifted his own shoulders a bit, a gesture I knew so well. "Looks as if we have a job to do," he said. "That boy of ours and my little business." He opened the door.

Chapter 2

THAT CHRISTMAS, DICK WAS IN CAMP, AND FOR THE FIRST time the family was not to be together.

But something else happened. Ed and I had been married twenty-two years and now we acquired a fourth child. It wasn't a baby. It wasn't even ours. It was just loaned, so to speak. Charles was ten years old, and he came from London to stay with us for the duration of the war. "One more won't be any trouble," Ed had said.

I can't tell you what the excitement around our house was as we waited for him to arrive. It was the Sunday before Christmas. We had an open fire going, there were big tassels of pine on the mantel, and wreaths with red bows at the windows and the door, and the radio was bringing music. I wanted the house to seem bright and gay for the little guest. A friend of Ed's was to bring him. At last we heard the car draw up outside. "That must be Charles." Freddie almost fell over his own feet getting to the door.

It's hard to describe what I felt when I saw that little chap coming in, saw his narrow shoulders, fair head, and thin legs against the blackness of the night outside, as if he were coming to us out of all the darkness over the world. I put my arms around the boy's shoulder, drew him in, and shut the door. I saw a thin little face with wide blue eyes.

"So you're Charles? How do you do?" Charles looked each of us straight in the eye and shook hands quickly and a little stiffly. "Nice to see you," Ed said. "Come in and let

me help you with your things." "Hi'a'yuh, Charlie?" Fred
die pumped Charles's hand. (I'd never noticed it before but
Freddie was built approximately on the lines of a woodchuck.)
But it was Babs who took Charles almost literally off his feet.
You never could tell about Babs. The year before, she was
tilting every baby carriage in the street to get a peek at the
baby inside, but this year she had been saying children were
a bore. Perhaps Charles was just the right age to appeal to
her; anyway, he went straight to her little old heart, and was
no sooner well inside than she was giving him a hug that left
him almost breathless.

"Come on, chum, I'll show you where you're going to live.
Want to see?" They went upstairs together, the rest of us
trailing along like children going to a fire. Charles was terribly
excited to find that we had two bathrooms. "Then we can
shout to each other from our tubs!" he said. We gave him a
choice of Dick's room or a cot in with Freddie, and he chose
the latter. "Oh, you have a dog. Can I have him on *my* bed?"
This put Freddie under as great a strain as he'd ever been
under because he and Rags slept practically arm in arm. "Oh
. . . okay. Oh, sure, sure!" he said, and he even added gen-
erously, "Look, Rags likes you."

A few days later we received the news that Charles was
among the children chosen to talk on Christmas Day, by radio,
to his family overseas.

Could we bring him to the studio? *Could* we! We thought
at first we'd all go, but Ed said that perhaps that was too
many. "What if everybody brought the whole family?" So it
was decided that Ed and I would be the ones to take Charles
over in the car when the time came. Word reached us the
night of the Christmas pageant in the church. We always

seemed to have at least one youngster in the pageant. The year before, Babs was the Madonna beside the manger; this year Freddie was to be a shepherd in the procession.

All the way to the church Ed was very quiet. He looked troubled—especially when he thought I was not watching him. I knew in a general way it was the war. I just couldn't believe we would ever be drawn into it, but I thought Ed didn't feel quite so sure. I didn't see, however, why this should be bothering him, especially that night. Of course, there was Dick away at camp, living under conditions which made me worry a good deal about his health. A letter from him had described them.

" 'Up to our necks in slush,' " he quoted from the old song. "Our uniforms are something they had left over from the Spanish-American War. They take the shears and cut them off to make 'em fit."

He was joking, I supposed, but apparently things weren't any too ready for the new recruits. Their quarters were in a street of tents with a wooden walk along it. The tents were equipped with little stoves, but somehow the boys didn't seem to get the hang of them, and it was very cold. Worst of all were the conditions under foot. Dick's tentmate said, "If I hadn't gone to Princeton, I'd swear this was mud." But Ed laughed at me for worrying; it couldn't be that he was worrying about Dick's health. Nor did I think the fact that Dick was not to be with us for Christmas could account for his mood of depression.

"Is there anything especially wrong?" I asked.

Ed hesitated, then, "I had to let August go." August was Ed's foreman, an old German who had been there twenty years, even before Ed bought the business. "The government inspector who checks up on the shells," Ed went on in a voice so low I could hardly hear him, "thought I ought to. 'A little sand in the machinery,' he said, 'and where would you be?' I suppose he was right, but I don't know what August will do or how he'll live. It's a heck of a Christmas present."

I put my arm through Ed's and felt him twitch. Then he shook his shoulders as though in that way he could get rid of what weighed on him. He smiled down at me—at least with his lips.

"Speaking of Christmas presents," he said, "I was thinking of replacing Fido this year." The children had labeled my old fur coat Fido. They said it was spaniel fur. "I looked at Persian lamb," Ed went on, "but—I didn't get it after all. We've taken a lot of new responsibilities with this boy, you know."

"Oh, I'm glad you didn't," I told him. "Fido's good for a few years more. When I do get a new fur coat I want beaver. It's so soft and flattering. You'd love me in it."

Once in church, we sat down on the aisle. The youngsters were just forming the procession at the back: little girls we knew in angel dresses, three big swarthy young men in kings' costumes, and behind them the shepherds. Their cue was, "It came upon the midnight clear." As Freddie's shaggy little figure shuffled down the aisle, we were singing, "Peace *on* the earth, good will to men." My throat closed up. Ed and I reached for each other's hands. What would happen before there was peace on the earth? Later, as we were waiting for our shepherd, Ed said—almost fiercely, as if he were trying to hang onto something that was slipping away from him, "Let's make it a good Christmas this year. The best we've ever had. Let's have a *big* tree."

Babs and Freddie trimmed our tree. This was something of a concession on Ed's part. He was firmly convinced that nobody could do it the way he could. This was the first time he had ever been content to sit back and supervise.

Christmas dawned clear and unusually warm. The children scrambled down for their presents. We had bought Charles a chemistry set, a hockey stick, and a pair of ice skates. Babs gave him some dark blue socks she had knitted in a new spiral pattern and which she had originally intended for Freddie. "Not as good as the service wool I got for Dick's helmet," she explained, "but it *itches* just the same." We gave Freddie, among other things, a big book on magic and magicians and some trick apparatus he'd been wanting. Babs had a dress for tea dancing, and the rest of us—well—the rest of us had to hurry through our breakfast to be ready for the broadcast at eleven o'clock. There was a little tense look on Charles's face while Ed got the car out.

I'll never forget that broadcast. Ed and I were in a glass-enclosed observation balcony where we could hear the merest whisper from below but couldn't be heard. The British children sat in the studio at a long table, in a row, their thin faces eager, their manner attentive to everything that was going on. They were all sizes, from a big, serious-looking girl to a tiny, red-cheeked boy in a sailor suit, his baby face all smiles. He never spoke, not even to his mother overseas. He just kept on smiling. They wore earphones. The announcer carried a little portable mike which he held in front of each one in turn.

"Hello, London," he was saying. "This is America. Hello, Vancouver. Hello, Halifax! Just checking up to see if everybody is ready."

A down beat of the producer's finger and like an orchestra the studio went into action.

"Hello, Mummy." It was Charles talking.

"Hello, darling. How do you like America?"

"Oh, I like it fine." Charles's small voice was brave.

"What did Santa Claus bring you?" The voice at the other end was urgent and trembled a little.

"Oh, some skates and . . ."

"'Here's Charles's daddy," the London announcer broke in.

"Hello, darling." Only a great emotion could make an Englishman so affectionate in front of the whole world.

"How are you, Daddy? Are you having any bombs?"

"Not today." The man's voice was firm and cheery. "Christmas, you know."

"Charles's mother wants to speak again," said the announcer's voice from London.

"Hello, darling." Her voice shook my heart. "Have you anything you want to say to me, darling?"

"No, Mummy."

"Nothing—nothing, darling?"

"Sorry," came the announcer's voice. "It's time to say good-by."

"Good-by, Mummy."

"Oh . . ."

That small sound from distant London—that soft, despairing voice. I couldn't bear it. I got up and stepped out into the corridor and paced the floor until the time was up. What a world, in which children have to be sent three thousand miles to escape scientific destruction and yet can speak to their families at home almost in a whisper and be heard! I went down into the studio to find Charles. The photographer was pulling a plate from his camera with one hand. With the back of the other he was wiping the tears from his eyes. "And I'm supposed to be the hard-boiled guy around here," he said.

We hurried down to the car. Charles sat in front between Ed and myself. I was afraid he would cry, but he didn't. He sat there very quietly, just looking straight ahead. I could still hear that despairing little "Oh" that had come from Charles's mother when the conversation was broken off. If only I could have put my arms around her and said, "You can trust us. We'll take good care of your boy." And I had been fretting because Dick wasn't home, Dick, who was less than a hundred miles away.

The smell of turkey met us as we opened our door, and Freddie, all excitement, grabbed hold of Charles. "How was it, Charlie? Huh?"

"Oh, it was all right. It was *okay*!" Charles said. His voice was very steady.

I went upstairs and sat down to put my hair in order. Suddenly, in the mirror I saw a figure in khaki. Then there were two arms around my neck and crossed under my chin and someone kissed my ear. Only Dick does just that.

"Oh, Dick!" I said. "Oh . . ."

How tall and compact he was, just like Ed, though not quite as heavy.

"We got leave on three hours' notice," Dick said. "I didn't call up. Thought I'd surprise you."

We went downstairs together.

"See who's here!"

But Babs and Freddie were looking at me, their eyes wide with excitement.

"What are all of you up to?" I asked.

"Here she is, Daddy!"

Ed came out from his den.

"Come here," he said. He was hiding something—or trying to hide something—behind his back. Then he held it out—the most beautiful coat of soft, shimmering beaver. He put it around me. "Like it, huh?"

"It's beautiful. It's simply . . ." I couldn't find any more words. I felt warm inside as I stood there with all of them around me: Ed, Dick, Babs, and Freddie. Then a small hand crept into mine. And Charles!

Charles was saying, "I like it. It feels like my rabbits, the ones I had at home. I wish my Mummy had told me if they're all right." He sighed. Putting out his hand gently, he stroked my coat.

Chapter 3

I WAS SITTING IN FRONT OF MY DRESSING TABLE PUTTING on my hat, the one Freddie calls a cup and saucer, before going out to do my ordering. I had spent the early part of the afternoon getting ready for a visitor. He was a young lieutenant, just out of West Point, named Vic, a friend of Dick's, who had thirty-six hours' leave and nowhere to go, so, at Dick's suggestion, he was coming to us. I had fixed Dick's room for him, taking up a number of magazines, a silver bowl filled with apples and grapes, my own little radio, and a small red flowering plant in a white pot that looked gay and somehow just right for a man. I was looking critically at the face that stared back from the mirror when I saw Norah at the doorway, an empty wastebasket in her left hand, her right resting on the woodwork, and that resolute set to her wide mouth which shows Norah for the sound character she is.

"I was thinking, did you know Barbara was staying late today, going to a meeting?" she asked.

I didn't. If I was busy or out, Babs usually confided her plans to Norah. When she was small she told Norah everything, sitting on her lap in the kitchen rocker. Later, she and Freddie used to play hearts, evenings, with Norah and her young man. Babs had outgrown all that, of course, but she still was very chatty about her affairs as she went for her milk and cookies in the pantry.

"Is the meeting at school?" I asked absent-mindedly.

"It is not; it's in a hall it is. Arguing against the government they are, like in the trouble in the old country, home in Ireland," Norah said. "Them girls down the street that goes to a college took her. They should know better. But of course it's not for me to say." Her mouth closed firmly.

"Thank you, Norah," I said. "I'm glad you told me. I'll look into it."

All the time I was marketing—trying to think of things Vic might not have in camp, such as big juicy lamb chops, sweet potatoes, and chocolate pudding with plenty of cream—I was wondering what Babs was getting mixed up in. I was well aware that Babs was opposed to war. To a great extent, this was probably due to my influence. I had brought my children up to be gentle, to work for peace, to believe that violence is never justified and never settles anything, and now she *did* believe it. I was slowly changing my opinions, but not Babs. I wondered if this meeting was pacifistic in purpose and what Ed would say to his daughter's being present at it. I knew it would become an issue. I would have to face it somehow.

I looked at my list and crossed off "groceries." The next items were, "rubber bone for Rags," "see Principal at school about Charles"; the important and unimportant things in life are always jumbled together like that. I bought the rubber bone and then went to the school. It seemed that Charles was too advanced mentally for the sixth grade in which he had been placed—the English schools must be a little ahead of ours—but that he was too young for the seventh. The grade teacher thought he should have a project of his own and work on it in the shop during study period. You'd have thought Charles would want to keep away from airplanes after the raids he'd seen, but instead, he had his heart set on building a model Spitfire. I said we'd pay for the materials the school shop did not provide, and so that was settled.

I got home just in time for supper. Babs always sat next to her daddy at his right. Freddie was a little off center on the other side so his feet couldn't reach Charles's—just in case. Charles was on my left. Dick's place, on my right, was empty unless there was company. As soon as we'd all been served Babs began indignantly:

"What kind of a family are we? I think it's terrible letting Dick join an old army. And Daddy's factory making munitions to kill other people just like us. *I* think it's terrible. What's come over everybody all of a sudden?"

Charles looked anxiously down the table at Ed, a worried expression on his thin little face.

"You've got to fight back, Silly," Freddie said.

"No, you don't." Babs's voice was decided. "I just can't tell my friends about us," she finished.

I took this chance to ask her where she had been. She had gone, it turned out, to a conference of young women.

"And," she finished, "we're going to organize our friends and make the government give us money so we can all afford to get married if we want to, and make them promise not to use the Army anywhere but here in America. And we're to go ourselves and find out what conditions in the camps are. Gee, in the last war men at camp died like flies from neglect."

"Now wait a minute," Ed said a little sharply, "who told you that? Nobody in the Army ever died of neglect. They died of flu and so did thousands of people right in their own homes. Nobody with a grain of sense thinks the service men are neglected. Why, Dick's gained three pounds already."

"And learned how to make a bed that'll stand inspection," I put in.

But Babs was not to be diverted.

"I don't care," she said. "It's wrong to fight, and that's what armies are for."

Ed lit his pipe. I saw his hand shake just a little as it does when he's excited. I put a comforting cup of coffee at his elbow.

"You don't think your daddy is bloodthirsty, do you?" he asked. "Well, then, why did I give the government my factory to make shells in? I'm not forced to—not yet. I did it because I want us to be able to take care of ourselves if we have to."

"But, Daddy—"

"Let me finish," Ed said. "It's because I think we've got to stop an evil force working against everything we love, that's why."

"But they're people, just like us," Babs said.

"They're not acting the same way," Ed said patiently. "That's the point, darling. We must stand up for our way, not only because we like it best but because we think it's right."

"Well," Babs said, "I think it's wrong to fight about *anything*."

"Aw, nuts," Freddie put in good-naturedly. "Come on, will you? Charlie wants to play parcheesi. It's more fun with three."

They sat down on the floor in a corner. Then without any further warning Vic arrived. Service men are like that; they come and go dramatically, not telling you their plans. You open the door and there they are, and Vic came just that way.

We liked Vic. He sat in one big armchair, Ed in the other, talking about this war and the last. Ed told his favorite A.E.F. story about how when off duty he and another officer went for a stroll and found themselves behind the German lines, were taken before the German Staff and told to locate the American line on the map, and how Ed finally said, "Well, if I knew where it was I certainly wouldn't be here." And how they got back—another story. Vic talked with him with that combination of comradeship and respect boys get in the service and so seldom acquire outside of it. He told me about his people out in Texas and he grinned at the boys. But his eyes kept going back to Babs on the floor, half kneeling beside the parcheesi board, her legs trailing out behind her. Freddie and Charles had to say, "Your shake!" over and over. Babs was finding it hard to keep her mind on the game.

I sent the boys off to bed at eight-thirty, and at ten we all went upstairs. While Ed was busily locking up, Babs came in and perched on the foot of my bed. She had on a nightgown of raspberry-colored flannel with white woolly edging on the high neck and long sleeves. The vivid color made her eyes look very brown. She sat hugging her knees, her bright dark hair brushing her hunched-up shoulders and her feet in their white fur slippers sticking out like paws.

"What do you think of Vic?" I asked.

"He's a neat guy." She sighed. "I *would* get caught playing kid games on the floor and wearing socks. He's a lieutenant and Dick's just a private. I *wish* he'd worn his uniform," she added wistfully.

"I guess he likes to get back into his regular clothes now and then," I said.

She sighed again. "But I'd like to have seen him in it. Oh, well, I guess it doesn't matter."

"By the way," I said, "I don't think your daddy is so keen on this conference idea. You weren't serious about going again, were you?"

She sat bolt upright.

"Of course I'm serious. I'm going tomorrow night again. It's the last meeting. I've simply *got* to."

I hesitated. I could forbid her to go. I knew Ed wouldn't want his daughter there. But it would be hard to make Babs understand why. There *is* a difference between just worrying about what people think—I agree with Babs that would be silly—and not wishing a member of your family to get mixed up with a crowd whose ideas are fundamentally opposed to your own for reasons that have to do simply with your convictions. But Babs might be too young to see it. If she didn't, she would be scornful of our motives. I was turning this over in my mind while Babs looked at me with big resentful eyes, when Ed came it.

"Fade," he told her, "I want to get some sleep."

So the moment passed.

Next morning our guest slept late as we had urged him to, and so did Babs. Sometimes Ed teased her about the hours she kept on the days when there was no school.

"When we were kids we got up mornings," he would begin. "But maybe you could get up a little more each day, like a convalescent."

However, I never woke her. She was storing up energy for the time when she'd have to run a home of her own and get up with her babies and would need all her reserves of strength.

She and Vic sat down together about eleven o'clock to coffee, toast, and scrambled eggs made by Babs, while Norah helped me straighten up the rooms upstairs. I heard the two of them laughing and guessed Vic didn't seem so old any more; actually he was only twenty-two. That afternoon he invited the family to the movies, and of course Babs accepted and the boys jumped at the chance.

"How about you?" he asked with a smile, as the others were all putting on their hats and coats. "Aren't *you* coming? It's that man. You like him better than us. Well, we'll make him come, too."

But in the end it was Ed who went along, partly because he didn't want the youngster spending money on tickets for our whole family. I know Ed. I had hardly seen to the many things that needed my attention when there they were, back again. They'd all been rolling each other in the snow on the way home like five-year-olds. While they cleaned up I had a chance to tell Ed about Babs attending the conference. I asked him whether we ought to stop her from going again. He listened seriously, but he only said:

"Let's see, when the time comes."

Dinner was fun, and after it as we walked into the living room Vic said, more to Ed than to me:

"If I can persuade that daughter of yours to go out dancing with me, is it all right with you? I'll get her home safe and sound at any hour you say. I'm very responsible," he added.

"She's never been to a hotel, dancing," I answered first.

"But I don't know why she shouldn't go with an older man, like you."

Ed added, "It looks like a perfect solution for the evening."

I'll never forget Babs when Vic went in and asked her. She was so excited she almost wriggled. But she struggled to show *savoir-faire* in front of Vic. "I'd love to," was all she said.

"Well, then, let's go." Vic spoke with a slight air of authority characteristic of him. "We may as well have all the fun that's coming to us. I'll have to catch the twelve-thirty train to report for duty in the morning," he went on, "so if you'll excuse me, I'll just change and get my bag down in the hall."

"By the way," Ed looked at Babs quizzically, "didn't I hear something about an engagement you had—to go to a meeting with some girls?"

"The conference?" She did not look at her father. "I'll call them up. It really doesn't matter so much because I know everything they're going to say at the meeting and I agree with it already; they don't have to work on *me*." She disappeared in the direction of the phone.

I went up to Babs's room with her and helped her slip into a little flame-colored afternoon dress with a pleated skirt we had given her on her birthday. She looked in the mirror.

"Listen, Moms—" she began. "No, never mind."

"You can take it," I said. "It's in the hall closet with Daddy's dress suit."

She gave me a quick hug. "Oh, Moms, you're a darling. I'll be so careful."

She came along the hall wearing my new beaver coat, hugging it to her face as if it were the thing she loved most in all the world. At the top of the stairs she caught hold of my elbow. "*Sh,* look," she gazed down into the hall below.

Vic was standing at the bottom of the stairs in full uniform. Vic was arresting. He was tall and lean, with a brown skin and darker hair, blue eyes that looked black, and a smile that was, well, brilliant. He was wearing the new officers' blues with gold bars and the big insignia on his cap. Babs went down the stairs, folded her hands, and looked at him, not even trying to conceal her admiration. I packed them off with a key and instructions.

"As if he were a little boy," Ed said.

"She's a little girl," I answered.

"That's your coat." Ed's voice was accusing.

"I know, but it gave her just the feeling of confidence she needed so badly. And didn't she look adorable?"

"Could it be because she's our child we think so?" Ed asked.

But his eyes were suspiciously bright. Barbara is the darling of his heart.

In the quiet they left behind them I sat down at my desk and brought my accounts up to date. As I shut the book, Ed put down his paper. I saw he was still bothered by the argument at dinner.

"It's not that I want to keep Barbara from thinking for herself," he said, "but I don't want her mind made up for her by a lot of screwballs. Kids don't understand; they haven't the experience."

"I know." I shut my desk. "Once they get an idea they stick to it forever. Their opinions don't seem to be at all affected by what's happening in the world. And then they are critical of their elders for thinking we ought to be ready to

defend ourselves. They act as if you were something out
of the past, as military-minded, as old-fashioned as a character
out of the Rollo boys."

"That's about it," Ed said. "And could you possibly be re-
ferring to the Rover boys? Rollo boys!"

He was still laughing when his head touched the pillow
and he went to sleep.

I was awake when, on the dot, Babs and Vic came in at the
front door. I heard him go for his bag, say good-by, and dash
for the waiting taxi. It was scarcely a minute before Babs
leaned in at my door and breathed softly:

"Hi, Moms, are you asleep?"

I put on my bathrobe and went into her room.

"Listen," she said, "'we danced and danced and danced.
Just before we came home we had a regular supper, steak
and ice cream and everything. Oh, Mom." She gave me a
squeeze. "Stop picking up after me. I'll hang up my clothes
in the morning. Just *listen*, will you?"

"Did you tell Vic about the young people's conference you
passed up for him?" I asked.

"What do you think I am?" She looked at me, round-
eyed. "But I sort of brought him out on what we were talking about. And you know those kids are crazy. Vic showed me
how *wrong* they are. He's so noble. He wants to take *care* of
his country, not pick on it. Wait till I see those ignorant old
girls, will *I* tell 'em sump'n." She dropped into bed. "Open
my window, will you?"

She gathered the bedclothes under her chin and looked out.
Her eyes were very bright.

"He's coming back just as soon as he possibly can. I'm so
happy. I never thought I could be so happy."

The cool night air drew the curtain in toward her face. She reached out and touched it as if returning a caress, then sank down deeper into the bed.

"Well," she said, "good night."

"Babs home?" Ed asked sleepily as I entered our room. "Did she have a good time?"

"He's coming back, his very next leave."

"Well, that tells the story." He burrowed his head in the pillow.

"Or starts it," I said.

Chapter 4

OFTEN IT'S HARD TO KNOW THE RIGHT THING TO DO. There are two times, however, when I am never in doubt, one when taking care of babies and the other when trying to give the children an education. Dick had been to college and now Babs was next in line. So when she told us one evening in early spring that she'd been asked to fill out a paper at school telling whether she was going to college and if so, where, I said, "Of course you put down 'yes.'"

We were in the living room, Ed, Babs and I, in the lull after the boys had gone up to bed. A comparative lull, that is. Babs had reached the radio first and there was a dance orchestra on. I was knitting. Ed had given up his paper because Barbara was leaning over the back of his chair, her pink angora-covered arms around his neck and her pearls brushing his ear. Her brown eyes were fixed on the radio dial as if it were speaking just to her.

"And I put down I was going to Blake," she went on, "because that's where you snagged Daddy. That was right, wasn't it?"

I saw Ed's face change. It was as if it settled a little. All he said was:

"Do we have to decide that right now?"

"Goodness, no. Don't you adore this tune? They played it over and over again the night I went out dancing with Vic." Babs gave Ed a hug.

"Hey." He clutched something. "Look out for my pipe."

"Excuse it, please. Just listen to this." She gave a little lift to her shoulders, closed her eyes, and leaned her smooth cheek against Ed's rumpled hair. "Don't let's talk about college now," she said.

I went on knitting. I was making Charles and Freddie sweaters of the most heavenly delft blue. Before I picked the color I looked carefully at their eyes. Freddie's, although they've got the nicest expression, are sort of an onion green. I decided Charles's would be much prettier to match. I had just finished a row when there was a crash upstairs. I knew what that meant. Soon after Charles came I bought a double-decker bed thinking it would be not only a space-saver, but fun for the boys to have. It was! As they went to bed, Charles made Freddie play ocean liner, which meant that they undressed in utter darkness. Later, Freddie changed it to gangsters, which was more in his line. He would break into Charles's bunk by climbing up the ladder, and then the trouble would start.

"Barbara, you go up this time, will you?" I asked.

Babs is better with the boys than I am. Besides, I wanted to talk to Ed.

"Okay." Babs got up. "I'll show 'em."

I said, "You know, Ed, we *do* have to decide about college for her."

"She's only sixteen." Ed puffed a while in silence. Then, "Can't it wait awhile?"

"The children's affairs can never wait," I said, "that's the trouble. If we keep her out this year, she won't *go*. Something else will happen. I'm sure of it."

"I don't know that college is so necessary for a girl," Ed

said slowly, and since I knew that was not what he really thought, I asked, "What's happened?"

"I wasn't going to tell you." He put down his pipe. "But I may as well. You know my cousin Joe died out in Denver last month. Well, I had a letter today from Sally, his wife. It seems Joe's affairs were in a terrible tangle. It'll be a year or so before she can pull anything out, so she's turned to me."

"Isn't there anyone else?" I asked. "You've never even seen her."

"I suppose not," he said. "Anyway, I'm sending her sixty dollars a month. Joe would have done it for me." He got up and snapped off the radio. "You want your little girl to have everything," he said. "So do I, but this can't be helped. Well, I'll put up the car." He went out. I knew he didn't want to talk about it any more. Ed's feeling of responsibility is the very core of his character. I love him for it and I wouldn't try to weaken it. All the same, our children's whole future depended on what we gave them now. Besides, it should be part of the experience of growing up to get out with your own age awhile, between life in your parents' home and the one you make when you're married, and I wanted Barbara to have that experience. I said to myself that I'd find a way to send her somehow. Presently Ed came back, his face all smoothed out and smiling. "Gee, it's a wonderful night," he said. "Stars, breeze, everything. Let's move out on the sleeping porch? Want to? Come on!"

In the rush next morning I forgot about college. Babs was the first to leave. She always took a cold lunch and bought hot soup or cocoa at school. I put up some honey and peanut butter sandwiches, fruit, and cookies. In the hurry of getting breakfast Norah is apt to think old cold lamb and dry white bread is a noon meal for a child. The boys came home at noon. All I had to do for them at breakfast time was to see that they finished their food and got off. Once they were gone, I sat down for a second, peaceful cup of coffee while Ed read his paper. The sunlight poured in, falling just short of the table. Rags was lying with his paws over the threshold, only his nose in forbidden territory. Norah is very strict with Rags and doesn't allow the boys to give him any bits from their plates, and when they argue with her she says, "And has he ever had a sick day since I'm taking care of him?" I watched him sniff and then pretend to be asleep. I looked at the blue band and rosebuds on my coffee cup with pleasure as I always do. Suddenly I realized it; there *was* a way. "Ed," I said, "why doesn't Babs try for the alumni scholarship. Or is it alumnae?" Blake is coeducational, and I never know which to say. Ed put his paper down.

"We're certainly not going to ask people to help us," he said. "We're not that hard up."

"We weren't last year," I answered, "but this year you have Sally to support. And now we've taken Charles, food and clothing bills are bigger. There aren't going to be any fancy profits in business this year. So that actually we *can't* afford to send Babs to college."

"I thought we'd settled that for the present." His voice was flat.

"We agreed we couldn't afford it," I said, "but that doesn't settle it; not to me it doesn't. For twenty years you've given to the Scholarship Fund. Maybe it's our turn to get on the receiving end."

"Put and take?" Ed asked. "I guess the Scholarship Committee wouldn't see it that way."

"That's up to them," I answered. "And I'm just determined to give Babs a good education and at least a couple of years away from home," I added.

"I see you are." Ed looked across at me with a funny smile. "Well, go ahead," he said. "See what you can do."

It took a few days to get the necessary information and the blanks. I found Babs's marks were good enough and that she could enter Blake without examination. In the meantime I thought I'd go around and talk to the chairman of the Committee and find out what sort of questions they were likely to ask her. But the day I was going the boys came down with chicken pox. I kept them in their room and sent for Dr. Beard. It was early afternoon when he came. He was a big man. He came into the house leaning slightly forward, saying nothing, and just moved up on the kids until he cornered them and gave them a dig or a hug. They all adored him. This time he said,

"What's the matter with *you?*"

"It's the boys, not me," I answered. "They're upstairs."

He rolled back the lid of my eye. "Bilious," he asked, "or just worrying? You go to a bed for a day, and I'll give you something to fix you up."

I telephoned the stationer for a fifty-cent backgammon board and told the boys to teach each other how to play and on no account to go out of the room or open the door. I called the drugstore and then promised the doctor to rest for the remainder of the day. So I didn't have a chance to talk to Mrs. Heath, the head of the Committee. Ed said later that that was a lucky break, that it would have been the worst thing I could have done. Well, anyway, I didn't do it.

Instead I went to sleep. I woke to find Babs leaning over the foot of my bed.

"Goodness," she began, "what's the matter with you? Don't you feel all right?" She jounced cheerfully on the footboard. "Can I do something?"

"Yes," I said. "Pull up a chair and sit down." Babs collapsed opposite me and pushed her little round hat back on her head. "Now listen." I explained the situation to her. "And Sally is going to need just about what your tuition would cost," I finished.

"Why doesn't this Sally woman step out and get a job?" Babs asked.

"She probably will," I answered, "in time. But she apparently doesn't quite realize her situation yet. One of the bills she sent Daddy to pay was for a mourning outfit that cost seventy dollars."

"Goodness." Babs's eyes were wide. "Can't you mourn in something for sixteen ninety-eight?"

I had to smile in spite of myself. "Maybe not in Denver. But the point is if you get a scholarship you'd be helping your daddy out just that much."

"Gee, I'll try." She thought a moment. "Guess I'd better hoof it back to school and see what has to be done."

"And keep out of the boys' room on the way," I added. "Having chicken pox the day the Committee asks you to appear isn't going to help."

I had trouble—just a little trouble—with Ed over the paper he had to fill out. He took it with him to the office and from time to time he called up. Where was my mother born? What did I figure Charles cost us? How the heck could he tell what he was going to make next year? He'd grunt, say, "Wait a minute," then, "Never mind," and hang up.

"Well, I sent it in," he told me as he came in just before supper. "They certainly wanted to know your middle name. I don't know why I should have to tell a lot of people just what I make and how I spend it."

"Oh, Ed," I said, "that isn't important. Lots of people's incomes are printed in the paper, and what you do with yours just shows what a darling you are."

"Oh, yeah? You're prejudiced." But he grinned.

At supper I said I wondered what Babs had better wear and that I might buy her a little plaid suit so she'd look peppy and like promising material. Babs laid down her fork and looked at me.

"Listen, Mom," she said. "The idea is to save money, not spend it. Wait a sec." She left the table and ran upstairs. "The kids have more sense than you have," Ed put in. She came back with one of those little Mexican pigs. On it was a sticker marked "Joe College." "If you have any spare cash," she said, "give it to me. It goes right in here for a needy student."

I laughed. "All the same, nobody is going to give a scholarship to a girl with stringy hair and a sagging hemline. After supper bring me your navy blue dress. I guess you can wear it. But it will need something done to it."

"What I'm worrying about is the questions they'll probably ask me." Babs groaned. "I'll be just dumb enough to say all the wrong things."

"If you don't know, say so." I was anxious and my voice showed it. "Don't try to think up anything tricky."

"Don't worry, Toots, you'll do all right." Ed looked at her and smiled. His eyes are blue-gray but they can turn very dark, and they were almost black now. Suddenly I saw what meant the most in this to Ed. To me, it was getting a daughter to college, and, of course, Ed also wanted her to have an education. But to him it was essentially his girl against the rest. To himself I knew he was saying, "I'll bet she has it all over those other girls in looks, in personality, in brains, in everything." I saw it in his eyes. What he said out loud was, "You might do something about your hair."

"This?" Babs pulled a brown lock over one eye. "It *was* my pompadour, but I'm growing it. I guess if I want to grow my hair that's my business."

"Well, it's a heck of a business," Ed grinned. "Take it from me."

At last the day actually came on which the Scholarship Committee was to hold its meeting. When Babs came home after school, I went to her room as she was dressing. "Oh, Moms, do stop hovering," she began. "I'm nervous enough, already. I'll bet the day I get married you'll be leaning out in the aisle twitching my veil as I go by." But when I came in with her dress she was full of appreciation. "It's adorable. Thank you just loads."

At four o'clock she went out of the house, leaving as she always did an emptiness and a sudden quiet behind her, and just for a minute I wished she need never go away from home, even to school. Soon afterward Ed got home from the office early. Like me, he was very restless. We went up and talked to the boys. Dr. Beard came in and said they could go out next day. We tried to keep him just to have somebody to talk to, but he had a lot of sick people to see. Ed went down to the cellar and I went out with Rags. But finally we both came back and just sat down frankly waiting.

"Of course you won't hear today," Ed filled his pipe. "Don't expect that. There are always two or three interviews."

"She looked so darling. You didn't see her. I lined the little jacket of her navy blue dress with a red and white plaid and she found a purse to match. And that silly hat on the back of her head." I took out my knitting but I couldn't keep my mind on it.

"She's got the looks," Ed said. "I hope the school backed her up all right."

"Her language teacher sent me a copy of the note she wrote," I answered. "She said Babs wasn't an A student, but she was a B plus one. Doesn't that sound just like a teacher? Then she hoped, she said, in a way, that Babs wouldn't work for higher marks because she might lose some of the courage and gaiety with which she attacked her studies. Nice of her, wasn't it?"

"Very nice," Ed said. "That reminds me. I had a letter from Dick. Here, I'll read it to you: 'Dear Dad: Moms has written me about Babs. I hope she gets the scholarship. Tell her I am betting on her. If things were different I'd have liked to chip in toward her tuition, but $30.00 doesn't go far, even in camp.'"

"Wait!" I thought I heard the phone. No, it was a bicycle bell out in the street. "Go on."

"'I am enclosing a modest two bucks. I figured Freddie and Charlie might like to take our girls to the movies by way of celebration or consolation, if that has to be, but I hope not. Then if I were home you and I could sneak off and shoot a little pool, eh, Dad? Love.'"

"That was like him," I said. "He'd help if he could."

"Seems to me she ought to be back soon. What time is it?" Ed pulled out his watch. "Five-thirty-five."

"She couldn't be here yet," I answered. "You know, Ed, it's the first time she's ever really been out on her own. It made me think of the day she was five years old and we gave her a tricycle. Remember? There was a whole bunch of kids on tricycles and roller skates going down a play street. She fell in behind them. She saw they were going to turn around at the end so she turned first and came back ahead of them all. She looked so little. She rode up and said, 'I was the fastest and the best.' "

"I bet she's the best today." And he added, "She'll be in the class of 1945."

"We hope," I put in. The phone rang. Ed started up but sank back. "You'd better go. Take it easy!" as I almost slipped on the rug. It was Mrs. Heath, the head of the Committee.

"You'll get a letter, of course," she told me in her clear, clipped voice, "but I wanted you to hear it from me. Your daughter won in the first interview. Usually we see the candidates over and over again, but this time we hardly had sent them out of the room when somebody said, 'Barbara is my choice and I won't even consider anyone else,' and we all agreed."

"How nice of you to call me," I said. "It's just wonderful. She was worried about the questions. Tell me, how *did* she do on them?"

She laughed. "You'll be amused at this. We asked her why she wanted to go to college at all, and she said her family had made up their mind and it was the line of least resistance."

I went back to Ed.

"So she crashed through." There was a deep light in his eyes.

Out of the window, I could see Babs just turning into our street.

"Here she is!" I called. "Come on down, kids. She's coming and we're all going to celebrate."

They tumbled down over the stairs. I knew they'd been hanging over the top rail, listening. The door opened. Babs came in. Her eyes were shining, her hair was blown, and her hat was swinging from her hand. She glanced quickly at Ed and the boys in turn and then threw her arms around me.

"I got it," she said. "I don't how, but I got it."

Ed laid an arm across each of our shoulders.

"Just a couple of Blake girls," he said.

Chapter 5

I SUPPOSE IF I HAD KNOWN THAT WE WERE GOING TO HAVE TO help Sally, Ed's cousin's widow, I would never have entered Freddie and Charles for camp. But the arrangements had been made before word reached us of Joe's death. The head of the camp had been very generous about Charles. When he learned that Charles had been evacuated from London, he offered him the last of the so-called scholarships. We had paid part of the fee to put Freddie there for the same length of time, and under these conditions it was pretty nearly impossible to withdraw. It was agreed that they should go up when school closed and stay until the end of July.

The spring came and passed and summer followed. The little white crocus buds, looking like nothing so much as bits of snow left in the broken earth, the pussy willows, and the forsythia gave way to purple iris, old-fashioned yellow lilies, and the heavy red flowers of the trumpet vine around the back porch. The roses blossomed, marking the onset of summer. And then one day the camp station wagon came by and picked up the boys, and the house settled down to a routine of shaded rooms, lighter meals, and long, cool drinks on the veranda.

We were just finishing breakfast one Monday morning when the postman brought the required "no-letter, no-Sunday-night-supper" mail from the boys. The day promised to be hot, but the porch had just been hosed and the breeze that came through the dining room windows was fresh and felt of wetness.

"It seems next Saturday is Parents' Day at camp." I consulted the letter. "According to Freddie, all the boys' fathers and mothers will be there."

"Listen," Ed said, "we've sent them to camp. We don't have to go along and camp too, do we? I like it here."

I looked around, at the white flowers in the silver bowl on the table between us, the delft blue cloth Norah had put under it, the organdy curtains moving in the wind, the striped furniture covers in the living room beyond that always give the place a summer-holiday air. I like it too, I thought. Nevertheless, I wanted Ed to go. I always feel sorry for Ed, because he's gone all day and misses so much with the children. So as the big moments in their lives come along, I try to push him into the picture. I hoped he'd take this trip for both their sakes.

"Freddie also says the camp will serve supper for the parents," I went on, "and after that there will be a fathers' and sons' show."

"Hey," Ed said, "am I supposed to miss my golf, meet a lot of strange people, and then make a fool of myself in front of Freddie and that bunch of Indians? Not me!"

I hedged.

"Maybe that part of it won't come off. But I think we ought to go. The boys know we went to see Dick at camp."

"Dick's in the Army," Ed said. "That's different."

"Yes, but they can't see that. Their life seems to them just as real and just as important as Dick's, you know."

"All right, I'll go," Ed agreed at last. "But I won't like it much and I won't be in any show."

I went around the table to where he sat. He looked awfully boyish in his brown and white shirt and tan coat.

"You are a darling." I kissed him. "And right there, as usual, when needed."

We left the city early Saturday morning with Babs between us in the car. She had added herself to the party.

"We three go together or not at all," she announced. "Isn't that right, Daddy? Besides, Charlie is entitled to a parent. That'll be me."

She sat in the middle where she could dial the radio easily. She was wearing a waist with big tropical flowers on it, blue shorts, and a bow in her hair. I thought how nice it was to be Babs's age, simply to move from place to place without having to change either one's clothes or one's habits. The radio was rendering "Loch Lomond," with the melody dislocated from the setting in the way the youngsters think is so wonderful. Ed took his driving seriously and didn't talk, so we ticked off the miles to music, running farther and farther, past lakes bordered with little pine trees, up into the hills. We stopped only once, for lunch. After that Babs began chatting, for we were almost there.

"I bet good old Freddie is always one lap behind," she said, "still doing his flag-raising when the others have gone on to tooth-brush drill. And shouldn't we be finding the true north by moss and lichens, scout fashion, instead of using a sissy road map?" And then, "Wait! There's a sign."

A wooden arrowhead pointed down off the highway. A sandy road stretched before us, and in a few minutes we rolled into camp.

A cluster of cabins stood in a clearing among the pines. Beyond them was a shining lake. My mind went back to the camp where Dick was stationed—I had visited it one Sunday—an interminable village of wooden shacks standing stark on bare fields, buses pouring up full of peering people, curt military police at the crossroads, khaki everywhere, the queer impersonalness of it all despite the consideration everyone showed us. Camp life in the Army, you knew, was a means to an end, and the end had nothing directly to do with the personal affairs of the individuals in it. I was glad when a hail from the cabin ahead of us brought my thoughts back to this happy and sheltered encampment.

A big, good-looking boy of about twenty came out to meet us. This was Bill Grant, counselor to the Bearcats. Our boys were right behind him. They looked browner, and heavier, too, in their blue shorts and gray wool shirts. We were introduced to all the other Bearcats and then went at once to the Lair. It was a two-room cottage with ten beds, and everything was in a suspicious state of neatness.

"How do you manage with just one maid?" Babs asked. The sarcasm was lost on Freddie. I thought of the layers of miscellaneous objects Freddie always accumulated in his room at home. My admiration for Bill Grant was born then. Barbara's, I noted, dated from the minute we stepped from the car.

"How's about a swim?" she asked.

"There are regular swim times," Freddie said. "You don't just go in, in between."

"That's a necessary rule, really," Charles explained gravely. "They have to keep track of us."

"But I'm available," Bill Grant put in, "if you'd like to go now."

"She would," Freddie said disgustedly as they went off.

"Come on, I want to show you the Lodge. Our Squad has the care of it. That's where you give the show," he added, fortunately trotting on ahead; otherwise he might have seen Ed's face. The Lodge was a big room with a giant fireplace at one end and a low stage at the other. First they pointed out the trophies, then the boys stepped out to show Ed the baseball field. I wanted to inspect the little stage. I walked across it and through an exit into a small room beyond. It was sparsely furnished with a table, a mirror, and a property box. A tired-looking man about my age was standing there holding a yellow wig with long curls in his hand.

"Oh, excuse me," I said.

"That's quite all right." He turned around. "Are you a visiting parent, too? They wished tonight's fathers' show on me. Ever seen one?"

"No," I admitted, "but I'll bet they're good."

"They're terrible. We get together here after supper and without an idea among us try to whip up something by eight o'clock."

"How do you ever do it?" I asked.

"Listen." His voice was grim. "No one has ever measured the driving power of despair, but it's probably the strongest force known to man."

I laughed. "Ed's outfit had a 'drammer' they used to do, back in the war." I reached into the property box. "He wore one of these." I fished out a handlebar mustache and sat down beside him. "It went like this . . ."

When I went out, Ed and the boys were still on the baseball field. The next event was to be a fathers' and sons' game. I thought I would take this chance to find the rooms reserved for us, deposit our bags, and freshen up a bit. I would be back in time to see as much of the game as I cared to. People are always talking about the differences between men and women; there's one real one, between Ed and me, anyway. He honestly enjoys everything that has to do with a ball game and I honestly don't. I like the friends and the party end of it, but I just can't keep my eyes or mind on the players. I drove up to our cabin on a little hill back of the camp and cleaned up. When I came back our Bearcats had lost to the Panthers and their fathers. The men were putting their ties back on and brushing the dirt off their trousers. They looked pretty much all in but a cheerful postmortem was going on.

"Gee, Moms, you should have seen Dad," Freddie said. "He sure does pitch a mean ball."

"He was good, really." Charlie was enthusiastic. "Only *I'd* have loved it if he'd run *all* the way around and made a score."

Ed smiled ruefully, and my friend of the property box, who had joined us, grinned.

"You'll have another chance to score tonight," he said to Ed. "I suppose you know that we make spectacles of ourselves for the benefit of the small fry at eight this evening?"

"Not me!" Ed's voice was cheerfully decisive. "But I'll help you fellows from the wings."

We started down toward the lake for the water sports. A thin woman with tragic eyes walking along beside me asked if I'd ever been here before. I said it was our boys' first year. She pointed out her son, a nervous-looking youngster who loped by obviously hoping we wouldn't call out and stop him.

"Have you more than one child?" she asked.

"Three," I said, "four, counting an English boy who's living with us."

"That's my only one," she nodded toward the receding figure. "You see, my husband isn't living and Andy is all I have. I never can bring myself to let him run any risks so I thought perhaps I ought to put him with other boys this summer. But I worry all the time, especially about the water."

We went down the wooden steps onto the dock which jutted out into the lake. A little cove beyond showed a sandy beach, but here great boulders rose gray and stark out of forty feet of glittering water, only a little deeper in color than the sky. I don't know how much the natural beauty of this place registers with the boys now, but I'm sure that later on it will come back to them again and again when they're cooped up in shops or offices. I know I can be cleaning a closet, and let a southwest wind blow in and I'm sailing off the Maine coast of an August afternoon. I've got my elbows crooked over the edge of the cockpit and below, on the other side, green water is running astern over the rail. Certainly this lake was something to have at the bottom of your memory.

Now the sports began. Freddie was entered in the crawl and got off a perceptible half-second after the others, in true Freddie style. Andy, the nervous-looking youngster, took part in a two-canoe catch-as-catch-can contest. He stood in the stern and without using a paddle jockeyed for position by jouncing up and down, while his opponent, a much heavier lad, did the same. I looked at Andy's mother. Her eyes were fixed glassily on the scene and her nails were folded tight into the palms of her hands. At last her boy reached his opponent and with a quick thrust toppled him into the lake. He plunged in too, but in a moment both reappeared, and grabing the bows of their canoes climbed back in and began working in toward the shore.

"He can take care of himself," I assured her. She gave me a quick, shy smile.

Then suddenly there was a murmur and everyone looked up. On the top of a great stone, perhaps a hundred feet away, a little figure stood thin and straight against the sky. My heart stood still. It was Charles. Babs dropped from nowhere onto the dock beside me and grabbed my knee. I had a quick glimpse of Bill Grant beyond her. He was watching Charles with a tense expression, his lower lip drawn taut, pulling his mouth into an angular grimace. Suddenly Charles dove, a beautiful folding, unfolding, folding swan dive into the water already darkened by the overhanging shore. It seemed hours before he came up, well out in the lake, and swam easily in. There were cheers as he climbed up on the dock, trying his best to look unconcerned. Babs was beside him in a second and when somebody standing next to Ed said, "Your boy, eh? You must be pretty proud of him!" Ed didn't even think to explain the connection between Charles and us.

Perhaps because we had two boys in the camp, the Head sat with us at mess. By this time all the Bearcat fathers and mothers were old friends. The joke about Babs's coming as Charlie's parent had got around. Bill Grant had volunteered to act as the other half and they had Charles between them, pretending to fuss over what he ate, all three of them giggling like the children they really were. Freddie was quietly tucking away an enormous supper; he had to keep right at it to get in his three helpings to everybody else's two.

"We take a hundred and eighty quarts of milk a day," the Head told us.

"And I have to drink most of it," I heard Charles whisper. He much prefers tea. Four of the boys brought in the ice cream and Ed, watching Freddie carrying a tray, told the Head they were developing a co-operative side of Freddie's nature that we hadn't known existed.

Supper was followed by flag-lowering. I don't know what it is about seeing the flag hauled down that moves you so. It's like some lovely living thing making a ceremonial gesture. I was still swallowing hard when the boys went off in the direction of the Lodge and the men after them. I walked along slowly with the other mothers. They were very different in type, even, seemingly, in age. A slender figure in front of me in shirt and slacks looked no older than Babs and certainly fifteen years younger than the solid, cheerful woman in the red and white dress beside her. But we all had a common concern, our children, and each was almost as much interested in the other women's youngsters as in her own. We trailed along comparing notes as to new prowess and added pounds until we found our places in the Lodge.

The show began with Bill Grant at the piano and Babs beside him to turn purely hypothetical pages. It seemed silly, but I was a little nervous. It was just that I wanted Freddie to be proud of his father. One of the younger women had told me that her boys always writhed during the show for fear their father would make himself ridiculous. I knew Freddie wouldn't be like that. He'd take it for granted Ed would be good, and it was just that I wanted to be sure Ed was going to come up to expectations. My tired-looking friend was master of ceremonies and announced the greatest tumbling act on earth. A bunch of boys ran out and with many "allez-oops" built a pyramid with Charles on top and then tumbled off stage. There was a wrestling match and an exhibition of jujitsu.

The master of ceremonies then announced "the Great Event of the Evening, that smashing Broadway hit, *Eliza Crossing the Ice*. The curtains parted to show Eliza, a small worried-looking boy in a calico dress. Eliza was dragging along her child, a six-foot counselor swathed in a white nightgown and wearing the wig with the yellow curls. Suddenly the dogs appeared behind her, six small boys with gray sweaters pulled on over their hips and legs. Baying fiercely, they forced Eliza onto the ice—indicated on the stage by pieces of white paper glued to the floor. Eliza had almost reached the other bank when Simon Legree appeared. It was Ed. He wore a checked waistcoat over a white shirt, big green pants, and the handlebar mustache.

"Down, you curs," he yelled. "I'll get the gal myself."

With quick, gingerly steps he strode across the ice. He had almost seized Eliza when the dogs set on him and rolled him into the white-papered river.

There was a burst of applause stamped out on the wooden floor. There were calls for the cast. Nothing loath, the dogs came down to the footlights, crossed their paws and took a bow. There were shouts for Ed and he had to come on again and again, rolling his eyes and curling his mustache to the noise of boos and hisses. The show wound up with the "Great Baltic Chorus in the greatest of their native songs, 'Boola-Boola,'" rendered by all in loud, hoarse tones. It was clear that the fathers' and sons' show had been a complete success.

At last we were back in the cottage where we were to sleep.

"They're a wonderful bunch of kids," Ed said, "and I never met a better crowd of men in my life."

"The women are nice, too," I said.

"Funny thing," Ed went on, "their hitting on the Eliza story." Suddenly he looked up at me. "It couldn't be you tipped 'em off?"

"Does it matter?" I asked. "You were the hit of the show, and didn't you have a good time?"

Before he had a chance to answer there was a knock at our door, and Babs and Bill Grant came in.

"Don't worry," Babs called out, "it isn't tooth-brush drill. We just came with a message from the Bearcats."

"They want to sign you on to pitch for them next year," Bill informed us, "and everybody wants to make sure of a return engagement of Simon Legree."

He said good night and left. Babs went into her own room. Ed and I stood looking out of the window toward the Lair. The lights were off and all we could see were the treetops and the stars beyond.

"I was just thinking—just thinking something." Ed picked up his pipe. "It's hard to put into words, but so often things are a *little* wrong somehow when you wish they were just right. This kind of life is just right. It's as it should be."

"I know," I said.

"The boys have duties and plenty of responsibilities," he went on, "and they do the right thing because everyone's doing it and because they're busy and happy and strong."

"I think what they learn in a place like this must help them a lot later," I said, "especially in an army camp. Boys need to learn to be good troupers. Dick says so many of the men have a wonderful camp spirit. It helps a lot. They don't grumble about things. They make the best of everything, in fact they really seem to enjoy the life."

Ed turned away from the window. His face was very serious.

"Yes," he went on, "all the same, it's different. There's a shadow over an army camp. They don't see it. They're too young. But it's coming, across the sky."

"Don't." I shivered. "I felt it, too. It set Dick apart from us. Let's just be glad Freddie and Charles are having this kind of a life instead."

Ed pulled me down beside him. When there are tears in his eyes he would rather look over my head.

Chapter 6

NO AMOUNT OF ORDERS THAT NORAH WAS TO ANSWER THE telephone when the family was sitting down at the dining room table for a meal ever did any good in our house. Babs was always sure it was for her and not a bit anxious to let anyone else in on who was calling her. Freddie and Charles had friends, too, and if it was only for Ed or me, they liked to be the ones to say so. The ring of the telephone was always a match to a firecracker as far as peace at a meal was concerned.

Freddie and Charles had returned from camp in a distinct spirit of anticlimax. The household had fallen into the August doldrums. It was in this mood that we were eating our dinner one night when the phone set up that hasty and insistent series of sounds that always indicates something of unusual importance, or seems to.

At the whir of the bell all three of the youngsters were off like ballplayers sliding for the home plate. They came right back, however. It was for me, long distance, the army camp calling. In a minute Dick's warm voice was saying hello and how would I like it if he came home for a couple of days' furlough? That should have told me something but it didn't. Also Vic could get leave.

"Privates get furloughs but officers get leaves; and he would like to come along." I said we'd be delighted to have him, and then Dick went on, "Mother, remember a girl named Eileen? She worked in our office in New York. I thought maybe I'd ask her, too.... Yeah, she'll come....

No, I'll get in touch with her. By the way, I just sent a line to Dad at the office. Don't worry about anything. See you very soon, dear. Good night."

I put down the phone and went back to the table.

"Who's coming?" Babs looked up eagerly. "Oh, Moms, it isn't Vic, is it? I wrote him to."

"Who's the woman?" Freddie asked. "I suppose just another of those girls that's crazy about Dick."

Before I could frame an answer everybody was leaving the table. There was a program they wanted to hear. I sat at my place feeling rather than thinking that there was more Dick might have said and hadn't. Norah came in and began to clear away.

"You'd better take your day off beginning as soon as the breakfast dishes are done tomorrow," I said. "There won't be much chance to rest after that, not for the next few days, anyway."

Norah stopped with a fruit dish in her hand. It was clear that she had overheard the news.

"Thank you. I will, then. But I was thinking I'd make a batch of cookies first."

Dick had mentioned them in his last letter as the "Norah Brand."

"Fine," I said. "Get your list. We may as well plan all the meals now."

The uneasy feeling I had persisted. A strange girl, Dick's first real furlough, his writing Ed at the office; it was all unusual and a little disturbing. But getting down to housekeeping reassured me. It's always that way in a home. There's the next thing to be done and you do it, and it gives you a feeling that nothing can ever change. Besides, no matter what,

Dick would be here soon. I could see for myself how he looked and get an armful of him. We'd all be happy and that would be that.

Late the next afternoon I went up to Babs's room to see if the day bed had been properly made for Eileen and whether Babs had left her a bureau drawer or two and a little closet space. My mind was on the girl. I wondered if Dick was in love with her. It hardly seemed as if he would bring her way out here to us unless he were. Was she enough of a person for him and would she fit in with our family? Suddenly I heard Ed downstairs.

"Yoo-hoo, where are you? I've got a letter here from Dick." He came up and dropped into Babs's armchair and then jumped up again. "What on earth is this?" He turned and picked up a pink plush rabbit. "Isn't Babs ever going to grow up? Come on, let's go downstairs where we can be comfortable."

He took out the letter. It seemed there was a reason for the furlough. The boys were being allowed to visit their families because in a few days they were to leave for Texas. Texas! On the other side of the continent! This wasn't fun; this was good-by.

"And so," Ed finished, "I thought maybe I'd do something for the kids. I thought maybe we'd take them on a party, a real blow-out." He tried to make his voice sound casual; instead it was grave. "These things don't happen often and I thought we'd do it up brown. I'll order dinner in advance for the six of us, Dick and the girl, Babs and Vic, and you and me. Would you like that, dear?"

"Of course, I'd love it," I said, "if—but let's do it anyway."

"I know," Ed smiled, "it's going to set us back plenty. But they're pretty nice kids. We can't tell what's ahead for them and I'd like to give them a good send-off." He pulled out his watch. "Almost time to go down to the station." He went out to the car, taking the boys along.

Before I knew it they were back. Charles and Freddie dashed in first, tugging the bags, and went tumbling up the stairs with them.

"Here, give me hers," I heard Freddie say, "because I *may* marry her myself when I grow up if Dick doesn't."

The men came up the steps and with them a girl with wistful gray eyes, a wide sweet mouth, and a thin figure topped with curls. Like Charles, she had a fragile quality. I found myself kissing her very gently, as one does a lovely child. Then there was Vic, with his brilliant eyes and smile and his sure manner, and last of all Dick. We hugged each other, and he freed his arms to put one around Eileen and one around Babs. When Dick gets home he romps. It isn't that he does it physically, but his heart romps, the way a big dog does as he jumps around trying to welcome everybody at once. I held him off and looked at him. He was heavier, browner, more smoothly tanned, tougher somehow, the way hickory is tough. But it was the same boy. I turned and led them into the living room.

Dinner that night was a field day for all of us. Dick told us about the blue denim suits they had for fatigue duty such as cleaning up the barracks and cutting wood for fences and planting shrubs around the post, and about the man who, when they were issued to him in addition to his khaki, said, "All this and denim, too?" And the friendly "looie" who would send over word, "Inspection coming. If you've lost

anything, don't report it; borrow it from somebody else."
And about the old-time army sergeant who cautioned the new
recruits always to be nicely shaved because they must not
only look well "in the distant," but "near to, in case General Drum comes around for inspection."

Vic described with gusto the Broadway talent among the
enlisted men, who put on nightly shows, the Recreation Hall
with the cloth of silver curtains and the arc lights, and the
professionals who were to have semi-permanent duty there.
"Morale officers are something we never heard of in the
regular army," Vic said, "but maybe it's a good idea at that."
He promised to take Babs to the Officers' Club. "We can sit
on the back lawn under the colored umbrellas and wave at
Dick in the Service Club across the road. That's where the
privates are," he added, "but of course you and I wouldn't
know any of them."

Eileen looked up with a hurt expression in her eyes as if
Dick had been slighted. She really loves him, I thought with
a pang. And then realizing Vic was just having his little joke,
she began rather hurriedly to tell us about the changes at
the office, how everyone missed Dick and yet someone had
taken his desk and the water had just sort of closed up over
his place. Dick looked pleased, but thoughtful.

"Yeah," he said, "they say it's easier fitting into the army
than it is fitting back into a job when you get out."

All the time we were talking, Babs never took her eyes
off Vic. Dick kept putting his arm on the back of Eileen's
chair and leaning over from time to time and asking if she
was all right. Our children are the outgoing kind; you can
see their every feeling. But Eileen was reserved. She made
an effort to keep her eyes off Dick and, I thought, had

probably put up many a stiff fight with herself to keep her
mind off him. Vic easily dominated the table talk. He was
used to prestige, with girls as well as with soldiers. Freddie
and Charles quietly packed away their food and listened. I
looked across at Ed, so comfortingly grown-up that he could
forget himself in the interests of these youngsters. I saw he
liked Eileen. I liked her, too. She added something to the
family that we had lacked without knowing it, like the last
delicate ingredient that gives a dish its flavor. I wondered if
Dick was definitely tied to her and whether he would talk
to us about it.

After supper the four young people left in the car for
some place Dick knew. (Ed had planned his party for the
following evening, which was to be their last one at home.)
Freddie and Charles obviously felt left out so I suggested
to Ed that we take them around to a neighborhood movie for
the early show, and we did. There was a lot of love in it and
they complained, but there was flying and shooting, too, and
they liked that and came home content to turn in. I set the
alarm clock and put it in the hall, in accordance with a plan
I had worked out years before with Dick. The system was
this. I would set the alarm for half an hour later than he
expected to be in. When he got home, he would turn it off.
If it rang, it was time enough to wake up and worry. Unless
it rang, I slept the night through.

I awoke when they came in, however. It would have been
impossible not to hear them. They were harmonizing softly
in the lower hall, before coming up to bed and making silly
jokes like, "What do you do?" "I make trunks; it's an
empty life!" I heard them out in the hall, saying, "Good
night," and Freddie calling, "Keep quiet, will yuh? You're

waking up Rags." And, of course, Dick forgot the alarm
clock, and it started ringing and he had to stop it and do a lot
of explaining. But finally the whole household quieted down
and fell asleep.

The next morning there were some things the boys wanted
to buy, and while they were out Babs took Eileen over to
her school. So it happened that Dick came up to my room
and I did have a few minutes alone with him.

"That's a nice girl, Dick," I began.

"Like her?" He brightened.

"She's awfully fond of you," I said.

He moved his shoulders uneasily.

"I know. This is kind of in the nature of a good-by party."

"Really?" I tried to conceal my astonishment. "Nobody
would guess it. I'm sure she doesn't think so."

"Well," he said, "how can I make any plans on thirty
dollars a month? If we do come back, we'll have to start at
the bottom looking for jobs again. I guess girls will have to
wait. It's tough."

"Yes, dear," I said, "but don't *you* be. I don't know how
you stand with her, but if you do care about her, she ought
to be given a chance to wait for you if she wants to. I mean,
it would help her to know that she was a part of your life
plans."

"I suppose so." His tone was evasive. Then, "Trouble is,
I haven't got any life plans."

Suddenly, to my own surprise, my heart was on Eileen's
side.

"Just don't be careless, if you really love her, that is, or
you run the risk of losing her."

He did not answer, but he gave me a quick glance as if the idea that he might lose her was a new one.

"We'll wait and see how it works out," he answered at last.

"Things don't work out," I told him. "People make them work."

"Oh, well, as Vic says, the army takes care of the girl question." He tried to sound nonchalant.

"Vic is different," I answered. "He has a different attitude than you and your father. You're not the kind of men who kiss their girls good-by and go on just as easily to others somewhere else. Don't let the army change you from what you really are. You're really like your daddy. Somebody said that he was like an apple, sweetest near the core."

Dick laughed. "I bet it was you." But he put an arm across my shoulder and gave me a little hug as he went out.

In the very late afternoon we all got together in the living room. It would have been almost our dinner time—sometimes we still called it supper because the younger children did—and Ed was ready to issue his invitation.

"How would you all like to go to the High Hat for dinner?" he asked.

The High Hat was the swankiest place anywhere around with marvelous steaks and broiled lobsters and wonderful music and a roof garden where you could dance. Well, of course, everybody would adore to, and Dad was a prince. Babs said he always had the most wonderful ideas. "And just at the right moment," Dick added, flipping a lone quarter into the air. And Eileen called Ed a lamb.

"Well, then," he said, "go get prettied up and don't be

long about it. We might as well have all the party that's coming to us."

I had just finished my hair and was zipping on the black crepe dress that is my evening uniform when the door opened and Ed came in. He held a telegram in his hand. I wasn't alarmed, for all our family was at home and accounted for. Then I looked up and saw his serious face.

"It's from Ann," he told me. "Her husband has been hurt in an automobile accident."

Ann is his youngest sister, the baby of his family and his special pet. I remembered his telling me how when they used to go swimming as children he was always watching to see if that little head was above water and safely near the float. Business kept Ann and her husband on the move now. They were in Detroit and really quite alone.

"Poor Ann," I said. "I hope it wasn't serious." I hesitated. Then, "Do we have to tell the children? After all, Dick is leaving us for quite a while. It seems too bad to put any unnecessary damper on the party."

But Ed handed me the telegram. "He *may* die in a few hours. Of course, I could take the early morning train and say nothing tonight." He put a hand on my shoulder as if to steady himself. "After all, we ought to think of the boys, too."

I looked at the yellow sheet—a cry for help from a frightened woman.

"But I *ought* to go right now," he finished. Then, "I think I'll see how Dick feels about it."

He called Dick into the room and told him the situation. Dick's young face fell and then a look I had never seen settled on it like a mask.

"I guess we'll have to pass up the party this time. This is what you'd call in the line of duty."

"That's the way I see it," Ed said, "but I'm glad you do, too. You go right ahead without me though. Have your celebration," he added.

But Dick was pulling a timetable from his pocket.

"We'll stick with you." He studied the folder. "You and I and Vic can leave on the same train and have dinner aboard. Now, the New York Express comes through a few minutes earlier. If Eileen wants to make it, she can. Say, I'd better tell them before they get all dolled up in gold braid and froufrous."

I packed Ed's bag and tucked some bills into my evening purse. Ed brought the car around and I got in front with him. The two men and girls piled into the back. I could feel their dejection almost like a wave about to break as if it were my own; a little of it was. Eileen looked suspiciously near to tears as she said good-by. She kissed both Ed and me. Dick disappeared with her on the other side of the station. He came back only after the train had pulled out. He did not get into the car again, but stood moodily staring down the tracks toward the receding end lights. I noticed that something he had worn on his uniform lapel was gone; he must have torn it off and given it to Eileen. The incoming train whistled. He kissed me absent-mindedly.

"I'll write you about things," he said.

The three men got aboard. I saw Dick leaning to wave at a window and Vic's face over his shoulder and, at the vestibule door, Ed, who has never yet failed to turn and smile as he goes.

"Well, Toots," I said at last, for there had been no sound from the back seat, "how about getting in front with me?"

"Oh, Moms." Babs was out and in again in a second. "It seems as if every time people do what's right, it means some man goes away and leaves you."

"Yes, it does," I agreed.

"The Army just puts up Order 345 and breaks your heart," she went on. "It doesn't care."

"No," I said, "it doesn't."

"Moms," she asked at last, "do you think I could be in love?"

"You might," I considered. "But maybe the uniform has something to do with it, too. Don't you think so?"

"I don't know," she answered. "It feels like the real thing. It's very hurting."

I looked at her in the dim light. She looked very lovely in her summer dress and soft coat, lovely and very young.

"Let's not go right home," I said. "Let's you and me have a party. Would you like to have dinner with me at the hotel? We could sit right down and eat through all the courses from fruit cup to chocolate parfait and coffee."

She sat up suddenly and patted her hair.

"Can we have the *big* dinner?" she asked. "That would be the nuts!" She leaned against me. "Oh, Moms, you're the most *comforting* person!"

I started the car.

Chapter 7

IF I'D BEEN MADE CHAIRMAN OF SOMETHING, I'D HAVE RUN right home and told the family. Ed is different. He waited for just the right moment to spring the news.

We were on the porch in the cool dark. The stars were out. There was a smell of heliotrope from the garden. A tiny thread of music came from Babs's little portable radio.

Ed said, "Of course it's only because I have a boy in the Army, but you know there's going to be a big rally next week. Well, they've asked me to be the final speaker." Our town had been in the throes of raising its quota for recreation centers for the Service. The centers were to be run by six organizations under the general title of the United Services Organizations, which was being shortened to "U.S.O." The rally, Ed explained, was in the nature of a shot in the arm to the cause. "And I'm supposed to hand out the talk that does it."

"Why, Ed, that's an honor." I was delighted.

"Nonsense." He tried to make his voice casual. "They probably couldn't find anyone else. I'd feel like a fool getting up before a big audience. I might forget what I was going to say."

"You can read your speech," I told him. "The President does."

Babs broke in. "Now, Daddy, don't you dare say no. I think it's too exciting for words. I'll help you."

Ed laughed. "Thanks, darling, but I guess I can write my own." I knew then he intended to do it.

"Gee, it's a swell night," Babs said. "We could drive over to see Vic and get you your material first-hand." Vic had not been moved; he was still at the same camp.

"We could go see your brother," I suggested. Dick's outfit, instead of going West, had been sent to a more southerly state.

"They don't want a lot of vague stuff about what you saw on a trip," Ed answered. "It's just a matter of getting the facts, exactly like making up an office report."

My heart sank. I sometimes read important office reports for him just to check the commas, and I had a feeling that if this speech turned out like one of them, it wouldn't be apt to move the heart or loosen the purse strings.

It was Babs who spoke next. "Let's go see Dick, then."

There was a sudden scratching on the roof over our heads. "Boys!" I called.

There was a series of thumps, a silence, then a scurrying inside, and Freddie and Charles stood in the lighted doorway in their pajamas.

"We just happened to be out on the roof," Freddie began. "We heard you." He looked elaborately unconcerned. Charles was unstudiedly eager.

"May we go, too, probably?" he asked.

"Sure we can." Freddie gave him a quick dig with his elbow. "And Rags wants to come along." He leaned down and squared his fist in front of Rags's nose.

Ed fell into the trap. "We'll have to see about Rags."

"Then we can go! We can go!" They bolted, the dog after them.

"Well, why shouldn't they? Why not make them happy?" I asked.

Ed did not answer, but he reached out and took my hand.

Babs sniffed. "Hmm, lovey stuff. I guess *I'll* go to bed." The little thread of tune from the portable traveled away with her.

"They ought to be able to find somebody better than me to make that speech." Ed's tone was serious.

I leaned my head against his arm and looked for stars.

"You'll be good," I answered. "You'll be grand."

In the next few days he put all his spare time on the preparation of his facts. I realized this speech meant a lot to Ed. He was doing his bit. I was almost as anxious as he was. I was terribly relieved when at dinner one night he reported that he'd had his speech typed at the office and that it was reposing in his pocket.

"Come on, Daddy," Babs coaxed as we left the table. "Read it to us."

"Don't be silly, why would you want to hear it? Well." Ed adjusted his glasses. He looked a little self-conscious. "This is silly, but if you really do want to hear it—'Ladies and Gentlemen'—wait, 'Friends' would be better." He penciled the word in. " 'Friends: We are gathered here tonight to further the work of six great organizations who have united to help in building up *and* maintaining the morale of men in the Service. It is up to us, the people at home, to implement their efforts.' "

He glanced up. Babs waved a hand. "Will they know what that means, Daddy? I thought an implement was a thing like a hoe."

Ed smiled tolerantly. "They'll know." He continued: " 'To

accomplish this task...'" His voice went on firmly and evenly. After ten minutes or so he finished. He looked expectantly over the paper at us. We clapped.

"That's fine, dear," I said. "That covers everything."

"I think so," he answered modestly.

Freddie pondered, his chin cupped in his hand. "You could tell some jokes," he offered.

"I think this is much dignifieder, without jokes," Babs put in, "don't you, Moms?"

"It's a speech anyone could be proud of," I replied.

"Well, anyway," Ed finished comfortably, "I guess it's about what they want."

The next day we got off, Babs, boys, Rags, and all. The first part of the trip was like any other in the summer of 1941—fine roads but heavy traffic. The second day brought us into lovely country, but scenery got no attention from Ed. Every time I spelled him at the wheel he pulled the speech out and read it over, his mouth working, a little frown between his eyes. Eventually we left the highway and rolled down into camp, with all its interminable rows of packing-box buildings. At headquarters, the sergeant at the desk looked up Dick's name. "Company F," he said. "'First turn to the right, cross the railroad tracks, to the left again. Then ask— and you'd better walk!"

We soon saw why. The road was a footpath of reddish dirt baked into lumps. We crossed the tracks in front of a panting engine which had just pulled in with a train full of troops. We could see them marching away in batches. Here and there a few of them looked up and smiled, but some whose eyes met ours seemed not even to see us. The men on the streets at home look different, I thought. Their eyes are kind or sad or bold. But there were boys here who had a dead-pan expression that was utterly new to me. "Never let Dick get that look in his eyes," I prayed softly.

We found Dick's barracks—and Dick. It seemed queer to me that he couldn't come out without first getting permission and that he wore his cap in front of us. "Regulations," he explained, "not manners gone to pot." We stood on the step and got a glimpse inside the big dormitory room where he lived. Two or three men were idly reading papers, sitting on their beds. "Confined to barracks," Dick explained later, "for breaking regulations."

"Let's go somewhere and sit down," Ed said.

We sat on a rail fence. I told Dick about the speech his father was to make. Somehow it seemed necessary to justify our being here, where we were so obviously in the way.

"That's fine," Dick said to Ed. "Put it on thick. We certainly need some place to go besides the Exchange. I'll take you there."

The Post Exchange, or store, consisted of one room with a counter. It was thick with smoke and jammed to the doors. "Most of the boys push off for town Saturday nights," Dick went on. "But there's nothing to cheer about there, either. One lousy hotel, two beer joints, and a single bowling alley. The only fun is trying to get the drivers to race the buses, going in." He glanced at his watch. "Have to get back for retreat."

"Retreat?" Babs looked at him round-eyed. "Do they drill you for retreating?"

Dick laughed. "Watch that field. You'll see. It's the late afternoon line-up. After that I think I can get away and join you for some supper."

We had the meal in a mammoth hot-dog wagon near the edge of a field. The counter was lined with boys in uniform. After we had eaten there didn't seem to be much to stay for and nowhere much to stay. For a while we sat in the car, Dick in front with us holding Rags and rubbing the shaggy head absent-mindedly.

"You'd make a good mascot, old boy," he said. "Company F hasn't had time yet to get one."

I saw a startled expression in Freddie's eyes. He looked at Charles and Charles looked at Freddie. Ed and Dick were talking about something else when Freddie interrupted. Freddie spoke slowly but there wasn't a quaver in his voice.

"I think that would be fine," Freddie said. "Rags would like to be a mascot."

For a moment Dick was puzzled. He hadn't really meant it. He had never dreamed of asking them to give up their beloved pet.

"Charles and I," Freddie went on steadily, "would like you and the Company to have him."

I could see a protest hovering on Dick's lips. But Dick is like his father. He doesn't always put it into words, but he is very understanding. He reached into the back seat and shook hands with Freddie and Charles.

"That's swell."

We drove off, watching Dick walking away into the approaching night, back to his barracks, with Rags at his heels. He turned and waved just once. Freddie and Charles waved, but their eyes were on the dog.

"Good-by, Dick. Be a good dog, Rags," Freddie called. He was fighting hard to keep back the tears.

Ed drove on. Every now and then he would glance into

the rear-view mirror where he could see Freddie's and
Charles's solemn little faces. Finally he slowed down to a
snail's pace and half turned in his seat. He didn't say anything to Freddie or Charles. He just made a gesture with
his hand, like a salute.

On the way down we had picked a place to spend the
night. It was dark when we reached it now. Ed and the boys
went in to see about the rooms. Suddenly Babs said in a low
voice:

"Look, Moms, isn't that a man against the fence? He's
sick or something." Somebody was slumped against the
railing.

"Go get Daddy," I told her, "and keep the boys in the
house."

I backed the car until the light fell on the crumpled figure.
He was only a boy, perhaps nineteen or twenty, and he was
in uniform. He was talking to himself. I was glad when Ed's
voice behind me said, "What's going on here?"

"It's some youngster from camp," I answered. "I don't
know just what's the matter with him."

Ed crouched beside him. "Seven seas under," he told me,
"and probably had his pockets picked, too." From the grass
beside the boy's hand he lifted a wallet. "Yep. Empty. Come
on, feller."

The boy stirred. He said, "Put out that light."

Ed tugged at him. "Come on, I'm going to take you home."

"Tha's right," the boy sat up. "Mus' go home to my
mother. My mother sits up for me. I have a very lovely
mother."

"Sure you have," Ed said. "Come on."

The boy rose and moved toward the car. He lifted a foot

to the running board, then put it back on the ground. He turned and swayed majestically.

"Nope," he said, "can't go home. My mother wouldn't approve."

"Your mother will be glad to see you," Ed urged. "Get in!"

The boy grasped the edge of the open door and swung with it.

"Nope," he answered, "you don' know my mother." He sat down abruptly.

Ed pulled him to his feet. "Let's go back to camp. You know you're in the Army now."

The lad straightened. "Private Early," he said, attempting a salute. "Where you think you're going, Private Early? I'm going to get myself a girl and to hell with you. That's what I said. When I got off the bus there was a girl. Girl in a yellow dress. Hey, you, girl with the yellow dress!" He noticed me. "You're not the girl."

"You'd better run along to the kids," Ed told me. "I'm going to drive him back to camp."

"Wait." I ran up to the house. There proved to be no man about; the inn was run by a mother and daughter. They were kindly people. I explained the situation and went back to the car. "I think I'd better go with you," I told Ed. "Then I could drive, if necessary."

He hesitated a minute. The boy was in the back seat. "Maybe you're right at that. Hop in here with me."

For a while we rolled along in silence under the stars. A little fog rose to the level of the fenders, blanketing the road. We crept through it. Suddenly I heard the boy fumbling at the car door.

"Mus' find my girl," he muttered. "Had a girl . . ."

Ed reached back with one hand and gripped him by the shoulder.

"Listen, there's some warm milk left in the thermos. Maybe it would sober him up." I got in the back seat and held it for the youngster. He drank it unquestioningly. He slid down on the floor of the car, arms up, and put his cheek against my knee.

"You are so good to me," he said. "You're th' lady of all th' world." He ceased to move.

Well, it wasn't the easiest job, but we had his name, and Ed was cagey, and at last we put him in the door of his own barracks—no mean trick in the dark.

It wasn't until we turned into the driveway at the inn that Ed spoke. "Poor kid. Pretty sordid night off for a nice boy, isn't it?"

The rally was held in the high school auditorium. I was early and settled myself in the front row. The room filled up but the stage was empty. I began to get nervous. Where was Ed? Then I saw him, following the chairman. They walked on from the right with six other men and sat down. Ed's face was a little set, but he looked very handsome. His suit was meticulously pressed—I had seen to that. No one would have guessed he was nervous. I clasped and unclasped my hands. "If it only would begin!"

It did. The first half of the program was given over to reports. At last the chairman leaned over and said something to Ed. Ed nodded, gave a hunch to his shoulders, and adjusted his glasses. He put his hand in his inner pocket to take out the speech. I saw him look bewildered. His mouth pushed

into grim squares at the corners. He ran his hand frantically
through all his pockets. The speech wasn't there!

My heart did a power dive and crashed. I knew only too
well what must have happened. I had sent his suit to the tailor
just before supper and because I was in a hurry I had called
to Babs to get it from Ed's closet. The speech, of course, was
lying in the tailor shop. I shut my eyes.

The talk stopped. There was a burst of applause, and then
the chairman was saying, "I don't need to introduce to this
audience of friends and neighbors the final speaker on our
program." There was another round of hand-clapping and
Ed was standing out in front, alone.

He tucked the tips of his fingers into his coat pockets. After
what seemed an endless pause, he said:

"Ladies and Gentlemen. Friends—" His mouth worked
in a grimace. He stopped and looked fixedly at the waiting
audience. Suddenly his face relaxed. "I had a swell speech
all written down," he said. "It was full of facts and figures,
but I guess I forgot to bring it. Maybe it's just as well." He
smiled, but without humor. "Instead, I'm going to tell you
about a boy I met outside the camp where my own son is stationed." Then Ed told the story of Private Early, the boy
who had a lovely mother and who was lying drunk against a
rail fence in the dark, robbed and run out on by a girl in a
yellow dress. He finished.

"Well, I guess that's about all. Maybe now you see why
what we're trying to do needs to be done." He leaned forward. "We took that boy out of home and school or maybe
a job and dumped him down in the middle of nowhere. All
the gangsters in the country are getting to him as fast as they

can. The question is, who's going to get there first—we or they? We put him where he is. We can't let him down!"

There was a silence during which you could have counted the seconds, then the big audience burst into frantic applause.

"It was a wonderful speech," I told him, later.

"Well, at first I had a kind of a blackout," Ed said slowly. "Then I thought of Freddie and Charles giving up their little dog, and that boy! It came to me it was as simple as that; we can't let them down."

"Yes," I answered, "as simple as that."

Chapter 8

IN AUGUST 1941 THE DRAFT LAW WAS CHANGED TO EXTEND, indefinitely, the term of service of the younger men. Only the boys themselves seemed unaware of what might come. Like people playing a game under the lee of a hill, they gave no sign of seeing the storm whirling up the sky. An incident Dick told us illustrated this. One evening, he said, his company was assembled in the recreation hall to listen to a talk on army insurance. The officer explained how it would operate in case an epidemic in camp, for example, were to decimate the ranks. One soldier rose and asked seriously:

"Suppose we were actually asked to fight somewhere, would it also cover accident or death from that cause?"

Dick said the officer's face was a study. "At first he thought he was being kidded. Then he saw these dopes didn't realize it was primarily a war insurance."

Dick, however, had always taken the view that they were in for a long haul. Consequently, the minute the time was extended he had applied for officer's training. Now he'd been accepted and transferred to a Northern camp only a few hours away from us by train. A telegram had just reached me, saying that he was to have a brief leave. I was so happy I could hardly bear it. When Ed came in from the office I simply dove at him.

"Oh, Ed," I said, "Dick's coming home."

"Hey, look out for my hair," Ed said. "This doesn't mean the war is over."

"I don't care," I answered. "He'll be here any minute now and we'll all have fun together." Dick was always gay. He made everything swing.

A few minutes later he came in the door with his old quick tread. Freddie and Charles fell on his big brown figure. Not that they felt the way we did; they wanted to hear about Rags. Was he a good mascot? Did he go on maneuvers with them? Where did he sleep?

"He's fine," Dick said. "Never better. Most popular four-footer on the post." He walked into the brightly lighted living room. It was then I saw his face and something close to panic took hold of my heart. Usually his skin has a good color with ruddy undertones and his hazel eyes are clear and sunny. Tonight his cheeks had a queer yellowish tinge. There were dark circles under his eyes; there was a sort of desperate look in them. He knew that I had seen it. He said, "I'll take my bag upstairs."

I started after him. I had done his room over with new white curtains, bedspread, and pillow shams with wide embroidered ruffles. Not a very appropriate choice for a boy's room, perhaps, but it represented the greatest contrast to army bedding. Of course he wouldn't notice in detail, but I thought he might like the general effect. I had just sense enough, however, to turn back. I joined Ed in the hall.

"What's happened to Dick?" I was scared. "He looks as if he hadn't slept for nights. Something must be terribly on his mind."

"I don't know. He does look pretty seedy," Ed said, thoughtfully.

"Do you think he could be worrying because the draft period has been extended?" I asked, "and he has to stay in?"

Ed smiled down at me. He has a nice, tolerant smile.

"Dick wouldn't be broken up about that," he answered. "He went in expecting to stay as long as he was needed. You don't understand how a man would feel, dear. Perhaps they've been exercising him a little too hard."

"No," I said. "Somebody has crossed him up. If we can find out who, and how, we might be able to help him."

Ed put an arm over my shoulder. "Dick isn't a kid any longer," he told me. "He knows we're here. When he wants to, he'll tell us. If he never wants to—well, there's nothing we can do about it."

All through dinner the younger boys kept up such a fire of questions that there was no time to think of moods. Freddie sat with his shoulders hunched forward, his eyes roving over Dick's uniform. "Lookit," he wanted to know, was it true when they built planes they used midgets to work inside the wings? He'd heard there was a shortage of midgets. Wouldn't boys of around ten and eleven be about the right size? Charles asked in his clear, high, English voice—he never lost his accent, but merely added words like "okay" to his vocabulary —was the wheel of one of the big bombers really as high as a room? Dick told them all he knew.

Supper over, they looked at flight pictures in magazines until I sent them off to bed. After that Dick would not settle down. He turned on the radio, spinning the dial so you heard snatches of everything and felt as if you were going crazy. I brought my knitting and tried to be peaceful. I was making a rope-stitch sweater of tawny gray wool for Babs. It was fun to work on. The color was restful and the stitch went fast. Ed lit his pipe and relaxed in his big chair. Dick continued to walk around. He picked up the paper and glanced at the headlines, took up a book and put it down.

"Well, son," Ed said. "How are things going?"

"Okay." Dick did not sit down, but now he stood still and lit a cigarette.

"How do the men take the extension of the draft?" Ed asked.

"Well, it makes things definitely more serious," Dick answered. "They've stopped thinking ahead. They sort of live in the moment. Take Fred Haynes, my best friend in the outfit. *He* got married. . . . I guess it seemed like a good idea at the time."

A lightning flash of fear went through me. Had Dick done something precipitous that now was a weight on his heart?

"Fred's wife is a honey," he went on. "They call her Glo. She's living in a rented room in town about eight miles from camp. I guess it was seeing her and Fred like that sort of got me down."

"Because they're so happy?" It was more a statement than a question. I breathed freely again. Then Dick wasn't married. It was only that he envied Fred, who was.

Dick drew up a chair and sat down beside his father. "Yeah, I guess he's happy," he answered thoughtfully. "He's in love all right and she's crazy about him, too. It's just that neither Eileen nor I had ever seen two nice people in quite that sort of a set-up."

"Eileen?" I asked, surprised. I was seeing the girl with the honey-colored curls and wistful, gray-blue eyes in a new setting. "I thought she was still working in New York."

"She came to camp a couple of days ago," he said. "I . . . I had to see her. I made her promise to come pronto if I wired her to and she kept her word."

"She would," Ed put in. "She's that kind."

Dick glanced appreciatively at his father. "Yeah . . . well, we had dinner together at the only place in town you can eat, a little table d'hôte dive. Then we went over to Fred and Glo's and they threw a party."

"Was it fun?" I asked.

Dick hesitated, then, "It was awful. Glo lives in a furnished room, if you can call it furnished. There's a bed with a yellow pine headboard, two chairs, and a trunk to sit on, a drab old carpet full of holes, and a clotheshorse with Fred's socks and Glo's underthings drying on it right in the middle of the room. Of course she didn't know we were coming. Fred hadn't had any chance to tell her. She must have been just lying on the bed for hours; there was a deep hollow in the pillow and about a dozen cigarette butts in an ash tray on the floor."

"She sounds—I mean *it* sounds kind of messy," I said.

"Oh, she snapped right out of it when we came and tried to make it look like a real party," Dick explained. "She set up the glasses on the bureau and helped Fred unpack the piece of ice he brought in and put it in the wash basin. She squeezed the lemons, they whipped up some Tom Collinses, and she tried hard to make it all seem like fun. She was so nice and so gallant and the whole setting was so shabby, such a makeshift for a home!"

"Can't she fix it up somehow?" I asked.

"No," Dick answered. "Why should she? Fred might be moved tomorrow; it would be silly to spend any money on the place. Besides, they haven't got it. All I could think of was the way things are around here. I'm sure Glo came from an awfully nice home, too. I felt sorry for her."

"I suppose she doesn't mind, as long as Fred is with her." Ed puffed at his pipe.

"When he is—but he can't be there very much. It's a long hike back to camp. If the buses have stopped running, you can't be sure of catching a ride. Besides, there are plenty of times when he's on duty unexpectedly and has no way to get word to her so she just goes to a movie—I dunno, it got under my skin. I can't see it."

I kept on knitting. "You mustn't let your friends' troubles get you down too much," Ed said after a while.

"That isn't all," Dick went on.

Ed looked quickly at Dick and away again but made no comment.

"I guess in the back of my mind I've been counting right along on getting out of the Army this fall and marrying Eileen." Dick continued slowly. "Of course, I hadn't said anything definite to her. Then when this new draft law went through I went sort of haywire and telegraphed her to come out to camp. We talked a lot. . . . Eileen wanted to get married. I said I couldn't support her, and it wouldn't make sense for her to keep her job and live in New York. She said other people managed and she didn't care where she lived. She said she'd find the tent marked "Breton, D." and crawl right in. That's the way she is," he added.

Dick snubbed out his cigarette. For a time he stared off into space. Then, "I couldn't see it. We came as near fighting as we ever could come. It was after that we went to Glo and Fred's place. Glo told us what she does all day—makes coffee on the gas burner, washes out her things, goes to an early

movie—she was so surprised to find out you have to get in line
at ten-thirty in the morning—eats a thirty-five cent lunch,
takes a walk, looks in the shop windows, goes home thinking
maybe Fred will come. And she's such a nice girl, Mother,"
he said. "She has brains and background. What kind of a life
is that?" A bleak look came into Dick's nice eyes. "I couldn't
ask Eileen to live that way, not in a million years. When I
marry I want to start with a real home, no matter how small
it is, and I told her so. I want to be able to take care of my
wife."

"Sure," Ed said quietly.

"I kept on saying, 'Don't you see?' but Eileen didn't say
anything. She couldn't possibly care about me anything the
way I care about her, but you'd think I was some cold propo-
sition, acting like a stuffed shirt because I wouldn't marry her
then and there. Golly . . . girls haven't got any sense."

"A man has to take the responsibility," Ed said. "So of
course he stops and thinks."

"And now how do things stand?" I wanted to know.

"Well," Dick said impatiently, "of course everything has
more or less been called off. What could I do?"

"Then you aren't engaged to her? I mean, haven't you
asked her to wait for you?" I couldn't quite believe it.

"Of course not," Dick answered a little fretfully. "You
can't ask a girl like Eileen to tie herself up with no hope of
getting married. No one knows how long this thing will drag
out; it might be two years, it might be ten. I'm selfish, but
not that selfish." His mouth worked a little and his eyes took
on that desperate look again. "We just sort of left it in the
air," he finished.

Ed pulled at his pipe. "Well, son," he said sympathetically, "it's tough, but I think you handled it just right."

"So that's it," I said. My voice was empty. "You more or less broke it off and sort of left it up in the air."

I shut my eyes to the warm living room with its soft lights and gay colors and to the two men to whom it was home. I was picturing Eileen on the overnight train for New York, alone, looking out the window, at the stars, at the lighted towns slipping by, then seeing the dawn graying over the fields, over the Harlem tenements, seeing the darkness of the tunnel, and the big empty station, and starting back to work with nothing to cling to. It was a desolate little picture. I felt the hot tears against my eyelids.

"Oh, Dick," I said. "How could you? Will neither of you ever understand a girl?"

"What do you mean by that?" Dick asked. His tone was very short.

"Eileen came out to camp"—I tried to speak reasonably—"ready to give up her job and her apartment—anything, so she could be near you. She'd have married you and gone to Kansas or Georgia or Massa—Massachusetts." I almost stuttered in my indignation. "She'd have lived like Glo and been just as gay and just as gallant. And then all you had to say was, 'Well, sorry, but it's all off.'"

"But I couldn't let Eileen in for that—" Dick began again.

"Dick was perfectly right," Ed interrupted firmly.

"Oh, you're probably right," I told Dick. "You *are* right ... as long as things are as they are now. But, Dick—don't you see? Can't you see it, Dick? You've given Eileen nothing to pin her hopes on, nothing to hang to."

Dick looked blank. "Eileen knows how I feel about her. We have to let the future work itself out."

"Dick," I said softly, "a woman wants to be sure. She wants to be told right out in so many words. If you'd only said, 'Eileen, will you marry me the day I get my discharge from the Army?' she'd have something definite to work toward. As it was, you just walked off and wouldn't play."

"I never thought of it like that," Dick said after a long time. "Do you think that could have been why she cried so?" He suddenly looked panicky. "What had I better do, Mother?" He turned to me with a lost look, the way he used to when he came home from school, a little boy in trouble.

I said, "What has Eileen got now? She's got a man in the Army, being moved all around, goodness knows where, who loves her and who has decided not to do anything about it. What does it add up to? Nothing!"

"Do you think it would be the right thing to ask her to be definitely engaged, then?" Dick said. His face lighted up. "You know the present set-up isn't so hot for me, either. From where I sit I can see Eileen might easily meet somebody too old for the draft and just the right age to have a good job and give her everything. Don't think I haven't thought of that one," he added grimly.

"Of course you can ask her to be definitely engaged," I put in hurriedly. I was so afraid that Ed would get in first with another noble-minded comment. (Ed is noble-minded. He really is.) "You just put it up to Eileen and see what *she* says."

Dick grinned. It was the first cheerful expression I had seen on his face since he came home. "She might say 'no' after the way I've acted."

I got up and started for the stairs. I had had an inspiration. "In a way, your mother's right," I heard Ed say. "It would give you both something definite to look forward to and work for."

In my room I took down from my wall a picture of Dick in his uniform. I had just had it framed and hung—but that was not what I was after. In the wall behind it was the dial of my own little safe. I opened it and took out an old ring box of purple leather tooled in gold. I went downstairs.

"Here," I said to Dick, "this is your grandmother's engagement ring. She left it to you to be given to your bride-to-be. I thought of taking it out when you and Eileen were here that week end, but I didn't think you were sure. I think —I know, now, this is the time for you to have it."

Dick took it from me gently. He stood turning it around in his hand under the light. "I never saw it, did I? It's really a beautiful diamond. It's so very white, isn't it? I like the gold, too. It brings out the stone."

"It's an old-fashioned kind of setting"—I looked at it, thoughtfully—"but in a way, it represents what you were trying to tell Eileen. It stands for a real marriage, a home, children, roots in the ground, all the things your grandparents gave your daddy and me, the things you want to give *your* wife when the time comes."

"Can I really have it for Eileen?" he asked. "Do you think it will speak for me?"

I put my hand gently on his hard shoulder. "There are things—other things—about you that speak for you, too," I said.

Chapter 9

WITH DICK'S AFFAIRS, TEMPORARILY AT LEAST, IN A STATE of equilibrium, I turned my attention early in September to the task of getting the younger boys ready for the opening of school. There were trips to the dentist. Charles's teeth in particular were in none too good shape, and he emerged with a gold brace and a letter of instructions. "Keep brace scrupp-ou-lously clean," he read aloud. There were clothes to be bought. They wanted new straps for their books and new shoes.

Finally I got them fixed up and back to school. Next on the waiting list was Babs, headed for college. We spent evenings sewing name tapes on her underthings. I outfitted her with the tweed coat, sweaters and skirts, saddle shoes and socks, which have been college uniform ever since I can remember and probably always will be.

"Don't take anything up for your room," I advised her. "Not yet, anyway. You want to see what's there and consult your roommate. Maybe the girl who had the room before you will want to sell you her curtains, which will save you a lot of trouble."

"But don't buy the radiator from her." Ed grinned. "It comes with the room."

And so, at last, she went away to Blake, with money in her pocketbook for these expenses, and I wrote her problems off as settled.

At first she was undoubtedly excited and happy. Then,

gradually, I detected a change. I tried to tell myself it wasn't so, but I knew it was. I waited for a moment when I would have a chance to talk it over with Ed. The moment came one night at the end of dinner. We were sitting across from each other at the table. Norah had brought a big cup of coffee for him and a little one for me. Freddie and Charles had finished supper and run away to listen to a radio program dear to their hearts.

"Ed," I said, "what do you suppose is wrong with Barbara?"

Ed was peacefully tamping down the tobacco in his pipe. He stopped, the pipe in mid-air.

"Wrong?" he asked. "I thought after we got Babs safely into college we could relax."

"It's something about her letters lately," I answered slowly. "I can read between the lines. I—well—I'm sure something is preying on her mind."

"What, for instance?"

"That's it. I don't know," I answered, slowly. "There could be so many things. Every now and then you hear about some youngster being so worried she has a nervous collapse."

"That doesn't sound like Babs to me." Ed smiled and reached his hand across the table for mine. "Aren't you imagining all this? The kids are always on your mind. It would do you good to forget them once in a while."

I had tried that. You know how it is with something you don't want to think about. In the daytime you can put it from you, but during the night it comes back. I had been waking in the gray morning, turning over Babs's life uncomfortably in my thoughts like a child trying to fit a block in a space where it won't go. I knew there was something that she did not wish or did not dare to tell me.

"Maybe she finds the work too hard," Ed said presently.

"Or it could be Vic," I answered. "He's so much older; I'm always so afraid he won't realize how young she is. He must know a lot of other girls, and Babs could be hurt very easily."

"Maybe she's carrying the torch for somebody else by this time," Ed said hopefully.

"Perhaps," I answered, "but I don't think so."

"Why don't you call her up?" Ed asked. "Tell her we'll drive up to see her Saturday. We may as well get the facts on this, if only to set your mind at rest."

I went to the phone, and presently a small clear voice was saying, "Barbara is out, Mrs. Breton. This is Patty." Patty was Babs's roommate. "No, I don't know just where she is, but I'm so glad you're coming up. You know, Mrs. Breton, I think she's very worried. She has awful nightmares..."

I put down the receiver. "She *is* frightened about something," I turned to Ed. "It may be all imaginary, of course. I remember once, freshman year, I thought I was dying of some incurable disease and I nearly went crazy with anxiety. On the other hand, it could be something very real." Ed looked troubled. "She needs us, dear. I'm glad we're going to her."

I'm always excited driving over the last mile to Blake. First you see the chapel spire above the maples and then the college itself, the familiar granite buildings interspersed with others, new since our time, of pink brick with white trim, put up in the boom years to accommodate the increasing number of students. There is a kind of integrity about it all. Youngsters couldn't have a better place to be, I told myself, with the outside world the way it was in the year 1941.

Kenwood, the freshman hall where Babs lived, was a frame house at the edge of the campus. Its western windows looked out over a graveyard. We turned into the drive, Ed honked the horn, and I leaned out expectantly, waiting to see Babs flying down the steps with that eager way that always quickened the tempo of living. Instead, a little gray-haired woman with a shy smile and faded eyes came down to welcome us.

"The girls are at class, but they'll be home for lunch. I'm in charge of the hall," she added, "and I hope you'll stay and have something with us."

I thanked her, trying to conceal my disappointment. "I am Mrs. Breton and this is my husband. We drove up because we thought Barbara seemed a little upset and below par," I explained. "I wonder if you've noticed anything . . ."

The little woman's face grew immediately serious. "I think she *has* been looking a little overtired," she replied. "I sent her to the nurse last week. The Hygiene Department will have a record of it."

"We'll just run over and take a look at that record," Ed said. "Nothing else has happened to Barbara, has it?"

The woman hesitated for a fraction of a second. "Well"— her manner was unwilling—"during the past week a young man I've never seen before has come here several times and asked for Barbara. He didn't look like a college boy or anyone who'd be a friend of your daughter's. He wouldn't give his name and several times he hung around until I asked him to leave."

Ed looked thoughtful. "I guess you try to take pretty good care of them," he volunteered.

The little woman flushed. "I love the girls," she said, simply.

The Hygiene Department was more elaborate than in Ed's and my day. It was housed in the gym. The instructor said, "My impression of your daughter is that she came to us in excellent health." She turned to a steel file cabinet and took out a card. "She was in to see the nurse last week, it seems." A little V formed above the bridge of her nose. "She *has* lost weight. We never like that." She shut the drawer and put the card on the desk. "We'll send for her the first thing Monday morning," she said "and give her a thorough re-examination."

We went out and got into the car again. "We might as well go over to the office and check up on her work while we're at it," was Ed's idea. We drove slowly between students sauntering from building to building. It came back to me how I used to feel walking along that very path past the syringa bushes, with Ed coming the other way headed for his class. A line from one of Synge's plays always went through my mind, "Himself, drawing nearer all the time, like the stars of God." And the bleak feeling when, sometimes, he did not come.

"I was just remembering how miserable I was until I was sure you loved me," I smiled at my husband. "It's awfully hard to be young."

"Think so?" Ed asked. His eyes followed a girl and man in soft sport clothes. They were hatless. The girl's hair was very bright. "I'll say it's hard to be old."

"But we have our home and the children and each other," I answered. "There's no uncertainty in our life, now, the way there was then."

"No?" Ed asked, "then what are we up here for? You're

just a dear little dumbbell, but you always were." He stopped
the car. We were in front of the old building in the center
of the campus.

We got out and went inside. To the right was a big oak
door with black letters reading, "Office of the President." A
middle-aged woman was standing at a high, narrow window,
watering a plant. We introduced ourselves. She looked sharply
at Ed. "Ed Breton?" she beamed. "My goodness, I used to
admire you when I first came here to be the president's secre-
tary twenty-odd years ago. I suppose you knew the old Doctor
died. Well, President Hood will be glad to see you." She
went into an inner room. The president came out. He was a
large man, a little flabby. His face, in repose, was like that of
a big child, marked by a somewhat anxious expression. As he
advanced toward us, however, he smiled genially.

"We've been a little concerned about our daughter, Barbara
Breton," Ed explained. "She isn't sleeping well and she *has*
lost weight. We thought she might be worried about her
work."

"Miss Breton?" The president was plainly searching his
memory. "She has an alumnae scholarship, hasn't she? We
watch our scholarship holders very closely. I'm sure if she
had fallen behind, her instructors would have let me know."

"It might not be her work," I ventured.

The president followed me or thought he did. "We try to
amalgamate the freshmen into the life of the school as soon as
possible," he said. "But we have misfits. Of course we'd like
to have a resident psychiatrist as the state universities do. It
will come," he added, rather ponderously, "it will come."

Ed and I exchanged glances. "Oh, I don't think that Barbara is a misfit." I spoke with conviction. "She's—she's very normal."

The president smiled sympathetically. "I'll see that she's called to the attention of the Big Sister Committee." He was used to parents. "That's our set-up for handling a situation like this." He took out a notebook and wrote Barbara's name down. "I'll have them look in on her first thing Monday. Now I want you to meet our Dean of Women." He placed a fatherly hand on Ed's shoulder and propelled us down the hall.

The Dean was a big, ambling woman with a matter-of-fact manner. She practically dismissed the president with a nod, took us at once into the inner office, and shut the door.

"Barbara Breton?" she asked, studying us with peering, kindly eyes through heavy lenses. "Are you sure you're not just imagining things? Sometimes parents are more of a problem than the girls," she added with a smile so warm it took the sting out of her words. "I'll make an opportunity to see her on Monday, but offhand I should say that Barbara was one of the best adjusted girls on the campus."

"I congratulate you on knowing your students so well." I meant it.

She gave me a quick glance. "That's my business," she answered briefly.

"Then I don't think it will be necessary for President Hood to turn the Big Sisters loose on her," Ed put in.

"Oh, is he going to do that?" The Dean laughed delightedly. "Well, if he is, you can't stop him. The Big Sister and Big Brother Committees are his pet projects. Good thing, too," she added. "Especially for the older students, makes 'em feel they have a real responsibility for the younger ones. Barbara can handle them." Without our realizing it she had been showing us to the door. Just briefly, her friendly face grew stern. "Don't think I minimize the possibility of something serious happening here which might even involve your daughter. People who watch over the young are sitting on dynamite day and night. But," she added, her face relaxing, "I hope you'll find it's nothing this time."

We rolled slowly down the tar road. Suddenly there was a shout. Arms flying, Babs was running pell-mell toward us, behind her a smaller girl with a mop of blond hair who must be Patty.

"Oh, Daddy! Oh, Daddy! Moms, this is Patty. How about a lift to Ken?" They both got into the back seat. I turned around and studied Babs. Her coral sweater warmed her face, but she was thinner and there were hollows under her cheek bones. It wasn't like her not to meet my eyes, and as I watched her she looked the other way.

Ed wanted to take them out to lunch, but I knew their house mother expected us there, so we went in and met the girls and were ushered to the table. Ed forgot about grace and said, "Oh," apologetically, as he realized he was talking into a hush. The lunch consisted of tomato juice, slices of pineapple on lettuce with little mounds of cottage cheese, hot rolls and a choice of tea or cocoa. I saw Ed, who is a ham and eggs man, watching hopefully for coffee. I avoided his eye. Barbara sat near the window. Every now and then I noticed that she glanced out as if watching for someone. Once when a man came up on the porch she started to rise, dropping her napkin. But she sank back when she saw that it was the boy with the newspaper. The girls made a great fuss over Ed. They had found out that he used to be the head of the house in his fraternity and it was plain that they intended to go there later with him.

As soon as lunch was over he filled up the car with them and drove off while I went up with Babs and Patty. Their room, they said, was simply palatial, as they showed me the curtains and the armchair they had bought from the Students' Exchange. And then I had to see the view to the west, the low stone wall, and the graveyard.

"It's a great place for late dating," Patty said. "First off, when we used to hear noises there at night, we thought it was the dead. But it wasn't. It was just some man and girl getting over the wall."

"Speaking of dates," I asked, "has Vic been up?"

Barbara did not look at me. "A couple of times." Then, after a perceptible pause, she added, "I wrote you."

"Isn't he the dream man?" Patty broke in. "How I could go for him!"

At the moment I wished she would go—anywhere, and give me a chance to talk with Babs alone. Had Vic thrown her over? Who was this boy who kept trying to see her and why wouldn't he give his name? I realized almost for the first time that there might be things in life one could not fix for one's children, things they must face alone. I felt an ache like hunger around my heart. As Patty chattered on, I tried to concentrate on what she was saying. Suddenly Babs said, "I'll be back," and slipped out of the room before I could do anything about it. "It's just that she talks in her sleep all the time lately," Patty went on in a hushed voice. "She rattles on and on about the fifteenth and Vic, and she dreams about people that are coming to get her and wakes up scared and wants to know if I'm awake. I'll say I am," she added emphatically.

I tried to get more out of Patty, but that was all that she knew or all she would tell me. I couldn't help it. A sudden feeling of panic came over me. Of one thing I was now sure; something was definitely wrong and it was serious. I knew that because Babs always confided little troubles in either Ed or me. I got up. I wanted to find Ed. Ed would somehow know how to handle this no matter how bad it was.

"You're coming back, aren't you, Mrs. Breton?" Patty said. "We're having some of the girls in. Babs and I are giving a tea for you and Mr. Breton."

I told Patty that of course I'd be back, and left, only half conscious of Patty busily getting out the teaballs, lemon, crackers, and jelly which were to provide the refreshment. I didn't know where I'd find Ed. I had a notion that he might be at his fraternity house on the north side of the campus, but I discovered him studying with interest a tall cypress that was his class tree. At Blake, every graduating class plants a tree on the campus. I suppose they do that in other colleges, too.

"How that thing's grown!" Ed said, looking up at the cypress.

"I'm frightened," I told him. "Something's very wrong with Babs. It isn't like her to have nightmares. It isn't like her to keep anything from us, and she *is*."

Ed rubbed a hand across his chin. There was an odd look in his eyes. He started to say something, then stopped.

"You've seen her," I said, "you've seen Babs and she's told you."

Ed nodded.

"Is it about Vic?" I asked. "Did Vic hurt her? Or is it somebody else?"

"It's about Vic," Ed said slowly.

"What happened?" My two words seemed just like one.

"Well—" Ed began, then stopped again.

Across the campus came Babs's clear voice, "Hi there!" The next instant she was right between Ed and me not waiting for either of us to say anything. She had a small box wrapped up in tissue paper in her hand and was tearing off the paper. There was a lovely cigarette case inside the box which she held up in front of me. Vic's monogram was engraved on the case. "Isn't it simply gorgeous?" she exclaimed, bouncing up and down. "Don't you think he'll love it, Moms?"

I know I must have looked dazed. I said something, I can't remember what. I don't think it mattered much to Babs, anyway. She was too happy. She flung her arms around Ed and hugged him. Ed grinned at me over her shoulder. Babs let go of Ed. "I've got to go now," she said, "and help Patty. Come on over as soon as you get through sentimentalizing over your old tree."

I looked into Babs's eyes. I'd never seen her face so radiant, her eyes so shiny.

"Oh, Daddy," she said, "now I haven't a care in the world." And then she was off.

It took me a while to recover my powers of speech. The relief was almost harder to bear than the strain had been. "What happened?" I finally managed. "What was wrong?"

"Well," Ed said, with tantalizing slowness, "it was a matter of finance—the sort of a thing that only the old man could straighten out." He put his arm through mine and started to walk with me toward Kenwood Hall. "It seems," he continued, his eyes twinkling, "that Vic's birthday is on the fifteenth. You know, in addition to her regular allowance you had given Babs twenty-five dollars for incidental expenses, furnishing her room and so on. Twenty-five dollars is a lot of money to a kid that's never had more than two or three dollars in her purse at one time."

Ed never irritates me, but he came as close to it then as he ever did. He was so slow with his explanation.

"Babs saw that cigarette case and her heart was set on giving it to Vic for his birthday. It cost twenty dollars and she paid ten down. In the meantime the college clamped down on her for some books and things, and when it came down to paying the other ten dollars she didn't have it. Knowing the way things are she didn't like to ask us for it, and next thing she knew, the store began sending a collector around. She was frightened to death." Ed tightened his hold on my arm. "It wasn't silly," he said gently. "Look at how scared we've been all day."

I stopped walking. Ed stopped, too. "What's the matter?"

"I was just thinking, Ed," I said—my voice wasn't very steady—"I was just thinking that half the world is fighting —men swept by hatred and bitterness are dying everywhere. I suppose one ought to think of that. But I don't care. When I saw Babs standing there, her eyes shining, saying, 'I haven't a care in the world,' well . . . right now I haven't a care in the world, either!"

Chapter 10

I'D ALWAYS THOUGHT OUR CHILDREN WERE PRETTY NICE people. That went for Dick, Babs, Freddie, and Charles, too, who was almost one of our own now. Perhaps, I told myself, the weather is getting the better of me; the raw November days were hard to take. Whatever it was, they'd seemed like different kinds of youngsters, selfish, thoughtless, indeed, in the case of the younger boys, almost brutal. It was as if, having undertaken the job of making them gentle and considerate, I'd found out I'd flunked miserably on the whole assignment.

Take Dick, for instance. Dick had never forgotten an important occasion in the family before. Yet when we celebrated our wedding anniversary that year, we didn't hear from him. All that morning I looked for a letter. By afternoon I was watching for a telegram. In the evening I listened for a phone call. None came. Ed had merely laughed and said, "What's he got to do with our anniversary, anyway?" But I was definitely hurt.

I was mulling this over in my mind as I edged my way home, through a sleety rain, from the Red Cross rooms where I'd been rolling bandages. As I turned into our street I met Norah, outward bound on her day off. I backed into the rain which came down slanting and relentless like the undercut of a whip, beating Norah's gray coat around her sturdy figure.

"You're late getting out," I said. "It's half-past four."

She looked at me with serious eyes, sea-blue like the brim

of her hat. "The boys is home from school and up to some deviltry," she answered. "I didn't want to leave the house alone with them."

I told her to run along and felt her pass like strength going from me. I buffeted my way alone toward the refuge of the porch. It was then that I met Melissa. Melissa is our big black cat. Ordinarily mad dogs wouldn't have forced her out into weather like this. Yet as I lifted my head she came sideways through the window, dove drunkenly into the barberry hedge, and vanished, a dark streak, into the wind-swept garden.

I knew it was useless to try to get her, so I went into the house. A queer, strong odor filled the hall. From somewhere above came a thumping noise, as if a big dog were flailing the floor with his tail. I hurried toward the stairs. Charles's voice came down to me from the bathroom. It sounded tight and high. "You killed Melissa, that's what you did," I heard him sob. There was a succession of thuds.

"Boys, boys!" I ran for the bathroom. I could see Freddie driving his fist crazily into the air and Charles struggling up from the floor. As I reached the door he squirmed past me, head bent, but not so low that I could not see a red welt across his white cheek. "You just wait till I'm bigger," he shouted. He ducked under my arm, fled to his room, and slammed the door. I could hear his gasping sobs.

I turned on Freddie in a sort of rage. The rotten egg odor was almost overwhelming. A litter of test tubes and colored powders lay scattered about. I recognized them as part of Charlie's chemistry equipment. In the tub an overturned wastebasket rested in a welter of towels over which Melissa had evidently clawed her way to freedom. "Now, Freddie," I began almost choking.

"Aw, Moms," Freddie was sulky but, unlike Charlie, he was coherent. "I didn't hurt old Meliss'. I was just trying to see if I could bleach her hair. Aw, gee, you gotta do experiments in chemistry. Gee!"

"Freddie," I said, "go to your room and stay there. It isn't Melissa I'm worrying about." Nor was it. Freddie and Melissa have always treated each other like equals, and I was unsentimentally sure that Meliss' could take care of herself. "It's Charlie. He's . . . he's sort of a guest, and anyway he's shorter than you are. How *could* you hit him? Go right to your room and stay there."

"Aw, gee," Freddie began. "I can't go now. Not right now. I gotta feed my rabbits. I *gotta*." He went out and down the stairs like coal sliding over a chute. I followed hot after him. I was determined to have this out with him then and there.

At the foot of the stairs I was stopped by the ring of the doorbell. It was the postman. "I guess you'll be glad to get this, Mrs. Breton," he said, "I think it's from your daughter." I tore open the special delivery letter. There was to be a dance Saturday night, Babs wrote, and when Norah went out could she mail Babs's yellow evening dress? And could somebody please press it and see that it was all in perfect order? Because Babs would get home just in time to put it on. Home from what or where, she did not say.

Well, I told myself, that was to be my little job. Norah was gone, the boys had their homework to do, and I certainly wouldn't ask Ed to go out later in all that rain. *I* would have to go, of course. I found the dress, plugged in the electric iron, and set to work. There were dust marks on the hem and, oddly, I noticed a bunch of burrs which I removed rather thoughtfully. At the end of half an hour or so I had the dress pressed and packed in tissue. I went into the living room to write the label for the parcel, and just then Ed came home.

It's a funny thing about Ed. Over all these years—that anniversary was our twenty-third—I've never failed to have a sense of mounting excitement when the front door opens at five or six o'clock. I listen. Is it really Ed? If it is, everything seems safe and secure. There are no loose strings, no untied ends in my mind. Only this time I felt no relief; rather, that I must make him worry with me.

I told him about the boys.

"But, dear," he said, "all kids fight. What we ought to do is to get 'em some boxing gloves and a set of the Marquis of Queensberry rules."

"How can you be so casual?" I burst out. "And that reminds me," I went on querulously, "Dick hasn't taken time even to drop me a postcard."

"Dick was never much on writing." Ed shifted the subject. "What's the parcel?"

"It's Babs's dress. It seems she can't wear any of the three she has up there because George has seen them all; so *I've* got to go out and mail it."

"You're just making a martyr of yourself," Ed's voice had an edge to it. "You're not going out to the post office in all this rain. And neither am I," he added firmly.

Suddenly I began to cry. "They're all so inconsiderate! I don't know what's happened to them."

Ed looked at me a moment in silence. "What's the matter with you, tonight?" he asked. "Usually you're the one that finds excuses for the kids." Then, as I went on crying, "Have you got that pain again?"

I nodded.

"Get your hat and coat," he ordered. "I'm going to take you over to the doctor right now. You're no use to us this way," he urged when I did not move. "And you know everyone around here depends on you."

Well, once you see a surgeon and there's anything to be done, things move very fast. The doctor looked at me across his desk with grave, unyoung eyes as if measuring my ability to withstand shock. "It might be serious," he said. "It might not; but we must be ready." He would operate on me at the hospital on Saturday morning. Ed and I went home holding hands like frightened children.

Ed was far more worried than I was, about serious things, that is. I was worried too, largely, however, about the family. If Freddie and Charles fought as they did when I was at home what would they do when the lid was off? How would Babs manage with no one to understand the importance of things like parties and evening dresses? And was I to go under ether simply forgotten by Dick?

"I still can't see why he hasn't phoned," I complained, once we were home again. "And do you think if I did mail that dress tomorrow morning it would possibly get there on time?"

We were sitting at home in the living room. Ed gazed at me fixedly. A queer smile twisted his face. He said, "Let's forget the children for now."

And then before I could realize it, the operation was hours in the past and I was lying in a fog while Ed, leaning above

me, told me over and over again that everything was going
to be all right. I had gone a long, long way, to a region that
was very, very cold and I had gone there all alone.

I hadn't been afraid to go. Ed had stood beside me holding
my hand as I was sinking off into space. I had held on tight.
Absurdly, I had seen the unmailed evening gown lying on
the desk, then Freddie's face as he lunged at Charles, and
there was something about Dick, Dick.... Now I was
lying in a green-walled room. The light was softly shaded,
but I could see Ed standing at the foot of the bed behind a
narrow table with roses on either side of him. That was
comforting. Then some load settled heavily on my conscious-
ness. What was it I had been thinking? Oh, yes, the children.
What was it that had been wrong, that I had been afraid of,
before they put me to sleep?

I moved my head. The person sitting beside me was Dick.
His arms were resting on the edge of the bed and both his
hands were holding one of mine.

"You scared us 'most to death. I just barely got here. We
were off on maneuvers for ten days; I only got back last
night," he explained.

"So that's why you didn't call up." I turned my head toward
him.

"Sure, we were miles from everything. You didn't think I'd
forget your wedding anniversary, did you?" It wasn't a question, it was a statement. Dick had trusted me to understand
there would have been a good reason.

Ed opened his mouth to speak but closed it instead and took
a turn around the room. I followed him with my eyes and for
the first time noticed Babs. She was sitting on the floor near
the window, knitting.

"Babs," I said weakly, "isn't this Saturday night? What about the dance at college?"

Babs put her knitting down on her knees. The bright yarn fell between her feet stretched out in front of her. "Oh, that," she said. "As if that mattered." She leaned forward and looked up at me, her face an anxious glow. "Feel all right now?" she asked.

"I feel fine," I told her. "Where did all those beautiful roses come from?"

Babs picked up her knitting with a pleased smile. "George sent them. He picked them all out himself."

I lay looking at her. There's nobody like her, I thought. She's so comforting. She just sits and knits and loves you.

At this moment the door was pushed timidly open. I saw a familiar gray coat and blue hat and Norah came in. Close behind her, like a couple of puppies running to heel, were Charles and Freddie.

"How do you feel now, Moms?" Freddie asked. Then, "Lookit, we brought you sumpin'."

Norah laid a large box on the foot of the bed and removed the cover. "It was all with their own money," she said. "Like somethin' the boys and I seen on Joan Crawford in the pictures." She brushed aside the rustling tissue and took out a baby blue bed jacket edged with down.

"Like it, really?" Charles asked anxiously. He stroked it tenderly, as if it were a little bird.

"I thought you'd rather have bathroom scales." Freddie's statement was really a question.

"This is just what I wanted," I assured him. I could feel my eyes blurring. Freddie and Charles had been promised a pup as soon as it was old enough to leave its mother—and as soon as they had five dollars. They'd earned some of it. Some they had made on the bottle "concession," which meant they returned the empty bottles and kept the deposits. Norah had a word to say about this later. It seems when they were ready to buy the bed jacket, they were still short one dollar. After pondering the shortage, they had found a way to make up the difference. What they did was simply to squirt the seltzer out of the fresh bottles in the pantry so they would be empty and returnable.

"Poor Mr. Breton, and him coming from the hospital, wanting his drink, and not a bit of seltzer in the house," Norah finished, torn between disapproval and laughter.

Ed saw I was too weak to show all the appreciation I felt. He took the bed jacket and tucked it back to under my chin. Then he stepped off and gazed admiringly at the effect.

"What do you think of yourself now, Mrs. B?" he asked.

I looked up at him. His face had strange lines in it. They must have been put there by twenty-four hours of keeping watch. But his eyes were familiar and shining. I looked around at these utterly darling people who were my family.

"I think I'm in luck," I said.

"Gee, Mom, wh

anxiously.

"I'm sleepy," I a

"Oh, is that all?"

Charlie, come on. C

the back page of the

"Sure." I settled

"It's pretty bloo

Charlie, shoot."

Charles hooked h

the paper in his han

" 'Mr. Grimsby—

up here. Oh, yes. 'N

gloomy mansion wit

dear," he said to a

wool wrapper knitt

" ' "Why no, my

lady who was none

" ' "Well, then,

" 'Mr. Grimsby

sion down to the f

Lying right there

next to the coal sh

dered.

" ' "Come here,

" 'This mystery

removed and the p

of a man or a woma

tery,' " Charles fi

"Do you think

face intently.

Chapter 11

I DOUBT IF FREDDIE WILL EVER MAKE A REAL NEWSPAPER-man. To do that you've got to put your paper ahead of your heart, and that's just what Freddie, even at twelve, can't do.

It all began as a business venture of Bingo Berry's. Ed and I and the children were eating our Sunday dinner. Ed had just finished telling them that when he was little he thought chicken meat was all neck because, being the smallest one in a big family, it was all he ever got, when Bingo came. Bingo is a sharp-boned boy with black insect eyes who invariably arrived on the back porch on Sunday while we were still at the table and stood, quite undeterred by weather, looking in through the glass at us as if we were inmates of the Zoo.

"Come in, Bingo," I called. "Norah, I'll need another dessert plate."

Bingo entered and drew up a chair a little back of Freddie. "Have some ice cream," I said. "There's chocolate sauce."

"Okay," he said condescendingly. He did not even look at Ed or me. "Say, you kids want to be on a paper?"

"What sort of a paper?" I asked. "Is it school work?"

Bingo favored me with a hot, disdainful glance. "Naw. It's a weekly, five cents the copy." He looked sideways at Ed. "It's going to be called 'The Flash.' You kids kin be reporters," he told Charles and Freddie.

Ed filled his pipe and tamped it down. "We used to get out a paper," he said, "when I was in grammar school. To sell it, you need one good story, something that has human

"It's just horrible," I answered, "and I believe you boys *like* people's heads being cut off. You're—you're terrible."

"I guess that'll make people want to buy 'The Flash.'" Freddie relaxed, satisfied.

For the next few days I forgot about the paper. Babs's beau, George, had offered to drive her home from college on Saturday afternoon and take her back Sunday, preliminary to putting up the car. "Giving up the old ice wagon is my part in the defense program at present," he had said, cheerfully, "but we might as well give the old tires a last whirl."

I was at home alone when they arrived. Norah had made some cookies with little nuggets of sweet chocolate in them, and we had the usual array of dark drinks in small bottles accompanied by straws on a tray in the living room.

"Oh, Mother, cookies!" Babs sounded as if she lived on bread and water at college.

"I dream about those," George added.

They sat down at right angles to each other. Suddenly I had a curious feeling that they were a little team, those two. Babs had always been either so frankly casual or so frankly adoring of men before, that the previous boys had impressed me as just part of the furniture of life, useful in growing up. But George—well, I didn't know. Their easy, uncasual manner together struck me. They are perfectly at home with each other, I thought, as people are who really love each other very much and equally well.

"George," I asked suddenly, "what are you going to do after you graduate?"

"I don't know. I'm headed for medical school, but maybe I'll try to get into the flying corps." George's young face was serious.

Freddie's head appeared unexpectedly over the rim of a

armchair. "Hey, can we put that in the paper?" he demanded.

George's blue eyes danced. "Publicity, eh? Not this time, buddy."

"It's one we're getting out," Freddie explained. "It's called 'The Flash.' Want to hear the news items so far?" He consulted a scrap of paper.

"Sure. Spill it," Babs told him.

"'The popular Miss Norah O'Toole of 112 Elm Street will go to the St. Patrick's Day dance at Erin Hall with Mr. Michael Shaughnessy, well known motorman on the Main Street Line. They won a prize last year.

Mrs. Edward Breton of 112 Elm Street, who takes the First Aid course, has learned how to cut off a jugular vein.

Mr. Edward Breton of 112 Elm Street has been appointed air raid warden. Call him when puzzled.

Baby carriages and bicycles repaired at 112 Elm Street. Ten cents a wheel.'"

"Hey," George said, "where are you going to put 'em?"

"In our yard," Freddie announced. "That's an advertisement," he added, hastily penciling something on the sheet.

"Not in *our* yard, you're not," I said.

Freddie studied my expression as if it were the weather, without a trace of resentment. Then, "Okay," he said, "I'll take it out, but we *could*-a made a lot of dough."

Well, we had fun and the paper again slipped from my mind. We took in the movies, Babs and George insisting that we all go with them. When we got home, I shooed the boys directly off to bed, or so I thought, and even got Ed upstairs, which was a little more difficult. Ed loves to sit around with the youngsters and doesn't seem quite to grasp the idea that

George doesn't come expressly to see him. He told me once, "His face lights up when I come into the room. He likes another man around." But I got him upstairs at last.

The next day went all too fast and the late afternoon came and Babs and George were gone. It was then I found Freddie industriously picking out something on the old typewriter which he had dragged in front of the window seat.

"More news?" I was just trying to be friendly.

"Oh, boy, I'll say so. Listen, Mom," he looked up darkly, "I think Babs and George are going to get married."

I must confess I jumped.

"Freddie," I said sharply, "how do you know anything about Babs's affairs?"

"Well, gee, Mom, we needed some news that was a surprise," he said. "I thought George was getting goofy over Babs so last night I came down and sat on the stairs and I saw him kiss Babs good night."

"Well?" I asked.

"Well, Mom, isn't he going to marry her? He kissed her, didn't he?" Freddie said, indignantly.

I stood looking at Freddie. His honest little face was turned up toward me inquiringly. It wouldn't do to seem cynical. But it wouldn't do to let him go ahead and spread his conclusions either.

"Freddie," I said, "in the first place you were a perfect scrounge to listen, and in the second place if they are engaged, we've got to wait for them to tell us."

Freddie gave the typewriter a shove. "Oh, heck." He went off.

Next day "The Flash" came out, complete with ads, The Grimsby Murder Mystery, a Pet Column, and Newsy Items, but with nothing about affairs of the heart. It was an immediate financial success. Bingo had a dollar and a half in paid-up ads and Freddie had ninety cents from the sale of the issue. But I knew somehow that in killing the "human interest" news I had robbed the copy of some of its dreamed-of punch.

For the next few days all that Freddie and even Charles, in his quiet way, ever talked about was the paper. They had great plans for the next issue. To what they were running they were going to add a crossword puzzle contest, the prize to be a year's subscription to "The Flash." Ed listened, his face straight.

Bingo said, "What we really need is a scoop, something special that will make everybody in town sit up and take notice."

I could never quite make up my mind whether or not I liked Bingo, but I couldn't help admiring his drive, his untiring determination, and when, three nights later, he came in quivering with excitement, I was more conscious than ever of the fierceness in him. He took time out to say "Hello," to Ed and me very briefly, then beckoned Freddie and Charles to join him on the couch. After that there was much whispering.

Ed sat there smoking his pipe placidly and reading his paper while I was busy with the boys' socks. I did glance up once when I heard Bingo's voice rise, saying, "It's the biggest thing—a real scoop. We've got to get out an extra edition, an *extra,*" and then his voice fell. It struck me that there was excitement in Bingo's eyes, in his voice, but that somehow it hadn't communicated itself to Freddie. After a minute or two he got up from the couch and went out of the room.

For some time Bingo and Charles sat there, not saying anything to each other. Charles was very reserved, not the sort of a boy to take much to Bingo, and I think that Bingo considered Charles hardly worth noticing. More minutes went by in silence.

Ed looked up from his paper restively. When the boys raise a rumpus he doesn't mind at all, but when they're quiet it sets him to wondering.

Bingo said, "What's keeping Freddie? We've got to get to work on the paper."

"I'll see," Ed said. He started to get up from his chair.

"I'll call him." I don't know why I didn't simply go to the foot of the stairs and call him. Instead, I went up to his room. Freddie was sitting on the bed with a look in his eyes that I had never seen before, a funny, distant look as though he were confronted by something that was beyond his experience. "What's the matter, Freddie?"

"Nothing, Mom, nothing. It's just—"

With Bingo downstairs, it was perfectly natural for me to assume that whatever troubled Freddie came from their recent conversation.

"What is it, Freddie? Has it something to do with the paper?"

"Sort of," Freddie said, dully. "Bingo wants to get out a special edition, an extra. He's got—he's got a great headline. It's—" Freddie gulped a little. "It's—HAROLD MORRISON IS DYING."

I said, "Oh," and then I couldn't think for the moment of anything else to say.

Freddie said in that same unhappy tone, "You know Harold Morrison, don't you, Mom?"

I sat down on the bed beside Freddie and put my arm around his shoulder. Yes, I knew Harold Morrison by sight and I knew that Freddie and his friends didn't like Harold.

Nobody liked Harold. It was hard to say why. Perhaps it was the way he looked. His hair was thin and silky; his clothes were too nice. Perhaps it was because he insisted on sticking around when he wasn't wanted. Perhaps it was because his manner was too domineering, too unco-operative.

"I'm sorry about Harold." I knew it was inadequate.

"It would make a great headline," Freddie said. "Harold—I guess Harold's father is about the biggest and most important man in town. Only—"

I held him tighter. "What, dear?"

After a while Freddie said, "A couple of days ago some of us went down to Miller's Pond. We didn't want Harold to come, but he tagged along. There were some kids down by the pond, Mom, chasing an old stray cat, throwing sticks at it and rocks. It got hit in the back and it couldn't steer itself and it fell into the pond. Charles and I and the other kids just stood there feeling kind of sick, not doing anything. Only Harold—he yanked off his coat and jumped into the pond after the cat." Freddie fell silent for a moment, then, "That pond is deep, Mom, and Harold can't swim so good, the way Charles and I can. But he got the cat out. That's how it was," Freddie went on, "and Bingo went over to Harold's house tonight to get a personal interview about how he saved the cat, only he didn't get it. The butler told Bingo that Harold was in the hospital with pneumonia because the water was so cold, and—" Freddie's voice suddenly choked up and he stopped. After long, long seconds his head dropped to my shoulder and it came with a rush:

"Mom, I don't want a headline for 'The Flash.' I just want—I just want Harold to get well." He cried as if his heart would break.

Chapter 12

Y OU WORRY," ED SAID. "AND IF THERE'S NOTHING TO WORRY about, you start something. You say yes instead of no to the children, and then when they get into deep water you come running to me for help." In the meantime, according to him, they had been perfectly safe and all the uproar had been over nothing.

But had it? Often, I would watch Freddie whizzing home on roller skates. True, he'd miss a car on one side and a truck thundering down on the other. But both were there. He really was in danger. I knew it and my heart had been tearing along like a sewing machine. Ed was exactly the same, especially where Babs was concerned, but of course, he would never admit it. He always pretended I'd been fussing about nothing.

To get back to where we were when we started talking about my fears, Babs was at home for the Christmas holidays. She had gone up after dinner to take a shower. The first thing college life had done, apparently, was to upset the routine which at home meant baths before meals, not after. Ed and I were due at the Smiths' for an evening of bridge. We were in our room getting ready to start. Ed was studying the angle of his jaw in the mirror and I was at my dressing table giving my hair a final upward pat. Babs appeared at the door wrapped in a tufted bathrobe with a scarlet border.

"Mind if I come in?" she asked, sociably. She plumped down on my bed and drew up her feet in front of her. It was clear that she considered Ed and me practically as roommates.

She began, " 'Member George, Patty's brother? He's a sophomore at the University and an awfully important man on campus. Well, hold your breath. He's asked me there for the dance next Friday night. Isn't that *superb?*" she added hurriedly.

Ed stopped studying his jaw and caught my eye in the mirror. His look was not encouraging.

Babs hugged her knees firmly. "There isn't a single reason why I shouldn't go," she said.

I considered saying she was too young and rejected the idea. After all, she must grow up some time. "It's an expensive trip." I did not look at her. "It must be three or four hours by train."

"If that isn't just like this family." Babs sat up, stiffly. "All they ever think about is money. All right, I'll pay for it myself."

Ed went by and gave her a pat on the head. I knew he was thinking, With what? but all he said was, "Come on, Moms, we're late now. I'll get the car and you be ready."

Babs came over and sat on the floor, looking into my face. "You're awfully pretty," she said. "What I could do with your profile and my brains! Listen, Moms, I could borrow it from you and pay it back out of my allowance. I've just got to go. He's the most adorable man."

"Who, Vic?" I asked, teasing her. I knew Vic hadn't been in the foreground recently.

"No, George," she said earnestly. "Oh, dear, I fell for that one. But George is really more my type. Vic is kind of a worn-out shell of a man," she went on. I digested this. Vic is all of twenty-two or three. "George and I like the same things;

we're both crazy about skiing and rhumbaing and malted milks. Oh, Moms, I just *depend* on you."

"I'll see what can be done," I promised.

Ed and I talked about it all the way to the Smiths'. "My first impulse was to say she couldn't go," I told Ed. "It was hearing her talk about George that made me change my mind. Really, I'd like to see Babs interested in someone nearer her own age than Vic."

"True." Ed paused. Then, "I don't want to seem mean about it, but it's just after Christmas, you know, and the kids got their share. What's more," he went on, seriously, "we're in a war now; in what may be a long one. I somehow don't feel that in these times it's right to throw away a lot of money on parties even if we had it, which we haven't."

"I agree with you," I said. "It's only that Babs is just the right age for that kind of fun. We had it, you know; don't try to tell me we didn't."

"It was different then," Ed answered slowly. "At least that's the way it seems to me."

So, next morning, I told her we'd decided against it and why.

Babs stared at me with great tragic eyes. "You mean I can't go?" she asked. She sat very still, thinking hard. Then, "Don't say no, not yet." She rushed out of the room and a few minutes later out of the house.

At noon she came flying in and threw both arms around me.

"Guess what!" she began. "Ben Gunther and another boy are driving there and they're going to take me. Isn't that wonderful?"

"Who's Ben Gunther?" I asked. "I don't know him."

"Oh, Mother, yes you *do*. At least, I don't know him,

either, but you know who he *is*. I had his father in Math at high school. Ben graduated a year ago, and he and another man are going back stag. They're *perfectly* nice boys. So can I telegraph George?"

"I don't know," I started. "I'll have to see—"

"Oh, Mother, you're so *vague*," Babs said. "Ben is going to call you up. He'd be terribly hurt and surprised if you said no after all the trouble I went to to get somebody to put the idea of his taking me into his head. You can't refuse now." The phone rang. "That's probably him."

It was. A pleasant masculine voice came over the wire. "I'll drop by on my way home tonight," it told me, "so you can see who's running off with your daughter."

It was that bit of thoughtfulness that decided me. "All right, send a telegram to George," I said, "and put him out of his misery. Then let's look at your clothes."

I was always amazed at the amount of energy Babs consumed in preparing for a party. She would be intense and irritable even over her nail polish. Once when I didn't know where her evening compact was and said so, she burst into tears. "No one ever helps anybody around here!" However, Norah left her cleaning and came up to press Babs's dress and everything was ready when Ben drew up in front of the house. Ed and I went out to see her into the little gray car. The bags were stowed in back. Overhead, the stars were very friendly and bright. The inside of the coupe was lighted. Babs looked warm and protected between the two big men.

"There's a basketball game tomorrow afternoon that I'd like to see," Ben said. "We'll start back right after that. We'll be here by ten o'clock, barring accidents." He snapped off the light and turned on the engine. Ed and I waited instinctively for a last wave, but no one looked back. Suddenly I was very tired. I had told Babs to call me; I would want to know that she had arrived safely. After that, I promised myself, I would have a good night's sleep.

It was half-past nine when the phone rang. Babs's voice was low and excited. "It's the most gorgeous place," she said. "All snow and music and men. Ben's a neat driver. We made sixty nearly all the way, and a lot of places it was just glare ice, too."

Well, she was there. You had to let them run some risks if they were going to have any fun. And it would be fun. I remembered going back with Ed to his fraternity house, the late lazy breakfast, the boys drifting in, the wonderful feeling that you were the object of your man's special concern. I was glad I had let Babs go.

Saturday night we took Freddie and Charles to the movies. We sent them to bed in double-quick time a little after nine; going quietly was part of the contract. Ed sat down in his big chair and read the paper. After a while he pulled out his watch.

"Babs ought to be home pretty soon," he remarked. "This Ben Gunther looked like a nice reliable boy to me."

He filled his pipe and started reading his paper again. Ed has a leisurely way of reading the paper, turning the pages slowly and creasing them carefully. Perhaps I only imagined it, but he seemed to fuss with it a good deal that night.

"Why don't you go to bed?" he asked after a time. "You look like a wreck. I'll wait up for Babs."

I told him I'd wait up, too; I'd like to hear about the party. Ed let the paper slip to the floor and looked at his watch again. That was the third time within half an hour.

"It must be slow going, what with all the snow," he explained very casually. He got up and walked around, looking at the books on the shelves. He took one out and put it back. If he'd only settle down! But he didn't. He turned on the radio. He was just in time to hear an announcer saying, "It is now eleven P.M. Eastern Standard Time. At the request of the State Highway Commission we give you a brief summary of prevailing traffic conditions on the principal highways. Route 23—traffic heavy as far as Elmsville, normal from there on. Snow heavy. Route 42—badly congested at Four Corners owing to an accident involving two cars and a bus. An unidentified person was killed and two injured. Just what—" Ed snapped off the radio.

I said, "You know how kids are. They probably started later than they had planned to."

"Besides," Ed said in a flat voice, "they'll be taking it easy because of the snow and the ice on the roads. My bet is that this Ben Gunther is a little on the cautious side."

I thought of Babs's telephoning me that they had gone up there at sixty miles an hour over those icy roads, but I didn't mention it. For a long time Ed sat there smoking. Then he began to talk to me. We discussed the Smiths' bridge—always a distracting, controversial subject—everything except Babs and how late it was. Ed's face fell into deep lines as I have seen it do only once or twice in all the years I've known him. He still tried to be casual, however. When it got to be after midnight he stopped talking conversationally and suddenly said, "There are other good roads besides 42." He broke off and gave me a quick glance. Route 42. That's where the accident had been. He went immediately into an elaborate explanation intended to keep me from following his thoughts.

"That accident accounts for everything," he explained. "So

much traffic congestion the cars had to be routed around some back road that was probably clogged up with snow and the poor kids have had to plow their way home as best they could. There's nothing to worry about."

He looked at his watch again. "After all, it is only half-past twelve and when you think of everything—" He said he'd get a breath of fresh air. I followed him to the door. The street was dark and empty. Suddenly, two blocks away, I saw the lights of a car coming toward the house. I held my breath. It reached the corner and then with a grinding of brakes turned into the cross street.

Ed said, "I think I'll take the car and go for a little ride. I feel kind of restless. I could go for some hot coffee when I get back, and a sandwich," he added, when I said I'd come along. Then he was gone.

I lay flat on my back on the couch for a time, my arms crooked over my eyes. If Babs hadn't been in an accident, where was she? Of course something *must* have happened. Maybe she was hurt. I looked through the years ahead as into a tunnel, a dark tunnel, then I roused myself. I was being a perfect fool. I went out to the kitchen and started the coffee.

It was a little more than half an hour before he came in again. He paid no attention to his coffee. He just kept walking back and forth.

"Where'd you go, Ed?" I asked him. I tried to keep my voice natural.

"Oh, just around."

"You went to see Mr. Gunther, didn't you? You didn't want to telephone from here."

"Oh, I was passing by," Ed admitted. "I saw a light so I dropped in. Old man Gunther hadn't heard from Ben. It didn't seem to bother him at all. He feels just the way I do. Kids can take care of themselves these days." He fell silent for a moment, then he exploded. "Damn it! You'd think they'd telephone or something. Kids have no consideration. Not that I'm worrying—"

"Drink your coffee, Ed," I said, "before it gets cold."

I'd never seen the minutes drag by so slowly as during the next half-hour. When the telephone finally rang Ed got up so fast that he knocked over a chair. I heard him say, "Yes? Hello. Hello, Mr. Gunther." He listened for a long time then he went on in a scarcely audible voice: "Yes. Very considerate of you. Do that, will you?" He let the receiver slip back onto the cradle and when he turned his face was drawn.

"What is it?" I asked. "What's happened?"

He tried to speak once before he managed it. "That was old man Gunther. I had told him about that accident on Route 42. He called up the State Highway Commission just to check up on how bad the traffic congestion up there was." Ed stopped.

"What else did Mr. Gunther say?"

"Nothing much," Ed said, turning so that I couldn't see his face. "He's going to let me know if he hears any more." Ed was concealing something and he knew that I knew it. He drank his coffee and sat down in his big chair and lit his pipe, trying to look as though he hadn't a care in the world. Again he wanted me to go to bed, but of course I wouldn't. Instead I went and sat on the arm of his chair and smoothed down his rumpled hair.

"If we only knew," Ed said suddenly, "what fraternity house she's stayed at, I could call up and find out when they left."

"I have the telephone number." I hurried to my desk. "I made Babs give it to me when she called up."

"Why didn't you say so? Where is it?" Ed was on his feet before I finished.

I brought him the slip. He was jiggling the hook up and down, trying to get the operator and after an interminable time he got the number. And after that it seemed to take just as long to get hold of Babs's date, George. Ed didn't do much talking. He just wanted to know when Babs had left. He listened. Then, "Right after the game? Are you sure?... Thanks. Sorry to have disturbed you at this hour of the night. Sure ... sure."

Ed didn't say anything. He just went back to his chair and sat there with his head in his hands.

"Ed," I said. I got down on the floor next to him. "What is it, dear?"

"They left at three this afternoon," he said in a monotone. "Almost twelve hours ago."

"But anything could have happened," I protested. "Maybe they couldn't get through and are spending the night at some farmhouse that hasn't a telephone. Or maybe the car broke down and they were stuck for hours before they could be hauled out." I tried to make my voice reassuring. But what had Mr. Gunther told Ed that Ed was concealing from me? Something about the accident, of course. Yet it couldn't have been anything definite or he wouldn't have phoned the fraternity house, he wouldn't be sitting here. "Ed," I said slowly, "what kind of a car was in that crack-up?"

Ed didn't look me in the eye.

"I've got a right to know."

"It doesn't mean anything," Ed answered. "There are hun-dreds of little gray coupés, thousands."

So it was a gray coupé that was in the smash-up. My heart began to pound. The clock struck three, then shivered to silence. I don't know how I heard that other sound—soft footsteps behind me. I turned.

There was Babs standing in the doorway. She had on a bright pink flannel nightgown. Her hair was in curlers on top of her head. In one hand she held a glass of milk, in the other a peanut butter sandwich.

"I woke up and I was starved," she said. "Hey, what are you two doing up so late?"

Ed was staring at her as though he were seeing things.

"We had the most gorgeous time. I was simply dying to tell you about it and then when I got home you weren't here," she went on accusingly. "I even thought of waiting up for you, but I was so fagged I just fell into bed."

Ed cleared his throat. "What happened—what happened to Ben Gunther?"

"Ben? Oh, I didn't come back with him," Babs said. "He stayed overnight. I drove down with another girl. Hey, look out! You're making me spill the milk." I had reached an arm round her waist.

Ed got up. His shoulders had the usual swing.

"I guess I'd better phone old man Gunther. He's a fuss-budget. Just like Mom here." He stopped long enough to grin at Babs. "It's just the way I always say," he said. "She worries too much. You know Mother!"

They both smiled at me as if worry was something neither of them could understand.

Chapter 13

LISTEN, MOTHER, WHEN GEORGE COMES TONIGHT COULDN'T we have big high candles on the table?" Babs asked. "It look so pretty and sort of formal." Babs was home during mid terms, her examinations having all been scheduled for the firs few days of the week. George was coming that afternoon to take Babs to the Club dance and to stay over until Sunday night. Everybody was relaxed and happy except me. I wa nervous. Here was Babs building everything on George' visit and I had news that might spoil the whole thing for her We were having a leisurely Saturday morning breakfast. Bab was carefully buttering each dent in a waffle. Ed had pushe back his chair and settled down with his pipe to read a comi strip with an air of earnest concentration. On the table the elec tric waffle iron emitted a gentle steam as Freddie and Charle crouched in front of it, waited for its glowing little red ligh to blink.

"Oh, and another thing." Babs lowered her voice an glanced toward the pantry door. "Couldn't you make Nora carry the plates out one at a time?"

"Norah has a lot to do," I answered.

"Yes, but you're letting her get awfully careless. And," sh went on, "couldn't we use those lovely crystal goblets—th ones with the crest on them that were your grandmother's What's the use of having spiffy things," she added, as I starte to speak, "if you just keep them put away in the top of an ol closet?"

"It isn't that," I said, "but there are only six of them and there will be seven at the table."

Freddie began to count places with his fingers. "There's you three, and Charlie and me"—he hurried on, afraid that I might say they weren't going to sit down with us—"and this George guy. That's six."

"There'll be seven," I corrected. "I didn't tell you but we have another guest. Sister is coming."

"Whose sister?" Charles asked politely. Having been in the family only a year, Charles was often in the dark.

"That's just a nickname. It's what they call her. She's going to spend the night," I added. An ominous silence settled about us. Even Ed glanced up at me dubiously. "Wait, I'll get the letter." I went to my little desk in the living room with almost a sense of escape. Perhaps by the time I found it Babs would have grown used to the idea. I came back and read the final paragraph aloud.

"And as Sister will be driving through Saturday, I'm wondering if you can tuck her in somewhere overnight. I'm particularly anxious for her to renew her childhood acquaintance with your Barbara. Now that they are both seventeen, they will probably find many interests in common and, I hope, be fast friends.

Affectionately,

Sue."

There was no comment. I felt the need of giving my friend and her child a build-up.

"Her mother was a regular leader in college," I said reminiscently. "Once she got us all to go in bathing in a trout stream in our teddy bears. Sort of streamlined chemises," I explained to Babs's raised eyebrow. "Sister must be lots of fun, too."

"I 'member her," Freddie offered. "She caught that snake for us. She snaps their heads," he explained to Charles.

"Clear off?" Charles asked admiringly. "Ooh! There, it's shut its eye." He opened the iron and extracted a waffle.

Babs pushed back her chair. There were angry tears in her eyes.

"I never saw anything *like* this family," she said. "How can you all go on as if it didn't matter? Sister—she's simply impossible."

"Now, Babs," I protested, "when you saw her she was only twelve. She's probably awfully nice now. She's just your age. Having her here will make it sort of a house party."

"Mother!" Babs said. "Honestly! How can you *say* a thing like that? George doesn't want to see a houseful of strange people. He's tired *out*."

Ed grinned. "He is?" he asked. "Will he be strong enough to dance, do you think?"

Babs ignored this. "And who's supposed to take Sister to the dance?" she asked. "We can't just walk out and leave her."

"Don't you know any other snake fanciers?" Ed's voice was teasing.

"It's not a bit funny, Daddy," Babs said. "It just happens to be the most important night in my life and I've got to spend it finding men to cut in on Sister. She just can't come this week end, that's all! I don't have to have her, do I, Daddy?" Her hot eyes met Ed's steady gray ones.

"Now, Babs," he said. "She's *coming* and there's nothing we can do about it. So you might as well make up your mind to be nice to her. It isn't as if you didn't have a pretty good time around here," he added.

A big tear rolled down Babs's cheek. "Nobody in this family's got any imagination." She ran from the room.

The feeling of tension did not lessen as the early afternoon passed and we were still waiting for our two guests. I busied myself in the dining room. Babs came down wearing a bright green dress. As a rule she brings with her a distinct air of relaxation. Today, she was restless. She went into the living room and began putting on and taking off records without hearing them through. Her nervousness was catching. I began to think of Sister somewhat apprehensively as I had last seen her, a raw-boned child, without charm. I hoped time had smoothed some of the rough edges.

I didn't hear the bell ring, but presently I was aware of a gay masculine voice saying, "Hi there!" I hurried out to meet George. He was tall, with a fair skin. His heavy camel's hair coat almost exactly matched his blond crew-cut hair. His blue-eyed gaze was smiling and even. He looked sure—of himself, of finding certain things in his friends and in their houses. "It's awfully good of you to take me in," he told us.

"The fact is, son"—Ed put a kindly hand on the boy's shoulder—"Dick's being in the Army gives us an extra room. Glad to have you here any time, whenever you want to come."

Babs's eyes told me this was crowding him. "Come on, I'll show you where you park," she said. The three of them went up the stairs.

It had to happen, of course, that Sister arrived before we had a chance to get acquainted with George. She came striding in the door, dropping a suitcase, a duffle bag, and an overcoat of brown tweed. She looked exactly as she had as a child, only bigger. She put out a lean, hard hand. "Hi-ya, Aunt Elizabeth," she said.

"Babs, dear," I called. "Sister's come. Sister's down here!" I waited for an answer from above, but none came. "Yoo-hoo, Babs! Here's Sister." I turned back to my guest. "Run right up."

Sister started, heavily laden. "Oh, *hello!*" Babs's voice came down, a little too near and a little too hearty. "Why didn't somebody tell me you were here? Let me help you." She seized the duffle bag. "You're back in my room with me. Hope you don't mind."

I trailed after them as Sister threw her things on Babs's floor.

"Now don't you worry about me. I have my sleeping bag," she said. She began unpacking, telling us how her mother had given her a car and her father'd given her a revolver and a hundred dollars and how she was driving to Texas, stopping with friends on the way. "Mother always makes me take one party dress," she explained apologetically as she shook out something in a dull Alice blue.

"That reminds me," I said. "There's a dance tonight. Would you enjoy going?"

"Oh, I don't mind. I'm game, if that's what you've planned on," she answered.

Babs gave me a look the meaning of which I couldn't quite decode, but I pressed on. "Why don't you call up Bill or Harry to go with Sister?"

"Now don't you go to any bother," Sister peered at me over the top of her glasses. "I don't care two pins if I don't have a boy along."

"But you can't—you won't want to walk into a dance without a man," Babs said.

"Then I'll go with Uncle Ed," Sister answered. "I'd just as soon go with him as some silly soph."

"All right, Mother, you tell Daddy, will you?" There was no mistaking the message of the glance this time. Babs was passing the buck to me. "As soon as you're ready, Sister, let's go downstairs. I want you to meet George."

I always think that no matter how youngsters explode in private, they're fairly well brought up if you can count on their manners in front of people. Sister was definitely a tax on Babs's social patience, but you'd never have known she wasn't Babs's closest friend. First Babs suggested bridge with one of us as a fourth. George brightened.

"It's about all we do week ends at the House," he said. It then came out that Sister had never played bridge.

"But," she offered, "I'm perfectly willing to sit down and learn."

George looked up, startled, and hastily suggested getting a football game on the radio instead. I went off to break it to Ed that he and Sister were double-dating with George and Babs, which I finally put over, but only by agreeing to go to the club, too, and look on. I couldn't help wishing Sister was a little more our kind, but I told myself she must be a nice girl underneath. Perhaps the dinner party, with all the family around, would bring her out more favorably.

When we sat down in the candle-lit semi-darkness of the dining room, however, Sister seemed subdued to silence. Babs sat between her father and George. Ed told his best golf stories. They are old to us but polished with many tellings, and no one could do them better. George watched him with attentive admiration. Norah's dinner was excellent—she *can* cook—and she clumped in and out three times with the main dishes. I saw that Babs was superlatively happy. At last I could relax.

But I hadn't counted on Sister's co-operative spirit or on her great powers of organization. The plates were being removed when she rose. "Come on, everybody!" she called down the table, "I know how it is with just one in the kitchen. Everybody take out their own dishes." She strode toward the pantry.

George half rose, politely, and stood, plainly at a loss.

"I think Norah can manage alone," I said.

At this very moment there was a crash. Sister had collided with Norah at the pantry door. "Holy Saints!" Norah stopped. "Whoops, hold it!" This was George trying to catch the door.

"Here," Ed said, "better turn on the lights."

The sudden glare revealed Norah, her organdy apron and uniform spattered with gravy and at her feet a litter of broken plates.

"I'm so sorry," Sister was exclaiming.

"It doesn't matter." I was answering Sister but I was looking at my daughter. Babs's haggard eyes took in the scene. There now hung over the room the disheveled air of the tag end of a children's party. The magic was gone. For the rest of the meal, Freddie and Charles set the pace with no competition.

Babs followed me to my room as I went to dress for the dance.

"Oh, Moms," she moaned, "that girl's ruined everything. George was bored stiff this afternoon. Then she had to go around being helpful and making a mess of my lovely dinner. How can I ever seem glamorous again?"

"Things like that happen in every house," I said. "Go bathe your eyes; they show you've been crying. You'll have a wonderful time tonight." But I wasn't so sure. Sister seemed to be one of those people with a genius for doing the wrong thing. George, I felt, might easily be the kind who would stand for so much and then lose interest. My heart hit zero.

Nor was it helped by an episode that preceded the dance. Babs was the last to come down and the four of us waited for her in the hall. George gazed at her appreciatively. She stood poised by the console table, her dress, a black bodice with a bright red skirt, giving her the air of a well-groomed gypsy. It was at this moment that Sister moved again.

"Wait," she drew out a handkerchief. "There's a bit of soot or something on your lashes." She poked at Babs's eye with a linen-covered finger. Babs flinched.

"Careful," George said. "She's only got one more of those things you're putting your finger through."

"It doesn't seem to come off," Sister commented doubtfully. "Say, have you got grease or something on your eyes?"

"Sure! She has to keep 'em well oiled to watch me with," George answered for Babs. He put his arm through hers. "Let's go."

The dance, however, started off propitiously. The big club room with its exposed beams is an attractive setting for a party. From my place near the door I could see a few feet into the sun porch, now dark, and across to the stag line stretching down the middle of the dance floor. Sometimes, looking on at an affair like this, I feel that in spite of the cut-in system the girls are having the better time. The boys in the stag line, the very young ones especially, are likely to be white-faced and anxious-eyed as if the whole thing was too much of a strain on them. There was certainly no strain on George, however; he was completely in command of the situation.

Again and again I saw him cut in on Babs, his face aglow. Between times he stood nonchalantly looking on. At last, just as I was beginning to worry, he remembered his manners and cut in on Sister. They moved in my direction. She might have been a piece of furniture. His gaze, over her shoulder, swept the floor. Just beyond me, they stopped. "Gee, I'm hot," Sister said. "Let's go out and cool off." George followed her courteously enough. She peered into the darkness of the sun porch.

"Full of people twosing!"

George pulled at her arm. "Let's go somewhere else, then." But she shook off his hand.

"I've got an idea." She stepped out into the darkness. "Anybody got a match?" she asked.

"Hey, here, I've got a match." George's face twisted into an anxious grimace as he realized what she was doing. She stretched her head back.

"*Sh,*" she said. "This is going to be fun. You got a match?" she asked, in the direction of a rustle of taffeta.

There was nothing that could be done to stop her. George drew up stiffly against the frame of the door. One by one, three couples came in, the girls sulky, patting their hair, the boys glaring angrily, red-faced and hostile. Sister rejoined him. "Did you see their expressions?" she said. "Wasn't that rich?"

The three boys who came in gathered immediately at the end of the room. They were talking heatedly. At last one of them snapped his fingers. I had never seen any of them before. At every big dance there are a few strangers brought in, by somebody, whom you *haven't* seen before and by the end of the evening hope never to see again. I had no idea that anything was brewing, certainly not anything so cruel. I did know, however, that George must be relieved. I got a signal out to Babs. She came dancing up on the arm of a boy named Tommy. I told her, briefly, the story. All of us turned, just in time to see the punishment being meted out for Sister's joke. The first of the three boys was going out on the floor. He stepped up to George and Sister, who were now dancing again and gave George the usual touch on the shoulder. As George fell back, so did he.

"Oh," he said. "Sorry, son."

He moved on. He was immediately followed by the second boy. As Sister and George moved off again he, too, tapped George.

"Beg your pardon," he said as George released Sister. "Didn't mean to bump you." He walked away.

"You fellows better watch where you're going," George put in. As he started dancing again a third boy started across the floor. A titter ran down the stag line. I saw the slow red rising on the back of George's neck. Babs's eyes blazed.

"Well, of all the mean tricks—" she began.

At this moment Sister, looking over George's shoulder, saw her third tormenter bearing down upon her. She dropped her arms and almost ran to where we stood. Her face was brick color and her eyes were teary.

"I'm going home," she said. "It was just a silly gag. I only meant it to be funny. Nobody needs to take me but, please, I want to go home."

It was at this moment that Babs and George came up to scratch and came up like thoroughbreds. Babs put her hand on Sister's shoulder.

"Tommy here was just asking could he meet you. Please

don't go home. I've got a lot of other friends I want you to meet."

"It's all right, Sister." It was George speaking gently as if he were talking to a child.

"May I?" Tommy had his arm around her.

"Okay," George said, "but we were having a good time."

Babs stood by the door that lead to the porch. She was very, very still. George looked down at her, plainly a little puzzled.

"It wasn't quite all my fault," he began.

"Of course it wasn't your fault," Babs broke out. "I should have planned for her for every minute. I didn't realize she had that kind of a childish sense of humor. I wouldn't have let you in for all that for worlds. I didn't know what she was like; until today I hadn't seen her since she was twelve."

George continued to look down fixedly into Babs's face. His eyes were suddenly very dark. "Sister's all right," he said slowly. "It's only that she's *still* just about twelve years old. So she isn't anybody you care about," he went on, "and all this time you've been working so hard to give her a good time. From the way you treated her I supposed she was one of your oldest and very best friends." When Babs did not answer he continued. "Most girls would have been very snippy and mean to a girl as dumb as that. I think the way you've acted is just about the nicest thing I ever saw anybody do." For a moment Babs looked up at him. "If I didn't like you before," he said, "I'd think you were just about tops now. Come on," he took her arm and they moved onto the floor.

It was hours later when we drove home, George and Babs in the back of my car. Sister and Ed had preceded us. Usually I'm very strict about making Babs come right upstairs. Tonight, I said to myself, I would be lenient. We came into a semi-dark house. It was clear the others had gone to bed.

"Don't sit up *too* long," I said. "Good night."

George and Babs stood together in the hall watching me go. Their eyes told me they were grateful for the few moments of grace.

"We won't," George smiled.

It was then I heard the voice of Sister. It came from the middle of the dark living room floor.

"I brought my sleeping bag down here so I wouldn't be a bit of bother to anybody," Sister was saying.

Babs looked up at George. Her eyes were very bright. She put out her hand. "Oh, well," she said.

Chapter 14

I DON'T SUPPOSE I SHALL EVER HEAR THAT HYMN, "NOW the Day Is Over," without living again through some of the most nerve-racking moments in my life, those in the middle of a Saturday afternoon in April on which Dick had planned to come home and marry Eileen. Norah brought in his letter while we were at breakfast and I read it aloud to the family.

"The men are being shipped out fast now that we are really at war, and I am sure to be moved as soon as I've finished this officers' training course. Eileen is coming up Monday or Tuesday and you girls can make all the plans but we thought we'd be married in church and take the Old Guard around to the country club afterward. Eileen especially doesn't want to put any extra work on you, Mother."

Married! Dick! My throat closed so that I could not swallow. But while my heart stood still my mind hurried on. There would be food and drink to be seen to, the church must be decorated, I'd have to get something to wear—

Babs's voice broke in, cheerful and excited.

"Saturday! Goodness! My goo'ness! I'm going to be maid of honor—they promised! And I'm not going to wear any old poke bonnet, either." She considered. "I think I'll have a kind of heart-shaped pancake hat with ribbons and frills. I want to look divine," she finished.

Freddie retrieved a bit of bread which the toaster had popped up into the air. "Nobody's going to look at *you*," he said.

"George is," Babs answered promptly.

"Will *he* be here?" I asked. I hadn't realized that George was quite so thoroughly entrenched in the family. What was more, although Babs was having holidays at that date I'd understood that George was not, the two colleges having with studied inhumanity staggered the vacations to overlap as little as possible.

"Of course he'll come. And, Mother," Babs went on, "I wish you'd sort of drop a hint to Dick about asking George to be his best man. I know George would appreciate it."

Both Ed and I glanced at Babs, but there was not a trace of humor in her brown eyes.

"But, darling, Dick doesn't even know George," I began.

"Suppose you let Dick and Eileen manage that," Ed said gently. He studied Babs as he often did, as though she was something he wasn't quite satisfied with but hoped to improve, like his golf stroke.

"And while you're all here," I said, "I want to warn everybody to be terribly thoughtful of Eileen, and that goes for you, Babs, and you, Charles and Freddie. I suppose her family must be way off somewhere, so we're all she has."

"Well, they needn't expect *me* to be in any old wedding," Freddie broke in. "I think it's a wet idea, anyway, a soldier getting married. Maybe they won't even let him come," he added brightly.

Used as I am to Freddie's reactions, what he said made my heart sink. Suppose Dick couldn't get here—suppose the war plans—I closed my mind. . . .

Eileen arrived on Monday morning. I waited until she had had a chance to unpack a little, then I went up to her room— she was sharing Babs's—armed with my pencil and the list

of things to be seen to. I don't care how simple a wedding is
it involves innumerable details, and I was determined to pu
everyone to work on them.

I found Babs lying across the bed, face down, a hypnoti
stare fixed on her little victrola, her red-moccasined feet weav
ing rhythmically through the air. The bride-to-be, in yellow
slacks and shirt, was moving around the room with an armfu
of lacy underwear.

"Babs," I said sharply, "for Heaven's sake, shut that thing
off, will you?"

"Mother! Relax!" She gave me a bitter look. "That thing
is Sammy Kaye's new record." But she reached over and
stopped it.

"Oh, please come in and sit down with us." Eileen lifted
her coat and dress from the armchair. "Babs and I were jus
talking about going over to the club to order the food. Then
I guess everything is done. We don't want you to have to
bother about anything," she added.

I stared. "Everything is—" I stopped short. "But, dear, the
club is just a house. It hasn't any chef or restaurant," I ex
plained. "We'll have to send the food over." I consulted my
slips of paper. "I'm going to put Norah in charge, and Henry
and his helpers will do the serving." Henry is the colored
man who acts as a waiter at all the parties in our neighborhood
"I'll send Freddie and Charles down to find him after school
Have you any preferences or ideas about food?" I asked
"You know, we may be feeding anywhere from eighty to a
hundred people."

Babs brightened and sat up. "A hundred? Would they ea
lamb stew?" she asked. "I just learned to make lamb stew fo
a hundred in my emergency course at college. I could get a
mobile kitchen and serve it on the lawn!"

Eileen looked troubled. "Can't we get little sandwiches all made, and some trick ices and let it go at that?"

"You could," I said, "but I think the people around here like something substantial. Norah makes a wonderful chicken salad, garnished with sliced tomato and alligator pear and home-made mayonnaise, and I guess she can do it, even for that crowd, if we give her a couple of days with nothing else to tend to."

"*Mmm*," Babs said, "and can we have those little round hot buttered rolls?"

"That would be just wonderful. But isn't that a lot of trouble?" Eileen sat down at the foot of the bed and looked at me with great wistful gray eyes.

"It takes a little planning, that's all," I told her. "And now about the invitations. I used our Christmas card list and cut it, and you can add your list to that one. It's too late for engraved invitations," I hurried on, "so I've ordered plain white stationery."

"Invitations are out, anyway." Eileen's tone was firm. "Not on the budget, I mean."

"But I've bought the paper," I said, "and Babs, you'd better go right down and start writing them now."

"And Freddie and Charles," Babs amended.

"Well, I don't know about them." I was doubtful. "They might make smudges."

"They can lick stamps and envelope flaps, can't they? Well! So don't give it a thought." Babs lay back, resting her head on her arms. "I'll do it, but not right *now*." She rolled over and began fingering a record.

It was almost more than I could bear. I felt as if I were pushing on the wind—a little soft summer wind.

"Babs . . ." I began.

Eileen picked a cigarette from her case. "Let's not have anything complicated," she said. "Let's just have it sort of simple and gay."

"Isn't it too wonderful?" Babs gazed at the ceiling with dreamy brown eyes. "Who'd ever think we'd be sitting here planning Dick's wedding?"

Eileen turned the ring on her finger. "It just can't be me."

I looked across at the smooth, cool-looking girl Dick was going to marry. I had a sudden intuition that in spite of her carefully casual curls and her studiedly casual slacks and shirt, she was very shy, a little afraid, and immensely grateful. She had none of Babs's unthinking confidence. For that she must lean on Dick. I picked up my lists. But all at once, I couldn't see them. I couldn't bear the fact that Dick and Eileen would have to be separated so soon. And here was I spoiling everything by fussing over a lot of dreary details. I would try, instead, to make the preparations fun.

"I'll tell you what," I said. "This morning, let's us three go downtown and order the cake. I'm giving it to you," I put in, as an anxious look came across Eileen's face, "and we'll pick out your bouquet, Eileen. This is my luncheon for the bridal party."

Ed had shown a distinct tendency to hide in the office. But we caught up with him that night and made him agree to take Eileen to see the minister.

Dr. Howard is the minister of our church. The boys go to Sunday school and I get to service—sometimes. It was evident that he did not remember Ed, and that he assumed he must be Dick.

"Is this your first marriage?" he asked. Ed was delighted at being mistaken for the groom. "Nice fellow, that," he said afterward.

Toward Eileen, Dr. Howard showed a considerate tenderness. It was plain he felt all the drama and pathos of this wartime wedding. "Marriage is a great adventure," he said. "Try to keep it so."

The intervening days and nights slid by. In spite of all we could do to ease the strain, we were dead tired. We had been on our feet incessantly. Because of the time element, many answers to the invitations came by phone. There were presents to be opened with oohs and aahs, and a mountain of excelsior to be moved away. There was Eileen's wedding dress, brought from New York, to be laid out on the bed in Dick's room. And there was Babs's astonishingly effective and inexpensive gown to be exclaimed over. At last it was the night before the great event. I joined the two girls and Ed in the living room.

"Now if Dick were only here," I said, "we could have the wedding."

Eileen sat very quiet, looking at the hand with the ring on it. It was tightly clinched. I felt the need to make conversation.

"I'll never forget *our* wedding," I went on.

"Thanks!" Ed grinned over the edge of the evening paper.

I said, "I just mean you looked like a perfect stranger. There you stood in the front of the church in your cutaway and striped trousers looking too stuffed-shirty for anything. I was terrified."

"Gee, that reminds me. I've got to wear that cutaway tomorrow, don't I?" Ed asked. "I got a letter from Dick at the office today asking me to be best man." He tried not to show how pleased he was.

"I suppose everybody feels the same way," Eileen remarked slowly. "But you begin to wonder. It's—you wonder if people ought to get married at all these days. It's not that I don't love Dick, but somehow—"

"There's never a right time for getting married or having children, for that matter," I answered. "What about the last war and the depression? Freddie came along right in the worst of it. Suppose there weren't any Freddie?"

"Ooh, just suppose!" Babs gave me a teasing glance. "What? No comeback?" she said. "I hope you and Dick have a baby right away," she told Eileen. "I saw the most adorable baby sweater I'll knit for you. Yellow, with his class numerals in white."

I glanced at Eileen but she didn't seem to hear. Her face was drawn; there were sharp angles near her nose and jaw. She would be all right if only Dick were here. Why didn't the boy telephone or something?

"Let's go up and look at your wedding dress and veil, shall we? It's only bad luck when you put them all on in advance."

Babs stuck an arm through Eileen's. We trooped up to Dick's room. The dress, gardenia white, with a little wired lace ruching, lay beautiful and immaculate before us.

"It *is* lovely, isn't it?" Eileen's voice had a wistful sound.

"Where's the bride?" Ed's voice came from the doorway. "Can you see anything?" he asked anxiously.

"Oh, Daddy, you look gorgeous in that cutaway." Babs drew back to admire him.

Ed patted his vest. "But can you notice anything?" He lifted the edge of his vest and displayed a formidable chain of heavy safety pins fastened to the trouser top and the inside of the vest.

"I thought up this contrivance to anchor the whole thing. I must have put on a little weight. Pretty clever, don't you think?" He pulled the vest down again and looked anxiously at each of us in turn.

Babs had put on the heart-shaped hat and now she tucked her arm through Ed's.

"*I* pronounce you man and wife." She began singing it with a swing.

Ed stopped short in front of Eileen, "Do you like champagne?" he asked.

Eileen's eyes grew very round. "I love champagne," she answered.

"Well, you're having it," Ed said. "It's a present from the best man. Argentine champagne. Very good, and it doesn't cost—" He looked at me out of the corner of his eye.

"You're all so darling. I don't know why, but I'm—I'm panicky." Suddenly Eileen dropped her head in her arms and began to cry in a queer desolate way that it hurt you to hear.

And then, thank God, the doorbell rang.

"Special delivery—for you, Eileen." Babs had gone to the door. "From the groom."

"He's coming, he's coming." Eileen devoured the letter. "He's got three days' leave. He'll be here on the three forty-five and get off the bus at the corner just below the church at four o'clock." She stopped and laid a soft-scented cheek against mine. "Oh," she said, "I'm—I'm so happy, I could die."

I don't know what it is about the day of a wedding that everything stands out in one's mind with a leaden, frosty clearness.

Breakfast over, I tidied things. Looking out, I saw that the garage stood open and empty.

"The girls are gone downtown," Norah said. "Miss Eileen

wanted some face powder. They said they'd surely be back in a couple of hours."

I stood rooted to the floor. It seemed perfectly impossible to me that on the morning of a wedding the bride-to-be and the maid of honor were out in their slacks, no doubt having a soda in the drugstore. I told myself maybe I was getting hardening of the arteries.

The hours between lunch and an afternoon wedding are endless. One doesn't want to be ready too soon, yet one cannot settle down to anything. I dressed with Ed, Freddie, and Charles all tieing their shoestrings on the floor in my room, all peering into my mirror. At last I went down into the front hall.

"Ed, you get right over to the church with Eileen," I said. I shepherded Freddie and Charles out the door, stopping only to pick up a bunch of telegrams. Ed would want to read them aloud with the champagne. Once in the vestibule of the church, Freddie said suddenly, "There was one for you, Moms. Did you see it? Wait." He pulled it from the pile.

I opened it. It was a night letter, sent the evening before, which had somehow gone unread. It was from Dick. Because of the recent war news, all leaves were canceled. I was not to tell Eileen for the moment. He would make other arrangements and call her when he knew what they could do.

"Freddie," I said, "go find Daddy. I've got to talk to him."

Inside, the organ began to rumble and then slid softly into, "Now the Day Is Over." The student organist was improvising around the hymn we used to love for its tricky tenor. "Shadows of the e-evening." I could hear the mounting theme in the left hand.

This day wasn't over!

Would it ever be? Why didn't Ed hurry?

"Hey! What goes on?" It was Ed. He had seen my face. "You look like the family ghost."

"Oh, Ed!" I seized his arm. "There's a telegram here from Dick. . . . He can't make it."

"Hey, Moms." It was Freddie, outside on the church steps. "There's Dick now! I see his uniform. He's comin' round the corner."

"Dick . . . Dick!" I rushed across the vestibule.

Dick sprang up the church steps.

"Hello, Mother. Hello there, Dad. Where's Eileen?" He did not wait for an answer. "Well, the Army has a heart after all, so I came right along. Didn't know what you'd have done—but then I looked out the window and saw the crowd. Hey, do we know all these people?" He nodded toward the rows of heads in the interior of the church. "And where's Eileen, anyway?"

"Eileen is just beyond that door," I pointed to the left, "waiting for you and Dad to get down in the front of the church where you belong. Run around to the right, both of you—and don't forget the ring," I called after them. "Now, boys, you two go down the aisle right ahead of me."

"Hi!" The hoarse whisper was from Babs. "We're coming out. All right?" The hyacinth blue of her dress stood out flower-like against the rough stone. Behind her was the cloud of white that enveloped Eileen. Somewhere overhead the last notes of "Now the Day Is Over" came to a stop. There was a definite lurch of sound from the organ, then it found itself and began, soft, strong, and steadily louder, "Here Comes the Bride!"

Chapter 15

"OTHER MEN HAVE FAULTS," BARBARA SAID TO ME ONCE, "but George is perfect."

She told me this one night I was spending with her up at college. She was wearing a raspberry-colored bathrobe that made a brilliant spot of color against the old blue of her quilt. Every now and then she bounced on the bed in sheer delight. She looked like a confident child in whose life nothing could ever go wrong.

Although it seemed to me then that George would have a lot to live up to, I didn't for some reason think of disillusionment coming to Babs through him. Perhaps this was because I had never met it myself. Ed had faults as a husband, goodness knows, like playing thirty-six holes of golf when we were expecting him home for dinner, but in the things that really matter he had never let me down. I realized that George was a dream man in Barbara's mind but I expected him to materialize, eventually, into a real person. I remembered once seeing our little city from the river at dawn, all pearl and gray against the sky, like an enchanted place. But when presently the cheerful sunlight revealed red brick and gray concrete, it was still the town I loved. I suppose I thought George's character would define itself like that without any shock, which shows how trusting I was.

And now Babs was home for a Sunday. She came whenever she could get a free ride down and hadn't a date. She was crouched on a chair in the living room. She must, I thought, be very tired; it wasn't like her to be so listless. I picked up the white seaboot I was knitting, plainly meant for an elephant's trunk, and sat down opposite her, trying to think of something to cheer her up.

"I see the Glee Club is coming down from the University to sing Friday night at that Service benefit over at Kingstown," I said. "Isn't George on the Glee Club?"

"Yes." Babs's tone was level.

"I thought he was," I went on cheerfully. "You're coming home that afternoon, aren't you?" (Vacation began that weekend.) "Well, be sure to bring your black taffeta dress. Everybody will be dancing at the Hostel afterward and that dress will be just right."

"Oh, Mother, skip it, will you? I'm not going!"

"Not going? But why, dear?"

"Because George didn't ask me. Because he's taking somebody else. A girl he met at a tea dance at somebody's house. She lives right near the University and he sees her all the time, and now you know all there is to know and I don't ever want to hear about it again." She ran out of the room. I heard her sob as she went upstairs. Then the door closed behind her.

"Ed," I said, catching my husband as he sat down behind the evening paper, "I want to talk to you. It's about George. He's asked another girl to the Glee Club Concert at Kingstown."

"Yeah?" Ed rustled the sheets and refolded them to the sports page.

"Yes, and I sent Babs and Freddie and Charles to the

movies so I could get a chance to talk to you about it alone," I went on.

Ed lowered his paper and stared. His nice gray eyes looked tired. "Listen," he began, "all day long I've got to worry about priorities and finding enough metal plate and turning out shells fast enough for the Navy, and when I do have a few minutes to sit down and relax with my paper I'm supposed to worry about who George has dates with. Sometimes," he finished, picking up the paper again, "I think women are crazy."

"That's just it," I said. "You have perspective. You can see that ten years from now it won't matter about George, but Babs can't. She's in a whirlpool of emotion. She's in love with that boy and she thought he cared about her."

"She'll get over it." Ed was calm.

"Yes, but, Ed," I argued, "if a first love goes deep it can make or break you. Oh, it's all right if people stay loyal to each other for a while and then gradually drift apart. Then there's no lasting hurt. But I've known people who were double-crossed in love at Babs's age who were left completely unsure of themselves. Even after they were safely married, they were always suspicious of their husbands or wives. I don't care if Babs loses George in the end, but I care a lot how much she's hurt. Babs adores you. You're the one person who can help her take this the right way."

Ed bent his head on one side and looked at me quizzically. There were sparkling lights in his eyes.

"I know. I'm a wonderful guy," he said. "The old come-on stuff."

"No, just a simple statement of fact." I retrieved his tobacco pouch from behind a cushion. "Here—is this what you're fumbling for?" I put it beside him on the table and went on, "But you've got to find some way to give her a hand." I did not wait for an answer. I knew him.

"What are we having to eat tonight?" Ed came into the living room. There was a swing to his shoulders which I knew from long experience meant he had plans.

"We're having beans," I came back, "just Saturday night beans."

"I thought as much." Ed went up behind Babs and put a hand gently on her curls. "Hello, sport," he said. "How'd you like it if you and I took Moms out to dinner?"

The restaurant Ed chose had just the right air of sophistication. The hunter's pink leather in the stalls, the little drum-shaped bar at the far end, the waiter with the world-weary eyes and the indefinable accent who bent over us, all combined to create the feeling that we were very, very cosmopolitan. Babs responded wanly.

"This is the nuts of a place, Daddy," she said. She looked around thoughtfully. "I suppose we three will just get old together, and keep on going out to dinner together, year after year."

"What's the matter? Having men-are-louses trouble?" Ed asked.

"Yes. I'm off 'em for life."

Ed smiled. "Well, Toots," he said, "I don't know what's happened, but if I were you I'd forget it. There are other men in the world."

"Not like George." Babs looked up with something startled and frightened in her eyes. "You don't understand, Daddy."

Ed considered her closely for a few moments without

speaking. There was no mistaking the misery in her voice and the shaken look on her face. Then, "Suppose you tell me what it's all about."

"Well," Babs began, "George used to come up to college every week end, practically. Two weeks ago he stayed away, without any excuse, either, so last week I asked him up for a freshman dance. We had a perfectly all right time only he did sort of go off into himself every little while and leave me waiting outside."

Ed nodded. "I know what you mean."

"Sunday morning he didn't come over until almost twelve. There's nothing funny about that because none of the boys got up till then. They all stay in one great big dormitory room. It's a whole floor over at the Inn," she explained. "There's just one extension phone and the rats always take the receiver off the hook, so we can't call 'em!" She paused indignantly. "Well, when they *did* come I spent all of thirty-five cents buying George a simply huge breakfast at the Tea Pot, where I can charge. Then I said we'd better get organized if we wanted to crawl in for dinner before they closed the doors and he said never mind, because he had to catch the one-thirty train and he went off and left me, just like that."

"Well," Ed said, "he probably had work to do."

"Like fun he did. I found out. He had a date all the time. Here I've been sitting home faithful as heck and George has been playing around with somebody else."

"I suppose you never have any other dates!" Ed smiled.

"That's different," Babs said earnestly. "Of course I do but they don't mean a thing and they're with boys George wouldn't mind my going out with. I could bear it if George walked out on me for some awfully nice girl. At least I think

I could," she added honestly. "But I just can't stand him fall-ing for somebody that isn't—isn't *worthy* of him."

"How do you know the girl isn't—worthy of George?" Ed asked.

"Oh, Patty's got all the dope on her. Everybody knows what she's like. Patty says nobody but a boy as sweet as her brother could be taken in by her. She's *oodles* older than we are and hard as rocks. Patty is just furious at him."

"Oh, well," I said, "she can't be very attractive then. The excitement will soon wear off, I'm sure. George is too nice to like a hard girl."

"I don't know." Babs was doubtful. "Patty says she hates to admit it but she really *has* a superficial something and she certainly has got her hooks into George. Oh, Daddy, what'll I do?"

Babs's eyes were turned toward Ed. I had seen the same look once in the eyes of a woman trapped by physical suffer-ing. Her gray dress and the rose leather behind her set off her warm, passionate face. I knew Ed was having trouble with perspective. He stirred his coffee, then:

"You can't do anything right now. You've just got to wait. You see," he went on, without looking at her, "there are two kinds of men. There's the man who's one person with his family and friends and another person when he gets away from them, and those aren't our kind of people. Then there's the man who's the same all the way through. He makes mistakes, of course, but he soon realizes them himself. I think George is that kind and if he is, he'll break this thing off—eventually. It's up to you to decide whether he's worth waiting for."

"What about my pride?" Babs asked.

"Well, what about it?" Ed grinned at her. "Which would you rather have, your pride, or George?"

"Oh, Daddy," Babs said, "I wish other men were as nice as you."

"Yeah, you've been listening to Mother again," Ed answered, but he got up suddenly and walked away.

"Daddy's so understanding," Babs said. She dug into her ice cream. "Do you think George really *does* love me, Moms?"

"Of course," I answered. But I wasn't so sure.

Even I was surprised when later in the week Ed divulged the fact that he had taken tickets for the Glee Club Concert, reserved a table afterward at the Hostel, asked a young man from the office to come along, and invited George by phone. George had stalled a bit at first and said something about being tied up, but Ed had swept his objections aside.

"Awfully nice young fellow is taking Babs," he had said. "I know you'll enjoy each other. And bring your date along if you have one. I thought we'd make a real good party out of it," he had finished blandly.

"Could anything be worse than this idea of Daddy's! What got into him?" Babs commented as she put the finishing touches to her hair. "All I pray is we don't run into George and his date."

I glanced at her. So Ed hadn't told her.

"After all I said the other night, Daddy doesn't even know what the score is," she finished. "Oh, well!"

Even I was bowled over by Ed's friend. I came down the stairs and there he was, smiling up at me, a tall young man in a dark blue uniform. He had light curly hair and sea blue eyes, with a quick smile glinting over something deeply stern, like sunlight glinting on the surface of the cold sea. He stepped forward, reaching for my hand.

"You're Mrs. Breton," he said, and, turning at a sound behind him, "This must be Babs. I had to come and see you both for myself. It's true, all they told me about you." He slipped an arm through each of ours. "We're going to have fun."

We sat down at our table in the Hostel, we three, while Ed, excusing himself, went out into the lobby. He came back followed by George and a girl. Babs's face went suddenly scarlet.

"Mrs. Breton, this is Jimmsie Warwick. Hi, Babs." George came around the table. "Glad to know you." He put out a hand to Jerry.

The girl called Jimmsie acknowledged the introduction with a casual nod and stood waiting beside her chair. I saw a handsome girl with honey-colored hair and skin that was the same shade wherever her chalk-white dress exposed it, with no detectable make-up except a vivid geranium color on her thin lips. She might have been nineteen or thirty. She was probably about twenty-four. She carried herself with insolent sureness.

"Well, George?" she said at last. But when George hurried back to put her in her chair, she did not look at him. Instead she favored Jerry with a sharp glance. Her greenish eyes were her least attractive feature, just a shade too close together, just a bit too opaque and, as Babs remarked long afterward, she had fixed them so she could look out but you couldn't look in. Jerry glanced briefly at her and she gave him a long, cool, answering look. Then she half-closed her eyelids. It was as if her glance and her lashes swept his cheek.

Jerry turned away. Babs was leaning forward, eager and un
conscious as a child, to look around him at George.

"Hey, lady," Jerry murmured, "I can't have you lookin
at anybody else. My manly vanity won't stand it. And why
are we wasting time, with music like this?" He led her of
onto the dance floor. Formal, almost stiff, at first, he grad
ually relaxed and bent his head until his cheek was restin
on Babs's dark soft hair.

George saw it. A deep, slow red spread above his collar
Jimmsie's gaze followed the smoothly gliding uniform.

"Well," she said without moving her eyes, "do I have t
ask to dance, too?"

They all moved past us in succession and to my surpris
Ed cut in on Babs. He was evidently not going to make i
easy for George to get to her.

During the little supper Ed had ordered I was aware o
fierce riptides of emotion around me. George kept puttin
questions to Babs across the table in an attempt to keep he
attention from Jerry. Jimmsie was obviously furious at Georg
for having brought her to us, and at Jerry. Plainly she coul
not stand having a man ignore her, especially in public, an
above all such an attractive one.

"You know, you haven't asked me to dance yet," she sai
in a low tone.

Jerry did not turn his head. "That's right."

She bit her lip, but he made no move even when Georg
and Babs swept out onto the floor and stayed there.

"Check, please," Ed said at last.

"Here," George began, but Jerry had already taken out
handsome initialed wallet.

"Oh, no," he said. "This is mine." He whipped out

ckage of bills thick as a book, riffled, rather obviously it
emed to me, through a layer of tens and twenties and
illed out one of the latter. I'd never seen so much money
gether in my life. I don't know why, but I glanced at
mmsie. There was something very thoughtful about her
ire. George saw it, too. He was watching her with a
w and older look in his eyes.

George drove us home. It was Ed who cheerfully pushed
abs into the front seat and Jerry after her, with some clumsy
ke about wanting Jimmsie for himself. When we got to
mmsie's door George did not move. Nor did he need to. It
as Jerry she handed her key to and he who took her up the
eps and let her in. As we waited for him, George took his
ind off the wheel and moved a little toward Babs.

"Where on earth did you get Jerry?" I asked Ed as we
ent to bed.

"I borrowed him," he said smugly.

"Borrowed him?"

"Yeah. From his wife. You see, now we have that Navy
ntract they send an officer down to inspect the factory.
hat's Jerry. He's been on convoy duty and I imagine they're
ving him a breather ashore to rest up in. His wife comes
r him every afternoon. They're terribly in love and I guess
e doesn't want to miss a minute with him."

"I still don't see how you thought of this party," I went on.

"That was her idea," he said. "Jerry's brought her in the
ffice a couple of times. She knows about you and Babs and
ways asks for you, and the other day I told her how things
ere. She was the one who thought of loaning me Jerry. She

said he would drive George crazy. Of course *she* thinks he
the most attractive man on earth."

"But all that money," I asked. "Where did anybody
the Service get a roll like that?"

"The bankroll?" Ed smiled, very pleased. "That was *m*
touch. It's part of my factory payroll and he'd better get
back to the bank first thing in the morning!"

It was then that Babs came floating into our room fro
answering the telephone. "That was George," she said dream
ily. "He called up just to say good night."

Chapter 16

"DO YOU REALLY THINK DICK WILL LIKE IT WHEN I GET IT fixed up? Do you think he'll be glad he married me and has a nice little home, even if it's no bigger than a minute?"

Eileen sat on the foot of the studio bed and looked eagerly up at me. In her red and bright blue plaid suit, a round white collar below her blond curls, she looked like a lovely child. Childlike, too, her wide eyes asked anxiously for a favorable answer.

I glanced around me. Late in April, just after his wedding, Dick had been transferred to the officer's training course at the same post, so instead of being with him for the week ends only, Eileen had given up her job, moved to the near-by town, and rented this ground-floor room as a home for the two of them. The gas log fireplace, the dark red wallpaper, the carpet with its sprawling flowers, showed it had once been a parlor. Now a bureau stood beside the mantel, the studio bed occupied one side of the room and to the right a gas ring, a sink, a refrigerator, and a hanging shelf filled with dishes and groceries were only partially concealed by an ornate screen. Since Dick had successfully finished his officer's training course, he would presumably serve here for three months, perhaps, if he was picked for instruction, for much longer. So Eileen had decided to decorate.

"He'll love the way you're going to do it," I said. "You just wait and see, when he gets home tonight."

"I've tried so hard to give this room an air." Eileen walked

155

to the bureau and stood straightening the objects on it: a picture of Dick in uniform in a blue leather frame, a square perfume bottle with her initials in gold. She turned to the bed and smoothed an invisible wrinkle in the crepe de Chine blanket cover. "I made this myself," she said. "I even sewed on the satin initials, and I bought this plant." She indicated a splashy green growth with great pointed leaves that stood in front of the window. "But now I can make the entire room over so it'll be just darling. All Dick has to do is to agree about the colors and the materials. I do so want him to like it. Oh, Mother Breton!" She crossed the room and gave me a soft hug. "Isn't it wonderful, just think Dick and I are really married and settled in a place all our own!"

My eyes, focused idly on the gas ring on top of the refrigerator, filled suddenly with hot tears. I thought of our house, of Norah's big sunny kitchen, Ed's and my bedroom with the sleeping porch and the pear tree beyond it, the cheerful living room with Freddie and Charles playing jacks on the floor and Babs in the big chair beside the radio. I glanced at Eileen, so eager, so terribly in love, making such a gallant attempt to create a home in somebody's dreary extra parlor. I felt distinctly irritated with Dick. Even if he *did* have so much to do all day, marching people around fields and that sort of thing, he ought to find time to be appreciative of Eileen's efforts. I told myself he must be made to take an interest. In spite of being married, she somehow seemed awfully pathetic.

"Eileen," I said, "I've never asked you about your family, but Dick has told me that neither your father nor mother was living."

"They were both killed in an automobile accident in my freshman year in college. They were driving back to Kansas."

Eileen looked down to shield the expression in her eyes and picked up a cigarette. "After that, there was just me. But I made some pretty good friends. I roomed with Twick."

"Twick?" I asked. "The girl who couldn't get to the wedding? Oh, is she the one who is here now, helping you fix things up?"

"Yes. I had an apartment with her in New York. She decorated our whole place there all by herself. Twick's so clever and knows so much. I wouldn't know where to begin without her. It was just like her to offer to come out here and do this."

"Let's see what she found this morning, the, the—" I held out a hand.

"Swatches," Eileen said promptly. "That's what decorators call samples of everything they use. Twick used to work in a decorating place. She knows all the words and music. These are the ones we liked best. Twick brought them from New York." She handed me a piece of gray wallpaper, an inch or two of reddish-brown carpeting, a bit of maize taffeta, and a scrap of heavy turquoise colored silk. "I'd have had a chaise longue of the turquoise, and used the corn color for draperies and a ruffled dressing table," she said. "It would have been lovely with an oak-leaf red rug and gray walls. But look at the red velvet fleur-de-lis wallpaper. It seems it is the pride of my landlady's heart, and can't be touched. So good-by to all this!" She gave the scrap of turquoise silk a regretful little kiss.

"What's that one?" I reached for a creamy sample with huge cabbage roses on it, smoothed it into the arm of the dingy chair. "It's really lovely." I peered at the price tag. "Whee!"

"I know, and you'd never believe how much it takes to cover

just one chair. And as for hangings and the couch . . . " Eileen stopped dismally.

"Yes, we'll have to count that out." I was firm. "I'm sure your Twick will be back soon with something we'll like better, anyway." I got up and started for the door. "I brought along my electric sewing machine. It's out in the car. Tomorrow we can buy the material and all get to work. Between the three of us, we'll have things done in no time. I also picked up the organdy bedspread and curtains from Dick's room at home, and a pair of silver lamps that came after the wedding."

"Did you?" Eileen's faced warmed up with a big smile. "Oh, Mother Breton, you're a darling! Let me go out with you and get them."

"What on earth!" I stopped on the back steps and stared. Across the back yard and down it, soldiers in khaki were sauntering along in twos and threes. "Are we barracks or something?"

"Oh, that's my landlady's war effort. She feels sorry for the boys out in that dusty camp, so she's turned her woodshed into a bath-tub room with lots of big soft towels, nice smelly soap, and hot and cold water. Anybody in uniform can take a bath here." She laughed. "One day somebody dropped his identification tag. Instead of sending it back to the camp, she mailed it to his mother! It made quite a stir. Hi'ya, Joe!" She dropped her voice. "That's one of Dick's buddies who *didn't* pass. He's back with the buck privates again."

"Was it such a stiff course?" I undid the trunk at the back of the car.

"No. But it was put into such a short time—seventy days. There was so *much* to remember, and the reserve officers were always talking in your ear when you were trying to give orders. A lot of men just couldn't take it. Here, give me some of those." We went back into the house, our arms full. "If Dickie hadn't been so smart, we wouldn't be sure of staying here."

Sure? Only the young are sure, I thought—and dismissed it. Why not be like them—gay, hopeful, and full of courage?

Going back to the room we found Twick. I saw a small, compact girl, becomingly dressed in navy and pink, with a somewhat indestructible air. She was pretty, like a certain china with rosebuds on it in a store window; it's only after you've looked at it for a while you see it's not quite as nice as you thought. Twick settled herself sideways in her chair, crossing one knee over the other, and spread out a new batch of samples.

"Oh, they really are lovely," I said. I leaned over the pieces of soft gray-blues in various materials. I really was excited. It would be fun to have a free hand—to start almost from scratch and decorate, even if it was only one room.

"Well, we'll get an interesting effect by using different textures." Twick studied the samples. "And at the same time, they'll be all right with the carpet and the red walls, which I hear we're not to do anything about."

"I think Dick will like these," I offered. "I think he'll like them better than the others. As a matter of fact, men are apt to hate yellow and they usually think flowered materials are awfully feminine. I know Ed does."

"These are so fresh looking," Eileen added enthusiastically. "They'll be just right with the organdy spread and curtains, too. Dick will think you're wonderful."

"Well, I hope so." There was a hint of exasperation in

Twick's even tone. "Your husband hasn't been very much help to date."

"Dickie works so hard." Eileen looked up quickly—her eyes defensive. "He's the *goodest* boy."

"Where is he?" I asked. "Isn't it almost time for him? I just can't wait." I hadn't seen him since the wedding. "Think of having a whole evening and then a week end together!"

Twick lifted the organdy curtains out of the box.

"If we hurry, we can have these hung before he gets here." She dragged a small stepladder from behind the screen. "Now, I'll hand you down the poles, and you and Mrs. Breton can run on the curtains."

It was then that Dick came in. He was tall and lean and— and stronger. Stronger than he used to be at home. He saw me. In two strides he crossed the room and gathered me up in a rocking hug. He turned to Eileen, looking down and touching her shoulder very gently as if she were something wonderful.

"You didn't tell me Mother was coming," he said. "Hi, Twick!"

"We're the decorating crew," she offered.

Dick's eyes went suddenly dead. For the first time I noticed the marks of strain at the corners of his eyes. He turned his head and stood looking out the window.

"You'll never know the old place." Twick sat down on top of the ladder. "D'you think you're going to go for this?" She held up a piece of blue.

"Yes. Sure," Dick said. But he didn't even look at it.

"When we get it all fixed up," Eileen put in, "it'll be just sweet, Dick. You'll like it. You wait and see. Just look at these materials Twick found."

Dick glanced at them briefly and nodded without saying anything. I'm as fond of Dick as any mother can be, but I must confess right then he gave me a feeling of exasperation. Even if he wasn't particularly interested, he could at least pretend to be. Eileen was so eager to please him. I started to say something but Twick cut in ahead of me.

"We're planning to re-cover that chair," she said, "with this. Don't you think that'll be nice?"

Dick said, "What? Oh, yeah. I guess so."

A little shadow swept across Eileen's face.

"Aren't you in'trusted, Dickie? Don't you care about your home?"

For a few seconds Dick didn't say anything. Then, very slowly, "You know, darling, I'd like to go on a party tonight —just one bang-up party."

Eileen brightened. "That'll be fun, dear. But let's decide about the color for the chairs first. You know it's awfully important. This is *our* house, Dickie, yours and mine."

Dick's eyes drifted about the shabby room. He glanced briefly at me. I had the strangest feeling that he loved this room—loved it so much, he didn't care if it was never fixed up. He reached over and took the samples that Twick had brought out of her hand, stared down at them, and absently fingered them. Then it came to me, I don't know how—all of a sudden, but I realized that something was wrong, desperately wrong. I went sort of dead inside. My own voice sounded queer to me as I said, "Dick, what is it, Dick?"

"He's just like all men," Twick put in. "Women do all they can to make a place look nice, and men don't really care."

Dick glanced at her. His mouth shaped itself into a one-sided smile, but there was no smile in his eyes.

"It isn't that I'm not interested. It's only—it's only—" He took a few quick strides until he stood beside Eileen, and put an arm around her shoulder. "It's only—" He stopped, and just stood there very still, holding Eileen tightly and looking down at her.

After what seemed like a very long time, he said, "I suppose I may as well tell you now." His voice was husky. "I was going to wait until a little later tonight, till after we'd had our binge."

Eileen's blue eyes turned dark as she looked up at him. "What is it?"

"Well, it's just—it's just— Look, darling, you've got to take this like a trouper. I've been trying to think for hours of some way to tell you this gently, but there isn't any."

"Dickie!" That one word was nothing but a soft little cry of distress.

"We won't need this place, darling—after tomorrow." He wasn't looking at Eileen now, just holding her tighter. "Mother and Dad will take care of you for me. I've got my orders. We're—we're leaving tomorrow."

Twick's awed, "Oh, gosh!" was drowned out by Eileen's cry. "Dick! Oh, Dick!" She twisted around in his arm and buried her head against his shoulder.

I heard myself say, "Where are you going, Dick?"

"I don't know," he said. "I guess—I guess it's kind of far— Australia, maybe."

I gazed at Dick, standing there, brown, real, near, so near I could have put my arms around him. I would have to tell Ed. My heart hurt inside, as if it had been struck.

Then, slowly, something happened. It happened to me. I saw us all, our family, as we had been, a little close circle,

lways eager to be at home, always glad, unconsciously, to shut
ut the world. Now the walls were down. We were part of
omething enormous that was going forward. Our neighbors,
ur whole country, stood together. Home wasn't just a cozy
est any longer. But it was a campfire—that was it—burning
n the open and its warmth was vital. Our job now was to take
are of Eileen—all the Eileens—and give them courage, to be
roud of Dick and of all our men, to set up to them, wherever
hey went, a supply line of love and pride—and, yes—of hope.

Dick's hand, the hand that was holding the blue and gray
watches, stroked Eileen's hair.

"I'll be back, darling. I'll be back sooner than you think.
We'll take 'em."

He tilted Eileen's head back and kissed her fiercely. From
etween his fingers the colored samples fell and lay like little
lags upon the floor.

Chapter 17

"YOU KNOW, MOMS," BABS SAID, "I JUST CAN'T BEAR THE way you run this house."

Babs and I were sitting together in the living room after lunch. It was a hot day at the end of June and I was taking this hour for the sedentary job of bringing the household accounts up to date.

"Listen, sweetie," I explained, "I thought Daddy was going to be out tonight, but he isn't. All I want you to do is to bring home a little cold ham. He doesn't like stew."

"Well, isn't that too bad!" Babs sat down and stretched her long legs in gray slacks in front of her. Her face glowed above the vivid green of her blouse. Her warm brown eyes studied me as if I were something she was noticing for the first time. "You know, you—you just *cater* to Daddy."

"Everybody has different likes and dislikes and you have to consider them." I took refuge in the puzzle of the grocer's slips on the desk before me. "What do you suppose an 'erk' is? It says, 'three erks, seventeen cents.'"

Babs crossed the room and looked over my shoulder.

"Cuks, short for cucumbers," she said. "And another thing. I just loathe the way you act about a few cents on a bill. It's so—so *small!* And still I'll bet you don't budget." She went back to the big chair and regarded me again. "You prob'ly don't *know* what you spend on food. Do you? Go on," she pressed, "I'm interested."

I told her the amount.

I looked up because of the silence. She was staring at me, a
new and speculative light in her eye.

"And at that we prob'ly all have vitamin deficiencies," she
said. "Hidden hunger. Malnutrition. I had it in Home Ec."

"You look pretty husky to me, every one of you." I went
on adding up figures.

"I'll tell you what I'll do." Babs got up and came toward
me. "You give me the week's money, beginning Monday, and
I'll run the house for you. I'm supposed to find a summer
project in the home." She patted me kindly on the head.
"Well, here it is!"

I have to confess that I handed the house money to Babs
on Monday with some misgivings. It takes a tidy sum to feed
two boys eleven and twelve, Babs, Eileen, Ed, and myself,
and Norah. It wasn't the money alone that gave me pause,
however, it was the incidental difficulties I knew were in-
volved. Our individual tastes in food, for one thing. My idea
of a home is that it's a place where, within reason, people can
live as they like. Babs would probably try to feed us what *she*
thought we ought to eat. Maybe Charles wouldn't get that
cup of tea he loves to have now and then. And Ed—well, in
twenty odd years of married life I've never been able to interest him in lettuce, and he simply won't eat any meat that's all
minced up. I knew that unforeseen things were bound to upset
a rigid schedule. It was only the Saturday before, for instance,
that just as we were going to sit down to a dinner of left-overs,
Ed had phoned he was bringing home two men from the factory and there was nothing for it but to send out hurriedly for
a steak big enough for nine people. But I set my misgivings
aside. This was my chance for a complete vacation from home
cares. Why not take it?

There was no sign of any wish to reform us, however, as we sat down on Monday night to the first dinner of the new regime. In fact, as Norah brought the food on, it was evident that Babs was making a definite bid for popular favor. The meal began with luscious melons, filled with cubes of all kinds of fresh fruit. Babs, sitting beside her daddy, beamed as these were followed by a huge platter of broilers, each portion a half bird reposing on toast and the whole bordered with succulent slices of orange and pineapple.

"Everything *looks* so appetizing." Eileen's voice was enthusiastic.

"I'm glad, dear," I said. Since Dick had left the country with his army outfit, and Eileen had been staying with us, she had eaten so little that I'd been worried about her.

"Like it?" Babs looked around almost tenderly at each of the family in turn. "How about you, sport?" She touched Charles's arm. "Getting enough to eat?"

"Is it a party?" Charles's small face was shining.

"No, it's the new management," I explained. "From now on, Babs is going to run the house. It's her summer project."

"I took a course." Babs's face was knit in earnest lines. "It's simple to feed a family right if you just use your bean. All you have to do is to give them *lots* of *every*thing at a meal. That way, each person finds enough that he likes that's good for him. It's called a very liberal diet."

"Sounds all right," Ed said. "What I'm interested in is how the budget comes out."

"Don't give it a thought." Babs's tone was light.

"I won't." Ed grinned. "Not until you get in a jam and come running to Daddy."

"Not me." Babs helped herself to another spoonful of ice cream. "Never in a thousand years."

I set down my coffee cup next morning after a late and leisurely breakfast in the sunny dining room, to hear sounds from the kitchen.

"Gosh sakes, Norah." It was Babs's voice. "Have a heart, will you? I just can't *afford* to get all those things at once. I've spent a *fortune* on this family already, and it's only Tuesday."

Norah's answer escaped me, but Babs's next comment came over strong.

"Well, now look, Norah. You've put down ketchup, and here's a whole part of a bottle. And scouring powder! I can hear it rattling in the box. And what do you need soap for? You've *got* some!"

"All right, but if you wait till you're all out of a thing, you won't have it when you need it. Just you ask your mother." Norah's voice rose.

I started for the kitchen. Perhaps, I thought, the new regime needed a little introduction. It was then I met Blimp.

Blimp was the dog Freddie and Charles had been saving up to buy ever since he was the roly-poly pup that earned him his name. I met him head-on because it was his hard head, hurtled toward me by a strong hungry-looking body, that hit my knees as I entered the kitchen. Freddie and Charles were close behind him, grabbing at his strap. I saw a gray-brown beast with hair that was at once short and shaggy. His wild look, however, was belied by the gentleness of his eyes. At the impact I dropped into a rocker. Blimp put a quick paw on my lap and gave me a rough lick. I got the impression he was tasting my face.

"Hello, Blimp," I said weakly.

"He likes you." Charles was pleased.

"I think he's hungry," I rallied. I took down a big dish an
went to the refrigerator, out of which Norah was taking ever
thing, preparatory to a good cleaning.

"Hey, you!" There was a scuffle, a sharp bark, and Bab
and Blimp went down together. There was a low moan from
Babs. "O-o-h! There goes all the rest of that steak left from
Saturday night." She got up, dusted her knees, and glared
viciously at Blimp as his teeth crunched on the bone.

"Here," I said, "for goodness sake! Take him out into the
yard." I handed Charles the dish I had filled with milk. Do
and boys vanished with the sound of scraping paws and
scuffling feet.

Babs turned on me. "Do you mean to say"—she screwed u
her face until one eye was tightly shut, and the other fixed me
with a glittering stare—"do you mean to say you've given tha
dog half a bottle of milk *too?* Do you know that this family
eats up five quarts every single day," she went on bitterly
"and you never told me a thing about it—the milk bill,
mean?"

"We have to have milk." I was mild.

"Okay, but we could launch a battleship with what yo
buy," Babs answered indignantly.

"I need the eggs right away," Norah interrupted. "I wan
to bake some custards. I told you this morning, when—"

"All right. All right. Keep your shirt on." Babs was evi
dently anxious, suddenly, to stop the argument. "I'll zilch
right down to the store and get them." She disappeared.

"She has to learn some time, Norah," I explained. "If any
thing goes wrong, just remember it isn't your fault."

Norah's kind face was set in stubborn lines. "All right, Mrs.
eton," she said, "but then let her not be putting it on me."
was plain that Babs had managed to lose her stoutest ally.
I went upstairs. When I came down again for lunch the
ntroversy over the dog had been renewed.

"You know what Blimps is supposed to get to eat?" Freddie
ked. "Here, gimme that paper." He snatched a smudgy
eet from Charles's hand. "He has to have one pint of milk
r breakfast, and two dog biscuits for lunch, and a big help-
g of mixed vegetables and chopped meat for dinner, and a
ove of garlic twice a week," he finished emphatically. "That
scourages worms."

Babs wasn't friendly. "You can buy garlic and dog biscuits
r your own dog. See!"

"We don't have to. See!" Freddie's voice was angry.
Blimp is family like anybody else, isn't he, Moms? You're
t goin' to change it, either."

"There are a lot of changes that could be made around this
ouse," Babs said darkly, "and someday I'm going to make
m."

Babs's troubles were brushed aside in my mind next morn-
g by the fact that Eileen was ill. When she had not come
own an hour or so after breakfast, I went up to her room. She
as lying in the single bed that used to be Dick's looking so
nall that at first I was not even sure she was there. Her head
as turned away. I went to the far side of the bed. I saw a hot,
in face, heavy eyes, and blond hair tangled on the pillow
ke a child's. I reached for her pulse. At first I didn't find it,
ven in that little wrist; when I did, it was light and very
pid. I brought my clinical thermometer, and at the end of
vo minutes by my wrist watch I took it out from under her

tongue and read it. 103°! I didn't like that; I didn't like
at all.

I called Ed and then Dr. Beard.

Meet him on the street, and Fred Beard is debonair an
impersonal. Once in the sick room, though, it's as if a curta
were pulled aside, revealing his character. He is gentle b
strong as steel. I left him alone with Eileen. It seemed a lor
time before he called me back and handed me two prescri
tions and wrote down the directions that I was to follow.
leaned over the bannister.

"Babs, dear," I called, "will you run down and get abor
four pounds of beef—round steak will do. I want to giv
Eileen some beef juice every two hours. And get some calve
foot jelly, the kind with wine in it, that comes put up in glas
She may be able to take that later in the day. And here an
the prescriptions. You can charge the things at the drugstor
to me," I added hastily. I had seen Babs's face.

That night Ed and I stood side by side as Eileen tosse
under the sheet.

"Where's Dickie?" She put out her hot little hand. She sa
us standing together in the shadows. She sat up. "I'm going t
find him." She reached for her slippers. "You took Dickie
She fell back on the pillow.

I disengaged my hand from Ed's. "I'm going to sponge he
off a little, perhaps it will quiet her." I wrung a cloth out o
lukewarm water and alcohol and applied it gently to her he
face. She turned in bed.

"Where's Mother?" she asked pleadingly. I knew she wa
talking, not about me, but about her own mother, killed in
car years before. "I want my mother." Her voice was high an
anxious.

"Mother's here; she's right here," Ed said evenly. He leaned over and touched her hair. "She'll take care of you."

Suddenly he put his arm around me impulsively. Eileen was ours now, somebody we were watching anxiously through a long night, as we had all our youngsters at one time or another—a part of the family.

"You get some rest," I said to Ed. "You have to go downtown in the morning and I don't. I'll stay here."

And then, just before two, Eileen fell into a deep sleep. Her breathing was even, regular. I put my hand on her forehead—it was damp. The fever was gone. Now it would be only a matter of a few days' care. I, too, went to bed. I put my head on Ed's shoulder. He did not even know I was there, but his solid back comforted me. I cried with relief.

It's a funny thing about life. When you're under a terrific strain, you're sort of noble and calm. The moment the strain lets up, something in you snaps, and all your weaknesses and irritability show forth. When we sat down to dinner Thursday night, Ed and I were in that mood. It was Norah's night out, and Babs brought in a big platter heaped with grayish-looking balls surrounded by clumps of watercress.

"No, thanks, Toots," Ed said. "I'll wait for the roast." It's an old gag of his and not a very funny one.

"How about some salad then? It's got grated carrots in it and lovely peanuts—and chopped watercress! Makes the eyes shiny and bright." Babs leaned down and looked at her father anxiously.

"Give mine to the rabbits." Ed smiled, without much warmth. "I'll tell you, I'll just have a couple of fried eggs."

"We're all out of them," Babs was bursting with indignation. "There was an old egg man came Tuesday and made me pay him for five dozen eggs—*five dozen!* I told him **not** to come back, pretty quick."

"Oh." Ed opened his mouth to speak but thought better of it.

"I can't think what this reminds me of," Freddie tasted his meatball critically. "Oh, I know," he brightened. "Erasers, when you chew 'em."

"There's only about a teaspoonful of ketchup!" Charles was thumping the bottom of an overturned bottle.

"Well, that's all there is," Babs said briefly. "And it's just too bad about you all griping, because I'm using up the beef I bought for Eileen's broth. I made these meat balls myself and it was a lot of work." She pushed her lower lip forward resentfully. It trembled a little.

"You're doing all right, Toots," Ed gave me a warning glance. "Matter of fact, I'm tired tonight and I'm not hungry."

"It's just that everything had to happen this week," Babs burst out. "Blimp coming and Eileen's being sick—of course I don't blame her, but she *is* a terrible expense to me—"

Ed got up from the table and patted Babs's head in passing. "Same way down in the factory," he said. "You get your costs figured and inventories all straight and even your priorities taken care of, and still there's a human element that's unpredictable." He went out of the room.

And then came Friday. The cold cereal breakfast was followed by a pot cheese and peanut butter lunch and a meager dinner of codfish balls. However, I'd made up my mind to allow no more flare-ups. Ed was right; Babs should be left to work it out in her own way. At nine o'clock the boys went to bed, and we grown-ups, as Babs used to say—Babs, Ed and I—

were left in the living room. Ed was absorbed in his paper.
Babs was sitting in a corner of the couch reading a letter which
she had already read several times since supper, a sure sign
she was bursting to tell us what was in it but hadn't quite made
up her mind to do so.

"Okay, my pet," I said at last, "what is it?"

Babs looked up startled. She was always completely surprised that her looks and actions gave her away.

"What? This? Oh, it's from George. He says he can drive
down in time for dinner tomorrow night and stay over Sunday."

"Well, that's great, dear—that's fine," I said.

"I knew he was coming, at least, I *thought* he was. I asked
him to. I've been trying for three days to save up so I can
give him everything he likes to eat over Sunday. I tried so
hard!"

"I know, dear." I thought of our being Babs's project and
of the meals we'd just had.

"I went to the store myself; I didn't even telephone. And I
got those pamphlets that tell you how to have cheap meals
with all the vitamins. It was me found out about beet tops
and mashed turnips." She jumped up, took her purse, and
sat down with it in her lap, her feet tucked up under her.
"I'd have been all right if I hadn't had all those set-backs."
She fingered a crumpled dollar bill and some odd change and
eyed it ruefully. "How can I give George anything good on
that?"

"Who's catering to who now?" I shouldn't have said it, but
I did.

"That's different." Babs's face was tight with anxiety.
"You've already *got* Daddy, so it doesn't matter what he eats.

But I'm not absolutely sure about George and it's very important." Suddenly, to my consternation, she began to cry.

I looked at her and my heart just ached. It was on the tip of my tongue to offer to provide the week-end expenses. But something stopped me. I glanced at Ed. His face was blank. I told myself firmly that this was one of those times when Babs must learn by experience; she must fight it out alone.

I went upstairs and collected a basket of mending. When I came down Ed was sitting as I had left him in the big chair. The compelling music of somebody's orchestra was pouring out of the radio. Babs was pivoting slowly in the middle of the floor. Dangling from her left hand was a five dollar bill.

"You're married to the most *wonderful* man," she said dreamily, "the most understanding, handsome, wunnerful man."

"Oh, no." Ed smiled deprecatingly. "Just part of the unpredictable human element."

Babs danced out of the room. Ed looked up at me. His eyes asked me to see how it was.

"Do you think," Ed asked, "you could interest that daughter of yours in some other project for the rest of the summer? Nobody knows how I hate beet tops."

Chapter 18

THE CONDUCTOR POCKETED HIS WATCH, WAVED HIS HAND, and swung aboard. The train began to move. The heat beat up from the wooden platform in visible, weaving curves. High above us two small faces peered through the car window for a last look. Freddie and Charles were off for Scout Camp for the month of August, by train this time, because when the tires of our car were gone none would be available.

"I hate to see them go," I told Ed and I walked back to the car. "It *will* be awfully restful, though, to be home with just Eileen and Babs. I intend to relax and enjoy the peace and quiet."

Ed slid in under the wheel.

"Listen," he said, "any time a week goes by in our house without a major crisis, I want to know it. Eileen is a restful girl, but Babs—" He swung to one side to avoid a yellow cat spinning along the road. "Babs lives on excitement. My belief is that she abhors peace and quiet the way Nature abhors a vacuum."

I sank down comfortably into the seat. Ed is the only person with whom I don't unconsciously use all my driving muscles—when I'm not driving.

"Well, you know how it is, with a girl like Babs. At seventeen, you're always either on the crest of the wave or so low you have to look up at a mouse hole. As a matter of fact, it's Eileen I'd be a little concerned about if I were going to worry right now, which I'm not. She doesn't seem a bit like herself. I think she's terribly anxious about Dick."

"Naturally, aren't we all?" Ed asked.

No word had come from Dick since he said good-by to Eileen at camp. Our guess had been he was on the way to Australia.

The car drew up to the pavement. I got out at our corner so that Ed could hurry on to the factory. They were still making munitions down there. Ed was always pushing to fill his war contracts and never had half the time he needed.

I went up the walk to our front door and there I met the postman. He stopped, his boots crunching the dry hot gravel. His weathered, grayish face wore a tired smile.

"I left a letter inside," he said. "It's from overseas."

I went into the organdy-curtained coolness of the living room looking for Eileen. Norah had just placed a green bowl with white sprays from the garden there. (Once when I was too busy to prepare an entry Norah sent a floral arrangement with cuttings from our garden to the Garden Club flower show and won the first prize.) But while my eyes were grateful for the flowers, my mind was not on them. I was impatient for the news.

I first saw Babs sitting on the sofa, staring intently across the room. Opposite her, Eileen sat holding a letter in both hands. It was a thin sheet covered with Dick's familiar, even handwriting. Eileen's face was a blot of white above the candy pink of her cotton suit. There were deep circles under her big gray eyes, but a look of strain I had noticed lately was gone now and she was half smiling. Dick was all right then. I could wait for the details.

"What is all this?" I asked. While George is often here to see Babs, his home is fifty miles away.

"He wanted a job in a munitions factory for the summer," Babs said, "so he went to see Daddy. And now"—her voice was a little too firm—"we're going to get married."

I sat down on the edge of the nearest chair as if something had struck my knees from behind. If Ed was startled, he didn't show it.

"Does George know it?" Ed smiled indulgently.

"Daddy! I knew you'd talk like that." Babs bounced up and down on the couch. "You'd just better make up your mind to this. I was never so serious about anything in my life."

"Neither was I." Ed drew his mouth back into a smile without any glow; it squared the corners. But all he said was, "Don't talk nonsense." He took his hat and went out of the front door. Wonderful in a genuine crisis, when he runs into one he thinks is trumped-up, Ed simply walks away.

"But everybody's getting married, Moms." Babs viewed her father's receding back indignantly. "You said so yourself the other day, and you said you thought it was a very wise thing, too. I heard you. Oh, Moms!" She came and put her arms around me from behind, crossing them under my chin just as Dick used to do. "*Talk* to Daddy, will you? He's so— so unlistening. You're the only one who can ever do anything with him. I just *count* on you!"

It may have been that direct appeal to me, or perhaps I am what Babs in a different mood would call "Mrs. Rat-trap for biting." But I could not help feeling I must give the possibility of Babs's getting married very serious consideration. I knew, too, although Babs didn't, that Ed had by no means dismissed the matter from his mind. Going off, he was more likely to be thinking it out alone. It would come up later and I must be ready with my personal decision and good reasons for it. Yet I could not come to a decision. Youngsters need guidance they need protection. But there comes a time when both guidance and protection may cramp and cut off something very lovely and very real that should have been allowed to live and grow.

I said this to Ed as we moved about our bedroom getting fixed up for supper. Ed caught my eye in the mirror. His own was stern.

"Honestly, dear," he said, "sometimes I wonder about you. You're just the kind of sentimental little nitwit who *would* encourage a seventeen-year-old girl and a nineteen-year-old boy to get married, stop their education, and spoil their future. And live on us, I suppose," he added. "I'm certainly not going to take care of George, and if I know George's old man, he isn't, either."

The door, which stood ajar, was pushed open.

"May I come in?" Without waiting for an answer, Babs crossed the room and sat down on the small straight chair between my dressing table and the tall bureau, in front of which her father was standing studying his face in the mirror. "Now, there's no use trying to get away, you two," she said. "I want to know why you don't approve of my marrying a perfectly wonderful person like George." She looked balefully at her Daddy, her face alive and glowing above the yellow-green of her linen dress.

"You're too young," Ed and I said together.

"I guess that's for George to decide," Babs's tone was meant to be final.

"Yes, but what about the future?" Ed tried to make his voice patient. "With another year at college George can finish the pre-medical course. He tells me he's decided to be a doctor. Then, even if he's drafted, he can come back when the war is over and study to be a surgeon, the way he's always wanted to. And when this war is over"—Ed's eyes stared thoughtfully at the opposite wall—"this country is going to need educated men in the worst kind of a way. What are we going to do for doctors if we haven't any men prepared to study medicine?" He worked his lower lip over his upper one. His face was grave.

There was no reaction to this from Babs. With almost a start Ed brought his eyes back to her, in a puzzled way.

"All right then," he asked, "what about George's own future? What's he got to give up to marry you? If you love a man, you must look ahead for him."

Babs's brown eyes filled up with tears. "That's not fair, Daddy. Of course, I love him. But lots of successful men never even went to college. Besides, why can't he go back to college even if he *is* married to me?"

"And take you along with him to the fraternity house?" If there was sarcasm in Ed's voice, it failed to register with Babs.

"We'll live here." She seemed surprised. "I've got my room. You'll just have George, too, all the time, this summer, and week ends, all next year. Won't that be *fun?*" There was an overtone of anxiety in Babs's voice.

"That's no way to start a married life," I began.

"Eileen moved right into Dick's room. I don't see why George can't move into mine." Babs's face was stormy. I knew the look. I'd seen it all through childhood days, whenever Dick was allowed to do something that she wasn't.

"But Dick's helping win the war," I began again.

"So is George." Babs's voice rose angrily. "He *wanted* to enlist, but the family made him promise to stay in college until he was drafted and fit himself to study medicine. That's why he was determined to work in a munitions plant this vacation; he wanted to help the war along. He's just as important as Dick is, and if Eileen can live here, I guess George can."

It was then that we heard the unmistakable sound of sobbing. Quick, gasping sobs they were and they came from Eileen's room. Babs's eyes met mine, full of remorseful surprise.

"Oh, gosh," she said, "I didn't know she was home. Oh, my gosh!"

Both Babs and I hurried to where Eileen lay flung across the bed. Her feet in gay little red pumps were hanging in space and her head with the tumbled blond curls lay on her crossed arms at the far side.

"Eileen!" I ran forward. "What is it, dear?"

Babs sat down on the pillow and leaned anxiously over the turned-down head. "*What's* the matter, crumb-bun?" she asked. "I didn't mean that about—" Her voice pleaded for a chance to help.

Eileen lifted a flushed face. Her gray-blue eyes were blurred with tears, but I saw at once that they were tears of excitement.

"I'm going to have a baby," she said. "I've just come from the doctor's. I'm so *happy* and I want to tell Dickie and—and he isn't here." She buried her head in Babs's comforting arms and began to cry again, but softly now.

Babs sat holding Eileen. Her mouth made small wordless sounds. She looked down with great commiserating eyes. She stroked the tumbled hair with a proprietary, motherly hand.

"Tell you what," Babs brightened. "I'll make you a whole baby's layout. Layout?"

She saw a puzzled look on my face.

"You know. A whole set of shirts and nighties and adorable little dresses with blue bows on them. Won't you like that?" she asked. She jiggled Eileen's head to be sure of getting her attention. There was no ignoring her and no resisting her interest. Eileen turned her face upward and even managed a smile.

And then, suddenly, there was a sound of loud barking and Blimp hurled himself along the lower hall and against the screen door. A familiar voice said,

"Hi there, Blimps. Don't you know who it is, old boy?"

"George!" Babs jumped up, electrified. "Listen, Eileen!" She leaned down and peered into the tear-stained face on her lap. "Let's tell *him* about the baby."

A faint grin rewarded her. "But not in front of me," Eileen said.

After supper Ed took Eileen and me to the movies. We wanted to entertain and distract her. We wanted, too, to put off for the moment the inevitable interview with George. We would feel better able to handle the determined young people after the movies, when it was cooler. A little breeze blowing in from the garden picked up some of the whirling mist of the spray on the lawn. But the heat of the afternoon still hung in the street. The artificially cooled air of the movie house was grateful and the pictures took us out of our own affairs. It was almost a shock, hours later, to re-enter the hot street, to see the garishly lighted shops, to pick up again the cable of real life.

We found Babs still up. She was sitting in the big chair in the living room with a kind of inner glow on her face.

"Where's George?" I asked.

"He's gone."

I saw there was more to come. I dropped on the couch, Eileen beside me. Ed stood tamping his pipe in silence.

"We've decided *not* to get married," Babs said.

"Well, well." Ed's voice was noncommittal.

"How'd that happen, dear?" I tried to keep my tone even.

"George is so wonderful!" Babs looked around at her audience of three and ended by fixing her eyes upon me. "You know, Mother, he's the wisest, far-est-looking man I ever knew. I said, now he had a job, we could get married right away. He said he'd been thinking about it. He said I had the best person in the country pleading for me—him!"

"Well?" Ed was biting hard on his pipe stem. He did not look at me.

"But he said he thought we were both too young. He said his father wanted him to stay in college another year. He's influenced a lot by what his father wants. I think that's a wonderful quality in a man, don't you?"

"Oh, yes! I do!" Ed's voice had conviction in it.

"And then"—Babs spoke as if it were a brand new idea—"he said, when this war was over the country was going to need doctors like nobody's business and he wanted to be prepared to go into medical school."

"I think that's pretty fine." I meant it.

"And then I told him," Babs's voice went smoothly on, "how we could live here while he was in college—I knew ou'd let us, really. And I told him all about how Eileen was oing to live here as long as Dick was in the Army, and how he was going to have a baby and everything."

"You did? What did he say?" Eileen's startled eyes were vide. It evidently had not registered that Babs was really oing to take George into their confidence.

"He thought it was a swell idea for you and Dick, but he aid *he* would want to make his own home for the mother of is child. And just now, he thought the best thing for him to o was to get all the education he could and then be free to go vhere he would do the most good for the country. And he aid," Babs finished breathlessly, "we were both young enough o wait a little while, and I think so, too. George is so—well, e's just *noble*." She looked at her father with shining eyes. Don't you really think he's about the most wonderful man ou ever knew?"

Ed looked down at the earnest upturned face. He took out is pipe and with his free hand he patted Babs's soft brown air. He could not suppress a deep sigh.

"George is worth waiting for," he said firmly. "George has ot stuff."

Chapter 19

"WELL," I SAID, "I GUESS WE CAN MANAGE A ONE DAY TRI
without a man along."

"Yes, but who wants to?" Babs looked appealingly at m
across the corner of the breakfast table, then renewed he
attention to the toast. "I'm making this for you, Eileen," sh
said. "I want my nephew to be a nice fat baby."

Eileen smiled appreciatively. One of the things she enjoy
most about living with us is the light-hearted protectivenes
of her young sister-in-law.

"Oops." Babs caught a slice as it popped up. "This is th
spookiest gadget."

"What do you expect an electric toaster to do," Ed aske
"ring a bell, like a sidewalk elevator?" He put down his na
kin. "Well, I've got to push off."

"But, Daddy, you really aren't going to let George go wit
us?" Babs made a doleful face. "That's a heck of a note. It
his last Saturday before college opens. I should think your o
factory could get along without him this once, so's he cou
take care of your wife and daughters for you."

Ed patted her curls as he came around the table. "I gue
you three girls can take care of yourselves, all right."

"That's chivalry for you." Babs ducked. "The America
husband and father."

Ed laughed. He had offered us the car and what gas w
in it to drive out to the lake for a last picnic and swim of t
season. He stood for a moment by my chair. "Here, Mon

better take the ration book. Couldn't get any gas last night. I'm entitled to some more but I tried three filling stations without any luck. If you see a chance to get some, do." He leaned down and kissed me. "You've got enough to take you out there and back all right if you're careful. All you've got to do," he finished, without even a prophetic gleam in his kind gray eyes, "is not to run out of gas on a lonely road."

Babs fixed him with a challenging look. "What kind of dimwits do you think we are?"

"I don't think; I know." Ed grinned and went out.

It really might have been an uneventful day if Babs hadn't spotted a roadside log cabin on the way to the Lake and insisted on going in for something cold to drink. Considering the bright daylight outside, the interior was extraordinarily dark. There was a bar along the far wall, and although it was only about eleven in the morning, there were a number of men in front of it. They looked us over as we came in, and I realized it was not an appropriate place for unescorted women. One of the loungers in particular impressed himself on my mind. Perhaps it was his outfit, a green and orange checked coat over colored shirt and slacks; perhaps it was his face, which was heavy, with an upper lip overhanging the lower in a broad V, or his black eyes, which had a concentration I did not like. Nor did I like the fact that he looked fixedly at Babs. I thought of explaining this to her and leaving with our glasses still untouched on the table, but decided not to. Plainly, she had not noticed him. Babs's greatest protection is the fact that such things don't even register with her. I would forget him, too.

It was almost noon when we turned down the dirt road that ran to the edge of the lake. A northwest breeze swept out of a brilliant blue sky piled with white clouds and darkened the water, driving it on in exciting little waves that slapped the shore. There was the smell of wetness and of dead leaves and of the earth along the bank. We could hardly wait to get into our bathing suits. Eileen and I swam rather sedately about in front of a short beachy stretch, while Babs dove from a great square boulder. As she came thrashing through the water an enormous old turtle with a shell like the seat of a wooden chair rose where she had been and peered inquisitively after her over the surface. Something about the horny, reptilian head was vaguely reminiscent. Suddenly I placed the expression—the man at the bar. Rolling in her crawl, Babs lifted her head and saw him, but she plunged on unconcerned. He sank out of sight. After the swim I lifted a small box of paper and kindling out of the car and Babs started a very professional fire.

"Here," Eileen said, "I can do something." She set the coffee pot on the stone next to the blaze.

"Hey, what goes on here?" Babs shielded her face and put out a quick hand to the pot as a yellowish smoke puffed up from it into the breeze.

"Oh goodness, that must be the extra box of kitchen matches." I stopped, contritely, then, "I packed the coffee and the lump sugar in the pot. There wasn't any water in it, dear. The matches were on top."

"Well, that's one thing *not* to tell Daddy." Babs laughed down at Eileen's rueful face. "And now, why don't you two just sit down somewhere and relax and let me cook the chops?"

At last it was almost time to go. I wandered about, picking autumn leaves and goldenrod.

"It's really kind of nice," I said, "not to have any men along. They never want you to stop for flowers. They always say, 'Where, dear?' when they know it was at least a half a mile back."

We talked about Dick, stationed in Ireland, and about George and how once he got back in the pre-medical course, he would never have a vacation again. Then silence fell. It's queer; in a house, it's sort of a relief to have men go out for a little while. You can get to a lot of things that would bore or bother them if they were at home. But you enjoy it because you know they're coming in again, presently, bringing with them a little sense of renewal and a little tightening up of morale. But going somewhere without them is different. Babs felt it, too. She sat up and stretched.

"Well, kids," she asked, "what do you say we push off for home?"

We were only about two miles from town when a gasoline truck swung onto the highway ahead of us. Babs spotted it first.

"Oh, boy," she said, "here's where we get that gas for Daddy. He'll be tickled pink."

"How?" Eileen turned a puzzled face toward Babs, who was driving.

"Listen, my pet." Babs leaned out and watched the truck, which seemed to be slowing down. "He's delivering gas to a filling station, isn't he? All right, we drive in right behind him and get ours. They can't say they haven't got any when we saw it come." The truck turned sharp right onto a dirt road. "He's taking the short cut over to route eleven. There's a filling station right where the road comes out."

"But we're going away from home," I began doubtfully.

"All in a good cause." Babs took the turn and bounced us down over the culvert. The car followed a soft road which ran across a swampy stretch and then plunged into a tunnel of woods. Bright patches of sky were visible through the leaves but a kind of twilight lay like a carpet on the gravel and the coarse grass on either side. The truck led us on. Suddenly, without any warning, our engine coughed a little and our car rolled to a standstill. Far ahead the bounding tail of the truck vanished around a curve. We were alone.

Across Eileen, Babs and I looked at each other.

"Well, we're out of gas," Babs said. "I guess we're not as smart as we thought we were."

A late bird gave forth a few high notes in the treetops and then was still. It began to seem very lonely indeed. I glanced at Babs, relaxed behind the wheel, looking thoughtful but unconcerned. I realized that she didn't feel the panic that was slowly rising within me. With difficulty, I kept myself from communicating it to her.

"Something's coming." Eileen peered nervously down the road.

Around the bend, so recently vacated by the truck, a small car was coming on. It was driven by a lone soldier. He stopped, his fender almost against our own. He was sandy-haired and khaki-colored all over and quite undistinguished-looking except for his eyes, which were a blazing blue and had a laugh in them.

"Hey," he called, "would you mind pulling out of the road so I can get by?"

"Sorry, we're stuck," Babs smiled.

He studied the situation. "I'll give you a shove." He nudged our car to the side of the road.

"Thanks." By this time I was standing by his running board. "Would you mind taking me along to a garage or at least to a telephone?" It would be better for me to go with the stranger and the two others to remain together, I thought.

He cast a somewhat disappointed glance at the girls then leaned over and opened the door. I climbed in and we drove off.

"I'm real glad to have you along," the soldier said. His name I had found out was Michael. "Matter of fact, I'm sort of whistling to keep up the old courage and I hate doing it alone."

"What's the matter?" I looked up in some surprise at this tawny boy who sat so tall beside me.

"I went home on a couple of days' furlough to see my grandmother." He explained she had given him this car. "I was supposed to report back for duty early this morning?"

"Oh, dear," I said, as he paused.

"But you don't know my grandmother. She's just a little bit of a thing, but she's awfully determined. She isn't going to have her boy 'all wore out.' She took away the alarm clock while I was asleep so I never woke up till almost noon time."

I did not answer. I was thinking about grandma and her little scheme and all the invisible cobwebs, set up by affection, through which men so often have to break to reach their posts of duty.

"Golly!" We swerved to avoid a turtle placidly crossing the road. A car coming the other way had missed it by inches. The turtle, the coupé, the driver, were a single picture in my mind as we drove on. And then I sat up stiffly.

"Wait, that man in the car . . ." I told Michael about the horrible man. "He was watching the girls while we got a coke in a roadhouse this morning. "I'm sorry," I finished, "but I've simply got to get out and go back."

"We'll both go back." He was already turning the car. "I'm A.W.O.L. anyhow. Protecting the ladies gives me a really good excuse."

Michael saw it first.

"Good Godfrey," he said, "what happened?"

Another car stood beside our own, but that wasn't what caught my vision. It was Babs bending over something by the side of the road. My heart stopped. Eileen? No, there was Eileen sitting on the running board. Hearing us, Babs stood up, distress all over her face. The boy named Michael and I reached the fallen figure in almost the same instant. It was the man in the orange and green coat and the arty slacks.

"What's the matter?" I asked. "Did a car hit him?"

"*I* hit him!" Babs said excitedly.

"But he's out like a light!" Michael was plainly unconvinced.

"Well, I didn't mean to hurt him. Honest, Mother, I didn't. Honest, it wasn't my fault."

"He must have followed us," Eileen put in. "He just came down the road and stopped and got right out and . . . "

"And he poked his goofy old face right in over the door at me, and Eileen having a baby and everything. Oh! 'Scuse me!" She looked meekly at Michael.

"Think nothing of it." Michael's face relaxed into a grin.

"So I gave him a push. I had no idea he'd go over so easy. I guess he hit his head on something. He just lay there with his eyes closed, like in a movie. I dragged him here over to the grass so he'd be more comfortable." Babs's voice dropped to a worried note. "You don't think he's dead, do you?"

At this moment the man rolled his head and opened his eyes. They were yellowish and devoid of expression, yet menacing, like those of a snake. He saw Babs, looming over him. He closed them with a groan.

"I bet a bird like this has got an extra can or two of gas cached somewhere." Michael was poking around the coupé as he spoke. He lifted the back. "I thought so. Two five gallon cans, both full. Here's where we take one."

"All right. But I'm going to leave the money for it." I counted out a little pile of coins from my purse then went around and put them beside the remaining tin. I smiled up at Michael, passing with the can in his hand. "I'm fussy who I'm indebted to."

Michael emptied the tin into our tank and put it back. "And now," he said, "we better get this guy into his car." He put his boot out. "On your feet." The man opened his eyes heavily and started to close them. Then recognizing the uniform he shivered just once, and got groggily up.

"How do you feel?" Babs studied him anxiously. "All right now?"

"Don't you worry about him." Michael propelled him toward the car. The man climbed, grumbling, under the wheel. Michael reached in and snapped on the head and rear lights. "Just in case," he explained.

We all walked back together to our car where Eileen was sitting, looking, I noticed, a little drawn. This had been quite a day for her. We must get home now. For a moment Michael, Babs, and I stood smiling at each other. It had been us against the intruder.

"Gee, it was swell of you to come back." Babs was all

friendliness. "The good old U.S. Army. Always there in case of need."

"We have a boy in the Service, too," I put in, "haven't we?"

Eileen's thin hand lay against the side of the car and I placed mine on it.

"Oh, yeah?" Michael's glance at Eileen was full of quick sympathy. "What outfit?" We told him. "We might meet up some time."

"If you do," I said, "be sure to tell him how you protected the women of his family." We got into the car. "Good-by now, and thanks for everything."

Michael stood with his hands on the door next to Babs.

"About that 'protecting' now," he said, "from what I've seen around here, you don't need us men much. You can pretty well take care of yourself."

"Oh, sure. But—" Babs turned her brown eyes toward his. "Well, all the same—we miss you!"

Something electric flashed in Michael's eyes, something brilliant, like light, and urgent, like power. It flared and fell away. Babs, giving all her attention to the road, started the car. When I leaned out to wave once more, Michael had turned on his heel.

And then we were going into our own driveway. While Babs put up the car, I walked slowly toward the house with Eileen. At my suggestion, she went upstairs to lie down. I entered the living room. I confess my nerves were badly shaken. It was not only the sense of danger met, although that had left a tremor behind it, it was also the sense of change, a realization of how fast our men were moving into action, of how casual and fleeting our contacts with them had to be, and of how girls of Babs's age really might have to take care of themselves for a long, long time.

I found Ed peacefully reading his paper to the accompaniment of the baseball news over the radio. He looked dear and familiar and dependable. In the dining room beyond Norah was filling the glasses on the supper table with milk. I dropped into my own small chair. Ed glanced up.

"Have fun?" he asked with casual kindness. "Anything happen?"

Did anything happen! I opened my mouth to speak, but at that moment Babs wandered in.

"Nothing special, my pet," she said. "Oh, yes, I forgot. We bought you your gas!" She leaned across him to spin the radio dial, yawning slightly.

Chapter 20

MOTHER, REALLY, YOU'RE NOT GOING TO TAKE ONE OF those silly courses and clump around the streets in uniform?" Babs's brown eyes met mine with deep disfavor. It was one of those warm days in the first of September. She was standing in the doorway, her tan skin warm and firm above—and below—the frosty white of her tennis clothes. "I hate this old war!" she went on indignantly. "It just spoils everything."

I looked at her, not knowing quite what to say. I had gone through many changes in my own mind toward the war. When it first broke out, in Europe, I didn't feel it concerned us. Next, it hung terrifyingly over and ahead, like something I remembered from one night when I was swimming in the ocean. The person beside me suddenly said, "Look!" Against the horizon there loomed an oncoming wave, so huge, so imminent, it shut out half the sky. Too paralyzed to try to escape, we simply trod water. Presently, however, we realized that it did not advance, that it was in fact an island seen in silhouette. In somewhat the same way, the war took shape. It did not move in toward us. Even when Dick was drafted, it did not come to us; he went. After that, I tried to avoid the war in my own mind. I behaved like a little animal who sits tensely quiet, hoping the big and dangerous thing will pass him by. I did not want to talk about the possibilities ahead, for fear what was put into words might come true. When Dick was shipped to Ireland and Eileen came to live with us I still shied away from it all. It was Norah who freed me and set me into action

I had finished breakfast one morning and she was standing beside me, an empty cereal dish in her hand, while we talked over the meals for the day. As I finished, she began: "It came over the radio last night, Mrs. Breton. We've all got to work for this war. I'd be no good for anything but housework. I'd never get the hang of it, except maybe to dig in the fields. But you've got the education, Mrs. Breton." She looked at me a moment, full and fair, her earnest blue eyes searching my face. "Bombings and sinkings, sinkings and bombings! A body gets tired of hearing about it all." She sighed. Then she went on resolutely, "But we've all got to help, if we're going to beat 'em back."

At dinner that night, I told the family my decision. I had enrolled to train as a nurse's aid.

"An old aid?" Ed smiled across at me. "Well, as long as you don't try any war work around our place, it's okay. I guess we can make munitions without calling on the women." (I wondered how long, but I did not say so.)

"Then may I run the house, Mother Breton?" Eileen asked. "I'm a demon marketer. I know all about poking chickens' breastbones to see how old they are and everything."

"I thought you looked at their teeth." Babs's tone was serious.

"That's horses, stupid," Freddie began. Babs grinned and Freddie saw he had fallen into the trap. To cover up, he went on hurriedly, "Just so long as you don't go learning how to take care of children. Harold's mother takes that."

And now Babs was registering her disapproval, not to say scorn, of a war effort. I wasn't bothered by anything Ed might say, because what he does counts so much. His is an all-out job for the government. The boys are small, but they're lined up with the Boy Scouts; at various times they've collected aluminum and waste paper and rubber. They're on call to carry messages in an emergency. (Ed says he's going to have a sign made to hang on the bicycle, "Freddie is ready!") But Babs's attitude troubled me. She seemed to regard the war primarily as something that kept her from driving a car, made the boys work all summer instead of sitting around on the porch, and stopped all her fun. I did not know how to make her realize each one of us had to be responsible, and, anyway, I was busy finding my own place in the plan for the war. I was excited about it and a little bit nervous. So I let her comments pass unchallenged.

Then it was next morning and Ed turned off the alarm.

"Is it really time to get up?" I snuggled down deeper. In the pear tree that brushed the screen of the sleeping porch, there was a great going-on of birds. On a twig directly opposite me, a sparrow sat ruffling and resettling his feathers. "Silly. As if he had anything to do," I said.

"Well, *I've* got to get down to the plant." Ed ran his hand over my hair. "But why don't you stay in bed? You haven't a thing in the world to do that can't wait." I lay contentedly watching the pattern of the leaves against the sky. And then I remembered. Nurse's aid began that day. I leaped out of bed.

We met in a bare room furnished with a desk, folding chairs, a white iron crib on one side, to the left, and a high, narrow hospital bed to the right. The instructor smiled in a kind but detached way. For her convenience, we were seated alphabetically. I took my chair, in the middle of the front row, realizing with something of a shock that I wasn't used to being out in the world. At home, everyone who comes in asks automatically, "Where's Moms?" Afterward, each one may go his way, but my being there is essential; it's what apparently makes everything all right. Here nobody would care, personally, whether I was present or not. I was just one in a row of women in a class.

I looked down our row. Next to me sat a handsome girl with a high color, a small tight-lipped mouth, and blue eyes so dark and intent that they seemed almost black. A really beautiful bracelet, wide and jeweled, with pale sapphires, fell below the sleeve of her sports suit. Her legs were gracefully crossed and her foot, in a honey-colored alligator pump, swung restlessly, so that the light caught the disk of a slave chain on her ankle. I found out later that her name was Lila. Beyond her sat a Mrs. Brown, a woman of at least fifty. She looked up seriously at the instructor. Her face was without make-up and deeply dented. Her figure curved comfortably under the dark blue of her cotton dress. At the far end was a girl only a few years older than Babs. I never mastered her last name, but her first name was Mirella. Her thin black dress was skin tight and she carried a worn bright red pocketbook. I wondered if they could make us all into something useful and how much trouble we would give them in the process.

"What would you do," I asked a few days later as the family was at supper, "if an emergency case was brought into the operating room and the doctor began giving you orders about assisting him?" I sat back pleased because, of all the family, only I knew the answer.

Charles abandoned his attack on applesauce and hot gingerbread to give me his full attention.

"I'd try to be very quiet," he said. Charles has a British awareness of proper conduct.

"Being quiet don't matter." Freddie withered him with a scornful glance. "The guy's out cold, anyway."

"*Doesn't* matter, shrimp," Babs corrected him. "Well, first, I'd wash my hands."

"You'd both be right up to a certain point." I knew now that a good instructor registers his approval whenever possible. "But what you would do is to *leave* quietly and let the doctor call for a regular nurse. He probably didn't notice that you were only a nurse's aid. An aid is not allowed to do operating room work."

"Well, s'pose Daddy's factory blew up?" Freddie asked eagerly.

"Or a bomb hit the hotel? That's what'll *probably* happen." Charles had heard about all that in England.

"That's different," I answered. "I'd be allowed to help if needed at the scene of a disaster."

To my surprise it was George who answered. George had come up for supper. He was hard at work as a shipping clerk in Ed's factory, and the effect had been sobering.

"I think what your mother's doing makes a lot more sense than most things," he said. "Wouldn't hurt you, angel, to know how to take care of people. Who's going to hold my hand when I need it?"

"Who wants to?" Babs's look was gay.

"Lots of girls." George was cocky. "Okay, when I get hurt, I'll open my eyes and ask for your mother." He turned to me and smiled. George's smile is engaging; it has sparkle.

"Oh, is that so!" Babs did not seem to be able to think of any better rejoinder. "Well, I can't be a nurse's aid anyhow; I'm too young."

"Then at least you needn't laugh at your mother's being one." Because George loves her and can't do much about it, Babs irritates him terribly at times. He tucked his arm through mine as we walked out of the dining room. "A lot of fellows think it's crazy," he went on, "their mothers going all out for the war, at *their* age." He looked at me without a bit of humor in his young eyes. "Personally," he said, "I think it does them good. Look at my mother's friends. Until this war came along, they never did a darn thing but play golf and bridge and shop. Personally, I'm all for it."

"I'd go a step further," I answered. "I mean, I hope it will help, indirectly, to *win* the war." I freed myself gently. "You're the one to work on Babs." I meant it, but I didn't know how well he would succeed.

A few days later the front row—we four—lunched in the hospital cafeteria together, invited by Lila. A few questions set us to telling about ourselves. Mrs. Brown was a widow. Her children had married and left home.

"I'm well and strong," she said. "There's a lot of good in me yet, and I thought I ought to help."

Mirella, the girl in black, was unmarried. She cooked for and took care of an ailing mother, a partially crippled aunt, and an exacting grandfather, all living on the ground floor and basement of a two-family house. It was evident she snatched desperately at any excuse to get out, even for a couple of hours.

"I was going to take interior decorating," she said, "or maybe be a dentist's assistant, but on account of I never could get time to do my homework, I never finished school."

Only Lila did not give any information about herself—at first. Presently the other two left, each having housework waiting to be done. Lila and I sat on. She lit a cigarette. "What's your first name?" she asked.

"Elizabeth."

"Mind if I call you that?" She smoked reflectively. "I'm a wreck, just making that bed over twice till I got it right; and they're going home to start in all over again. Really, they're simply wonderful. I never liked women. Maybe because they don't like me, either. But, honestly, I'm crazy about *both* Mrs. Brown and Mirella."

I considered Lila, so smart, so vulnerable under the varnish. "A course like this does teach you a lot besides nursing." But Lila's mind had gone on to something else.

"I don't kid myself that what I'm doing is going to win the war," she said. "But anyway, now, I've got some reason to get up in the morning."

"It *will* help." And then, not because Lila was sympathetic, but because she thought straight, like a man, I found myself telling her about Babs, about her attitude toward the present situation.

"You were probably peeking out of your baby carriage in the last war," I said, "but I was in college full of dewy-eyed ideals; we were very emotional then, about war. Now, we're different—people my age, I mean. We're filled with a deadly determination to finish this right and fix the world so everybody can live in peace in it. This is a grim war, even grimmer than the other one. We've all got to push with every ounce of strength we have, and instead of working to help, Babs acts as if the war were something that spoiled her life."

Lila looked up at me as if I were hard to understand.

"What do you expect at seventeen?" she asked. "It *does* spoil her life, doesn't it? My mother used to think I was terrible because when I was around that age I said I hated babies and was never going to have any. But when the time came, I did all right by my baby."

"You have a baby?" I asked delightedly. "How old is he?"

"He's—he's four," Lila said, "but I don't have him now. His father saw to that. He had money enough to fix it up good and tight." She ground out her cigarette with a sudden motion. "What do you say we get out of here?"

I was too stunned to do anything but shift the conversation back to safer grounds. I reached for my pocketbook.

"I have to get home," I said. "Babs has a college friend coming to stay overnight."

"Well, don't get in a state over Babs." Lila rose. "When the time comes, my bet is she'll produce."

In the weeks that followed, we finished our course and finally began our actual volunteer work in the hospital. Mrs. Brown was assigned to the men's floor, so we did not see her on duty, nor Mirella, who was on the roof with the crippled children. But Lila and I worked side by side in the women's surgical ward. Lila went about her task of bathing patients and making their beds with a kind of savage, unsmiling energy. She gave no confidences and received none, but although I fancied her charges were a little terrified of her, they looked more spruce and better cared for, somehow, than mine. Their pillows were straighter, more smartly set. My work seemed to be a routine of small jobs—moving the pillow a fraction of an inch or two under the back of heavy Mrs. McKlosky in the first bed, telephoning the grocery below the Rosella apartment to see how the five Rosella children were managing without their mother, giving drinks of water to Mrs. Grube, who wasn't going to recover, and so on down the line. Often I left for home so tired I wondered if I could make it. At one such time, I lay down on my bed without even taking off my coat. Babs's incredulous face peered in at my door.

"Gosh, Moms, what's happened to you?"

"Nothing, except that I'm all in." I opened my eyes and closed them again. "It's just I've been on my feet every minute all day."

She went away and came back with a washcloth wrung out of cold water. She laid it on my forehead.

"Well," she said. "Relax. Forget about the old hospital. By the middle of next week, you'll be through there, won't you?"

"My required time is up then, if that's what you mean," I answered.

"That's what I thought." She sat down on the edge of the bed. "So listen, Moms, I want to ask you something. You know that Service benefit next week? Well, George is taking me and I'm going to be in it. I'm going to wear white and be the 'New World.' I stand right in the middle of the whole cast, just before the final curtain. Isn't that the nuts?"

"It sounds wonderful." I tried not to sound half asleep.

"And listen, Moms. You get through at the hospital Wednesday night and the show isn't until Saturday, so I thought Thursday you and I could go out and shop for some lovely shiny material and Friday we could make it up. I know just how I want to look. I want the dress to sort of float and shimmer. I want to just take George's breath away." She paused. Then, "I *can't* do it alone, and Eileen's no help when it comes to sewing. Yesterday she was sitting in front of the machine trying to stitch a skirt with the tread up and wondering why it wobbled so. I just *depend* on you," she finished.

"I guess we can do it," I said.

"There can't be any *guess* about it." Babs's voice was anxious. "I've promised."

"All right, dear. And now run along." I closed my eyes. I added making the costume to the mental list of things that simply *had* to be done. Babs depended on me; I could not fail her.

And then came the final day of our required work. I ran up to catch Mirella while Lila went for Mrs. Brown, and we found a table together in the cafeteria.

"It'll seem funny not to come down here tomorrow," I said, "or *are* you coming?" For Mrs. Brown had looked at me in mild surprise.

"I'm taking a few days to rest up. I've found I can't keep going all day long, every day, at my age." She sighed. "But beginning next week, I'm going to give every morning to the hospital."

"I'm coming regularly one day a week," Mirella said. "The family don't like it much, but I told them what the doctor said, that the best thing old people could do for the war is to keep well so other people don't have to take care of them. With me gone, they found out they could do a lot more than they thought they could."

Lila and I walked back to the ward together.

"My friend wants me to go away for a trip next month," she said slowly, "but I don't know—" Two internes fell in beside us. As we ate our lunch, I had seen them on a patch of ground back of the cafeteria, one pitching a ping pong ball while the other went to bat with a furled umbrella. They had looked like irresponsible boys. Seen close at hand, they looked very responsible and very tired. An older doctor was standing by the elevator.

"I suppose you've heard; a unit of nurses is being called up from here tomorrow to go into the Service. That leaves us terribly short-handed. We can't run a hospital with no nurses." Suddenly, he noticed Lila and smiled. "You're one of the volunteers, aren't you?" he asked. "Well, at least we'll have you."

Lila hesitated for a fraction of a minute. She started into the elevator and then dropped back. It was always hard for her to remember to allow the doctors to go first. Then, as she followed the three men in, she said decisively, "Oh, yes, speaking for myself, I'll be on deck in the morning as usual."

That night Ed worked late at the factory as he often has to these days, and I went to bed right after supper, too tired to stay up and also too tired to sleep. Babs joined me, bringing a glass of milk and a piece of gingerbread, as if she had not had her supper an hour before, and settled sociably on the foot of my bed. As she ate, I found myself telling her about the two little student nurses on the ward, the many baths to be given and beds to be made by ten in the morning, and about the unit of nurses that had just been called up to join the armed forces.

"But what'll they *do* with all those regular nurses gone?" Babs asked. "Why don't they let you stay on and help?"

"Oh, they want us," I said. "Some of the women *will* stay on."

Babs viewed me with indignation, her hand with the gingerbread poised in mid-air. "For gosh sakes," she said, "I didn't know they'd let you stay, once you were through with your training course."

"Stay on!" I answered. "Why, the Army and Navy need all the regular nurses they can get, so the hospitals just *depend* on help from us volunteers."

"And do you mean to say," Babs asked slowly, "that you took all this training and then when they need you, you're just going to walk out on them?"

"But, Babs," I said, "we've got to shop. The tableau's only two days off, and I promised to make your dress. I can go back later, I guess."

"You know how to take care of people while the real nurses help in the war," she said, despairingly, "and instead, you simply stew about an old dress for a silly show. It's all you can think about. Where's your sense of proportion?"

"But, Babs." I sat up. "It was because I promised you. What could I possibly care about the tableau? It was just that I thought your heart was set on being in it and having a lovely costume."

"Well, I can unset it, can't I?" She put her glass firmly on the floor and stared back at me. Her face was very earnest.

"Listen, Moms," she asked slowly, "what do you think I am?"

Chapter 21

Y‎OU’D THINK"—FREDDIE BIT INDIGNANTLY INTO A LARGE cookie—"people’d co-operate around here." He glared at me.

"Specially ’cause we’re collecting stuff to make battleships ’n’ things." Charles’s eyes were anxious, as if he wasn’t sure I understood.

"Yeah. Well—" Freddie brushed the war aside, honestly. "The Bearcats need the money for sumpin’ special—what we get for the scrap." The Bearcats were the eight boys in Freddie’s Scout Patrol.

"But do you have to bring it all here?" I was indignant, too.

"It’s got to be in one place for the junk man. He said so," Charles explained patiently. "When there’s enough of it, he’ll come for it with a horse and wagon."

"So I told everybody they could leave it in our cellar," Freddie went on loudly. "I said *my* mother wouldn’t care. And now look how you acted. All the kids are mad. They went home just—just *discouraged*."

"But the cellar’s been painted . . ." I stopped, halted by Freddie’s expression. He knows where to hit. He was telling me I’d let him down, that I’d failed to meet standards which he and I share.

A few moments earlier, Eileen and I had been quietly drinking, respectively, a chocolate malted milk and a cup of tea and looking together at the fashions in the rotogravure section, which was still in existence then. After all, war or no war, we had to wear *something!* Suddenly, as if from nowhere, yet from all about us, there had come the most stupendous clattering and clanging. It was as if all the shelves in the pantry had sagged at once and let their burdens slide to the floor.

"Heavens!" Eileen winced. She ran to the dining room window. "Come look out the window."

I peered out. In a sort of whirlpool of flying yellow leaves in our yard, there was a huddle of boys. Freddie, Charles, Bingo Brown, and Harold Morrison were steadying something straddled athwart a wooden cart. It was, I saw, a squat little iron stove. The lids were already gone. As we watched, they pulled off a rusty length of stove pipe and tossed that, too, into our cellar. It fell with a bang. Like smoke from a steamer, a cloud of soot trailed its course.

I flew down the cellar stairs and went into action. After weeks of pleading, not to say nagging, I had persuaded Ed to part with most of the things accumulated there and had actually cornered Vincent, our colored handy man, until he had cleared out the place and given it a coat of white paint. Vincent comes by each week to see what's to be done, but getting him to do it is quite another matter. A gleaming cave-like room—pipes that could be painted Venetian red—a game table or two—I had my plans. And now . . .

Lying inside the double doors which opened onto the back yard were the rusty pipe, two stove lids which had caromed off the white wall leaving arcs of black, and an old storage battery, slowly seeping its acid onto the floor.

"*Boys!*" I ran to the door. From the yard above they peered in at me, an intent little circle. I saw Bingo's sharp-boned features, Harold's pale eyes and colorless face framed by soft blondish hair, and Freddie's round brown head beyond

Charles's too-expressive countenance and apprehensive blue
eyes. They stared as if I were something with a sting they
had stirred up by mistake.

"You've simply ruined this wall," I began.

Bingo knew the signs. He would never have been allowed
so much as to bring the cart into his yard.

"Aw, come on," he said, "let's beat it."

I found myself looking out at nothing but the sky.

I went upstairs. Freddie and Charles came in and followed
me through the kitchen, with a short pause at the cooky crock,
into the dining room. Now they stood staring at me with unsmiling eyes. Freddie's onion-green ones looked as angry as I
felt.

It's a funny thing about those two. Freddie is my own. He's
very like me, really. He's strong; he fights back. When we
finish, he bears no grudge and nobody is hurt. I would always
help him, but I am very slow to waste any sympathy on him.
When something happens to Freddie it's as if it happened to
myself. I could take it, so I know he can. But it's different with
Charles. Like Eileen, he's an object of my special consideration. I cannot take either of them as naturally as I do our children. It's the way it is when you go swimming with your own
kids and someone else's. You keep close to yours, but you don't
worry about them. You know if they get tired, they won't
hesitate to drag you down or even to rest on top of your head,
pushing *you* under. But that other child—you never know—
he might get scared and just drown there all alone. So it was
Charles who pulled at my heart. He stood there, very small.
His hands were grimy. He had rubbed his eyes, and now they
looked out, panda-like, from rings of smudge.

"It's no cinch carting all that stuff. It weighs just about

a million tons," Freddie was explaining. "And then you've got
to sort it all out and break off the wooden handles 'n' everything. . . .

Charles's mournful eyes were turned toward me. He said,
"Scouts get tired, too."

Suddenly I saw how small they were and how heavy the
work was. And, as suddenly, I was completely on their side.

"I'm sure Harold's mother would give you some things."
Mrs. Morrison is chairman of something with half the al-
phabet as its title. "If you want me to, I'll call her up."

"Then it's okay about the junk in the cellar." Freddie gave
me a quick, sideways glance.

"Oh, yes, I guess so." I sighed resignedly. It was plain
that from now on our family and the Bearcats were together in
this.

I should have been tipped off by the tones of Mrs. Morrison's voice and by the meditative "*Hm!*" with which she considered the situation before answering fully. But there was a
thin layer of agreeableness there that fooled me. Not only
could the boys take away a lot of metal gadgets from her
house—she was going to redecorate this fall—but at a meeting
of her committee that afternoon, she said, she would send word
to all the members that the Scouts were to pick up the scrap.

I left the phone definitely pleased. To date, Freddie and
Charles's war effort had consisted mostly in collecting posters
and buttons. Freddie wore the buttons in V formation on his
sweater. "Slap a Jap," they said, "Hit Hitler"—and the whole
was built on an extra large button at the base, which read,
"Remember Pearl Harbor." Charles had a few posters. I have
no idea how he got them. He especially liked a sticker which
he had on his door. It was shield-shaped and it ran, "Men in

Uniform, Hop In." What the boys were doing now, however,
seemed really worth while.

"Harold's mother sure did give us a lot of loot," Freddie
said a few nights later as we sat down at the table.

"She gave us Mr. Morrison's golf clubs," Charles offered.

"She did?" The carving knife paused in mid-air like a long
forefinger as Ed gave Charles a startled look.

"Yeah!" Freddie chimed in. "She said Mr. Morrison had
been needing a new set of clubs for a long time."

"Listen," Ed gestured warningly with the knife, "if anybody goes near my irons . . ."

"Don't worry," I smiled, "they won't."

"The junk man was telling us things aren't the same as
they used to be," Freddie went on. "There's a ceiling price."
He pulled out a piece of paper. "Here's what he's goin' to give
us. Seven cents a pound for copper, four cents for brass, four
and one-half cents for lead and four cents for iron."

"At that, the Bearcats ought to rake in quite a sum." Ed
took out a pencil and figured a bit. "Just don't tear down the
house."

"Mother B., I want to ask you something." Eileen and I
were walking up our street the next afternoon. "Is it honest
for those kids to keep the money they make?"

"Well, it wouldn't be right for Freddie to buy himself a
bicycle with it, for instance," I said. "But if people give their
scrap to the Scouts without asking for any money in return,
I'm sure they expect whatever the boys get to go for Scouting.
If the boys want to do something with it as a group, it seems
to me that's all right."

"It is? I thought maybe they ought to give the money to
the government, too."

"Well, they might if they were older. I think the big boys *re* buying war bonds. But you can't expect boys of twelve or so o be quite so unselfish. Older boys maybe, but not—" I hesi- ated.

"But not Freddie." Eileen smiled.

"Freddie's—he's very normal," I said, quickly.

"He certainly is. Well, since you think it's okay, I can tell /ou what they're going to do with the cash. I'm their *confi- iante*. They're going to build a den for their patrol, and fur- nish it, too, if they can."

"Oh, is *that* it? I wondered but I didn't like to ask. I gathered it was a secret."

"Oh, yes. It's very hush-hush. Swear you won't let on you know," she added, "and I'll show you where their den is now. Come on, you've got time. It's only a block or two out of our way."

Our street runs up a hill. At the top, the Morrisons live in a big brick house with a wide lawn and orchards at the rear. A narrow roadway runs back of the orchards, and beyond, the land falls away to the railroad tracks. We followed this road and stopped beneath a great oak tree. You could see it rearing skyward, from the train. It was more or less of a landmark.

"There!" Eileen pointed up to a platform perhaps thirty feet in the air. "That's their tree house. They sit in it and keep a lookout over the railroad station."

"But how do they get up there?" My eye traveled up twelve or fifteen feet of bare trunk.

"That's the big secret. Don't *ever* tell. See this?" She pointed to a length of white string hanging down next to the trunk. "They pull it and down comes a clothesline and after

that a rope. They climb the rope, then haul it up after them.
But they need an indoor den for winter."

I walked away.

"They've set their hearts on furnishing it," Eileen went on.
"They especially want a big wooden chest, like the one you've
put all the old toys in."

"Why do they need a chest?" I asked.

"Oh, I don't know, to hold a flag and all that hocus-pocus,
I suppose." But Eileen began to talk about the baby and I
heard no more about the Bearcats.

A week went by. After school each day the boys dragged
their carts to our cellar, carts piled with unmanageable mounds
of curtain rods, electric irons, old vacuum cleaners which had
to be taken apart, lamps and pots and pans, an umbrella stand,
and a little bronze-colored boy who up to now had held a
torch over a stairway. They leaned him against the back wall
of our house beside an old iron bed and a set of rusty springs.
I was glad when Freddie told me, on Saturday, the junk man
would call that morning. But it was almost supper time before
I heard his cowbell ringing in the street. (It was attached to
an iron bar that ran across the cart above his head.) He was
standing in the cart with the scales. He turned his emaciated
horse into our driveway. The boys directed him to the cellar
door, and by standing up and yawing at the reins, he backed
the wagon to a stop directly beside the opening.

Charles scrambled into the cart to help from above while
Freddie and the junk man passed up the material. A load of
curtain rods was piled on the scales. Charles reached out a hand
to steady them.

"Hey, young feller." The junk man reached up and pulled
at Charles's arm. "I'm not buying your hand, you know."

Charles stared at him, bewildered.

"He thinks you're pushing down, trying to make it weigh more," Freddie explained. Charles's face flushed. He looked as if he were going to cry.

"He wouldn't cheat." As I said it, the junk man turned and saw me.

"I ain't got nothin' against kids." He met my eyes. "They're nice little fellers. But in my business you gotta be careful."

He was small, like a gnome, with bright bird-like eyes. It did not seem possible that he would give the boys any real money. Yet, when the cart was loaded, the price figured, and the junk dealer's horse had clattered off down the street dragging the smiling little man with the cowbell and the jangling load for the ships and guns, the boys held $28.40 in their hands.

We could hardly believe it, any of us. The Bearcats were plainly set up for life.

And then, without a word of warning, the blow fell, a simple, single blow that wiped out their hopes and almost wrecked their faith in human nature.

It came like this. Reckless with success, Freddie and Charles had at last told us everything: how they could get a den and furnish it with benches, or maybe bunks, and even buy the chest. Now the two youngsters were sitting on the floor contentedly playing jacks. Suddenly the telephone rang. Eileen answered it and came back from the hall.

"It's Mrs. Morrison, to speak to one of the 'little boys.'" She pursed her mouth in a fixed smile.

"Aw, heck." Freddie went to the phone.

"What on earth is that thumping?" Ed looked up from his paper.

"It's Freddie kicking the door opposite him," Eileen whis
pered. "Something must have gone awfully sour."

"Hey, Charlie!" It was Freddie's voice. It sounded stran
gled. Charles scurried out. There was a prolonged muttering
another furious tattoo, then silence.

I went after them. Freddie was sprawled in the chair, hi
feet pushing viciously against the door opposite him. Charle
sat on the floor hugging his knees. His blue eyes were wid
and shocked.

"What happened, kiddoes?" Eileen was behind me, he
voice full of concern.

"We been gypped." Freddie did not look up. "That ol
meanie Morrison—"

"She says we're to bring the money right over and turn i
in to the sumpin'-or-other."

"There goes our den 'n' our bunks—'n' everything." Fred
die's lower lip was wiggling. "And she said she'd give us eacl
a little button. A little *button!*" His voice slipped up the scale

"She's taking our money for her old committee. Can she d
that?" Charles studied my face as if everything that lay aheac
hung on my answer. Now Freddie, too, looked up at me
betrayal in his eyes, like an open wound.

In a crisis like this I am worse than useless. I was confused
It seemed to me that the Scouts, not Mrs. Morrison's com
mittee, deserved the credit for the scrap collection, and tha
the money belonged to them. But the funds, however small
would go for her organization's work and it was hard to argue
against that. Then, too, she had solicited all this junk fo
them, and, finally, I knew that if she had decided to make the
scrap collection one more feather in her chairman's cap, the
boys were licked.

I stood looking at them. I thought, I'll give them that play

om in the cellar. I'll give them the big wooden chest, too. I
mforted myself by thinking of these tangible things. I would
ll them later. But not now. I knew that at the moment some-
ing far deeper than their disappointment about the den was
stake, if only I knew exactly how to handle it.

Then I felt Ed's arm on my shoulder.

"What's all this?"

We told him.

"Well, son," he said at last, and I had a feeling that he and
reddie were alone, that the rest of us weren't there. "Some
eople are like that. You meet them all along the line. It
akes you sick; they're just thinking how to get their names
the paper, or how to make a little more money, or how to
rab themselves a little more power out of the war." He
aused to clear his throat, but he did not do anything about
e tears in his eyes; perhaps he did not know they were
ere. "If you want to help your country, you've got to con-
ntrate on what needs to be done and forget about what peo-
le of that kind say and do."

He stopped as if expecting an answer, but the children con-
nued to stare gravely at him.

"This is the thing, and the rest isn't important," he said.
The Army and Navy need that metal scrap like nobody's busi-
ess. It could mean—why, it could mean the difference be-
ween Dick's having a gun to fight with and having to meet
he Japs bare-handed. You did your job; you delivered the
oods. That's what matters, isn't it?"

He laid his hand half doubled into a fist on Freddie's shoul-
er. It was a caress and a challenge.

There was a pause—not too brief to hold a loud sigh.

"I s'pose. Yes, sir!" Freddie said.

Chapter 22

IT WAS JUST GRAYING FOR MORNING WHEN I HEARD TH
soft shuffle of slippers past my door. My head went up, the
down again—my trouble is sleeping *too* well. Presently cam
another stimulus to my drowsy senses—the sharp odor of co
fee. I peered at my clock. Five-thirty. *Coffee?* I pulled on m
dressing gown and went downstairs.

"Oh, Mother B., I tried not to disturb you." Eileen stoo
before the kitchen table, holding a coffee pot. "I guess th
baby's coming. I woke up about three, and I've been keepin
track ever since. Here." She poured a cupful of coffee wit
a steady hand and pushed it toward me.

I looked concernedly at my gray-eyed daughter-in-law
What she needed now, what she ought to have, was Dick'
stanch right hand to hold to. Well, I thought, if ever
woman was fitted to go through the ordeal ahead alone, it wa
this calm girl. And then I saw her eyes. They looked ou
anxiously from her face as if something small and very fright
ened was cornered there.

I had intended to say, "Let's have breakfast before we wake
the doctor." Instead, I went headlong to the phone.

"Ed, Ed!" I put a firm hand on my sleeping husband'
shoulder half an hour later. "Get up. *Do* something! Eileen'
going to the hospital."

"No!" Ed sat up in bed. "Well, don't get all excited." He
fumbled for his slippers.

I went across to Eileen's room. Fully clothed now in her dark blue butcher-boy dress, she was standing with her ten fingers pointing upward. She had just enameled her nails in what was evidently a determined effort to remain casual and unhurried.

"Well, Sister?" Ed appeared in the doorway, neat in a dark red bathrobe. "I guess you don't need me?"

"We certainly do. We want you right with us." I was firm.

Eileen waved a red-tipped hand at him and then turned to survey the contents of her open suitcase.

"Oh, I know what I forgot! My long white satin negligee to wear today, before the baby comes."

Ed took the bag. "I'll get dressed." For a moment his eyes rested affectionately on Eileen. "I promised Dick I'd do his pacing for him, you know." The words were light, but Ed's voice—it's like a musical phrase built on just the right lower notes. It has everything you want to hear.

"I wish I could talk to Dickie, even for a minute." Eileen's thin hand twisted away from mine. She looked through the taxi window into the shadowy street. "You're both darling to me, but . . . "

I thought of all the things we had done for Dick that were really his to do. Picking out a Christmas present for his first girl; helping on his homework in a jam (I was pretty mad when we only got a B for our joint effort on "The Defense of the Panama Canal"); sending things after him to college— "I forgot my racket. Could you send it along, and be sure to put it in the press?" But standing in his stead at the birth of his baby was the toughest assignment yet. Well, he wouldn't have side-stepped this. That's the trouble with war, it shifts responsibilities where they don't belong. I felt we would have to account to Dick for the safe conduct of his baby into the world. If there were decisions to be made . . .

We went up the steps of the hospital and were swept at once into its brisk drama. We shared the elevator with a little gray man on a stretcher. His eyes were closed, as if forever. Getting out on our floor, we saw a pretty patient in a bright pink bathrobe. A little dark girl in blue was rolling a tray full of orange juice to the various rooms. On the maternity floor there is tension, and suffering, yes, and sometimes tragedy, but cheerfulness is the rule; the business there is life, not death or a compromise with it.

A nurse with a white mask across her face hurried by, a little blue bundle cupped in her arms. Her black eyes smiled out over the gauze.

"Ooh, a baby!" I wanted to have a look—

Eileen shuddered slightly. "Don't show it to me."

"I don't know just *where* we're going to put you." The floor nurse studied us thoughtfully. "For now, you can step in here."

Eileen stood irresolute, looking around at the high, narrow room. Should she unpack or not? Almost immediately, another nurse came in and took over.

Ed and I went out into the corridor. A couple of wooden benches flanked the business end of the hall. Seated on one, you could only stare into the faces of the people on the other. Directly across were a mother and daughter. The younger woman, a dark and pretty girl, was wrapped in an immense cotton robe of Madonna blue, labeled, quite superfluously, "Maternity." She sat on the edge of the bench. The mother caught my eye.

"Her first," she said.

I smiled, but I did not make any return confidences. I remembered, oddly, what a boy had told me about submarine duty. "When there's trouble ahead, about all you can do is wait for it. It takes a special kind of courage." The words ran through my mind as I considered Eileen's plight—"a special kind of courage." It was indeed. I glanced at my wrist watch. By now the nurse would be through with her ministrations. We got up—and almost collided with Babs, loping off the elevator. In a green corduroy skirt and jacket she looked like a very big child. We had not waked her and her loud whisper was indignant. "Hey! Nobody told me anything! Where's Eileen?" I led the way to the room.

"Hello, kid. Look what they hung on me." Eileen held up two sides of the blue cotton robe like a child lifting its nightgown. "And me coming here, so trusting, with my white satin negligee!"

"Listen," Babs said, "why don't you just tell them you've decided not to have a baby *after* all!"

Eileen smiled one-sidedly. "For two cents I'd give up the whole thing. Oh well"—she bit her lip—"if this is all there is to it, it isn't so bad."

"*Good* morning." Dr. Beard has only to come into a room to make you feel warm and taken care of. He stood looking at Eileen with a questioning smile. Abruptly, he asked,

"You people got anything you have to do?"

Ed said, "I ought to get down to the office." I wanted Babs to go home and eat lunch with the two boys, while I went downtown and found out how we could get the news to Dick.

The entrance to the army office was guarded by a big, blue-shirted Irishman debonairly swinging a formidable night stick. He challenged me. "And what can we do for you?"

I looked about the hallway. A man in khaki sat at a table at the other side. As well tell my story here.

"How can I send word to a man with the Armed Forces overseas that he has a child?"

He indicated the desk. It was a diversion to the corporal to give me the necessary information. I turned away to find the big Irishman still at my side.

"Congratulations." He smiled down into my face. "I hope the little one is like the mother."

I started to speak but thought better of it. Why set him right? The tribute was a bright spot in a dark day. I ate my lunch downstairs in the hospital, met Babs in the hall, and together we went back to Eileen's room. I thought perhaps I could divert her. I said,

"I wonder why they do things backward in a cafeteria. You come in at a counter full of bright pink gelatins, work your way past the goulash and wind up at the bean soup. The result is I only take coffee."

"D'you s'pose they're ever going to feed *me?*" Eileen asked. "They just stick you in a room, go off, and forget you."

"They can't do that." Babs bustled out. In a very few minutes a nurse came in with a tray of toast and tea. She stared curiously at Eileen, then went away.

"I found out about sending word to Dick," I went on. "Since we know his army post office, we can cable for only sixty cents. Of course, we have to use a regular form. There are two of them. Number 85, 'Son born.' Number 86, 'Daughter born.' You just can't have twins, that's all."

"Don't." Eileen winced. "Don't even suggest it. But," she added gamely, "we could send 85 *and* 86, couldn't we?"

The door opened again. Babs came in and sat down on the window sill, her feet on a chair.

"There's a girl I know down the hall. She had her baby yesterday, and she and another mother are still in the overflow room—right next to the place where the babies come."

"Do they *keep* you there?" Eileen's voice was anxious.

"It's just 'cause they're full up. It seems the night nurse thought they were ward patients and washed their faces at five-thirty. Ward patients are washed at five-thirty and fed at six. Private patients can sleep till seven-thirty so they eat at eight. Well, at six o'clock a nurse rolls in a great big tray of breakfast, takes one look at them, and rolls it right out again. There they were, with their tongues hanging out, till eight o'clock."

"We won't let them do that to you," I assured Eileen.

"Oh, you're going to get a room all right." Babs rested her chin in her hands. "It's just there's been a bottleneck in maternity."

I caught Eileen's eye. I saw that Babs's chatter had gone on about as long as Eileen could stand it. Fortunately, the nurse reappeared.

"Finished your tea?" she asked. "Because if so, the doctor wants you, and we need this room," she added pointedly.

"Are you sure you're going to be all right?" Babs put a loving arm around Eileen. "I mean, it won't be too, too awful, will it?"

"Well," Eileen hesitated, "I wouldn't pick it for something to do of a Saturday afternoon. But it's—it'll be okay." The nurse took her arm and they went out.

"Good luck, sweetie," I said softly. I knew we wouldn't see her again until everything was over.

Perhaps, I thought, Babs was as well out of this. I dispatched her to do the marketing for over Sunday. Why didn't Ed come back, I wondered. I would feel so much better if only he were sitting here beside me. Turned out of the room, I found a seat by the window at the end of the hall. Time passed leadenly.

It was perhaps a couple of hours later that Ed stepped off the elevator. He spoke to the nurse at the desk and then joined me. A man who had been drifting about the corridor stopped beside us.

"Waiting, too, eh?" he asked.

"Yes," Ed said, "but they tell me the baby is coming right along now."

"It's our fourth," the newcomer went on comfortably. "My wife phoned me at the office. She has 'em pretty easy," he added.

Something in me rose angrily against this man's casualness. He crossed the hall. Ed and I continued to look out the window where now the light lay level along the rooftops. Our eyes did not meet, yet I knew they were focused on the same event years before—the arrival of Dick, *our* first baby. I said,

"I don't see how people ever break up a family."

"They don't," Ed thought a moment. "They just—they just shut their eyes and pretend they've done it."

A nurse came out, looking for someone. Had Eileen's baby—? I started to rise.

"I probably should let the doctor tell you, but you have an eight-pound boy." She stood by the other man. "I think you can see your wife for a minute."

"Hospitals drive me nuts." Ed twisted in his chair. After a few minutes' interval, the father of four rejoined us.

"Have a cigar," he said. "It's another boy." He turned toward me. "My wife heard your girl was just going in to have her first, so she was careful not to make any noise. Didn't want to frighten her, you know."

I sat speechless at the incredible kindness of an ordinary woman who did not even know Eileen. To the man, it was all a part of the business of decent living, like the next thing *he* had to do. He pulled out his watch.

"Well," he said, "got to get home and fix supper for the kids on time or I'll get hell when I come back tonight." He hurried off.

The anger in me burned down into respect. "What good citizens!"

"Oh, sure. Salt of the earth." Ed bit an end off the cigar but he did not light it. After a while he said, "Everything's going all right with Eileen, of course." He tried to make his voice confident. "Nobody better than Fred Beard for a thing like this." Then he brightened. "Here's Babs." She was coming along the corridor stooping slightly as she always does, giving the impression of eager inquiry.

"Don't move." She crossed the corridor and climbed into a wheelchair. She spun it rapidly toward us, just missing a white-suited interne. He grinned and hurried by. From her outsized pocketbook she drew forth a royal blue sock.

"Wasn't that wool once Vic's helmet?" I teased her.

"That was *ages* ago. It's been a sock for George all summer."

Silence fell. A full and anxious silence.

Suddenly I heard the sound—a tiny cry, a tiny but very personal wail as a little somebody cried out to the world.

"*Sh!*" I said. "It's our baby."

Ed smiled at me as if I were a gentle lunatic. "It could be anybody's baby." But he pulled out his watch. "Four forty-five."

The sun was gone now. The lights came on, inside and out. Below us the city winked and sparkled. Babs continued to knit quietly. Ed consulted his watch again.

"Five-thirty," he said. "You see, that was another baby. That was a much older baby. I knew it couldn't have been ours."

And then we saw Fred Beard standing in the archway, one arm upraised, the hand against the wall, the other rested in a tired fashion on his hip.

"Hasn't anybody told you?" he asked. "Your daughter has a grand little girl. I thought you might have heard her crying."

"Is the baby all right?" I could just ask.

"But how's Eileen?" Ed got up.

"They're both fine. Wait." He turned. "I think they're bringing her out now."

Eileen was lying in a low bed on wheels. Her face was flushed and her eyes were sunken, but she lifted her hand just enough to wave.

I pressed forward. "Eileen, dear." But the bed had been swiftly rolled through a swiftly opened door that closed in my face.

"Looka here, Fred." Ed cleared his throat and tried to be casual. "We can't be too grateful to you—Dick not here— quite a responsibility."

The doctor put a hand on Ed's shoulder. "All that'll keep."

Eileen's door opened and a nurse beckoned to us. We tip-toed in. "Dickie, has anybody told him?" She turned her head toward us.

Ed stood by the high bed. "It'll all be taken care of the minute we get home." He picked up her hand and stroked it.

Eileen's eyes closed again. Then,

"Is my baby—is she really all right?"

"You'll see her for yourself, very soon." Dr. Beard stood at the foot of the bed. As if she had felt him enter, Eileen slowly opened her eyes and looked fully into his. Something held between them. Suddenly, I knew; we were not in this at all. Out of touch with Dick, Eileen was traveling on the beam of this man's strength.

We stole out and walked down to the nursery. On the other side of the plate glass door, the nurse wheeled a tiny basket toward us and tilted it for us to see.

"Oh, Ed." I took his hand.

"Isn't she adorable?" Babs bubbled beside me.

"Children that age all look alike to me." Ed tried to be blasé. For a long moment, he stood completely lost in the contemplation of his son's child. "We'll have to finish up this war so your daddy can come home and have a look at his baby."

We went down the hospital steps together. Suddenly I thought I was going to collapse; my knees felt as if they were about to give, to let me down.

"I haven't eaten anything since breakfast," I said. "Maybe we could stop somewhere—"

"Why, yes, if you want to, dear." Ed stood irresolute by the iron gate. "But I'll tell you— I'd like to go home," he said. "I'm tired out. I've had a pretty long, hard day."

"Of course you are," Babs said. "Don't forget—you're a *grandfather.* Come on, you two." She tucked an arm trium-phantly in each of ours and propelled us up the street.

Chapter 23

"IF BABS HAS FALLEN FOR THIS PROFESSOR FELLOW," ED SAID, "she must tell George." His gray-blue eyes were dark as they are when he is angry. "Double-crossing somebody in love is the meanest thing in the world, and no child of mine is going to do it."

"It's easy for an older man to fascinate a girl of seventeen." I put some toilet articles into my overnight bag.

"But I thought she was all fixed up with George," Ed protested. "George is a grand guy. He has brains and looks, too. Once the war is over and he gets to be a doctor, it's my bet he'll go a long way. And he plays a sweet game of golf." He sighed. That didn't mean much now. "What's the matter with that girl, anyhow?"

"Youth." I smiled. "Remember it?"

But Ed was not to be diverted. "Well, it's time she grew up." He started to rise as if he might go right down and begin aging her.

"Wait," I said, "let's see how it goes over the week end."

"I don't like it." But he sank back. "She isn't—she isn't true."

"She's true underneath, I think. Here, my bag is ready." I set it on the floor. "Give her time."

A couple of hours earlier the boys, Ed, and I had been eating our Friday night dinner. Eileen, tired with the care of the baby, had taken her supper in bed. Babs was at college. Presumably, that is. For it was then I heard her voice.

"Where's everybody?" The door opened and she came in. She was wearing a white sheepskin coat trimmed with scarlet bands. Her dark hair glistened with rain. Her feet were tucked into red socks and once-white moccasins.

"Oh, hello, Toots. What are you doing here?" Ed's voice was gayer than I had heard it in weeks.

"Sweetie!" I kissed her. Then, "You didn't come down on the train like that—no hat—no stockings—"

"I like the motherly welcome." Babs went around and took a seat by her daddy. "Hello, my pet. I got a ride."

"George, I suppose. Where is he, out in the rain?" Ed asked.

"No." Babs avoided his eyes. "Matter of fact, I came down with Professor Cummings. I'm in his Social Science class. *You* know, I *wrote* you about him." Her voice said we were supposed to have registered this but not to have made too much of it.

"How come a professor gets all that gas?" Ed's tone was just a little critical.

"He's saved it up ever since college opened for some emergency like this when he had to get himself somewhere. Arthur isn't a prosperous businessman like you, Daddy, with plenty of traveling money."

"Thanks." Ed's tone was grim.

"When *he* goes somewhere he has to take himself in his car. He was asked to speak at a forum dinner here in town on Manpower and the War. So he drove down and brought *me*," she finished with a pleased smile.

"Well," I said happily, "now you've come, you can stay over Sunday."

"I'd like to. Hi!" Babs grinned up at Norah. She looked at the plate of fish before her. "Gee, that sauce looks good. They make ours out of some sort of glue. But I have late permission and I've got to go back with Arthur tonight."

I made no comment. Babs finished and ran up to see Eileen and the baby. Norah brought the coffee into the living room. Ed sat back in his big chair. Babs rejoined us and she and I settled ourselves on the sofa. The professor, I knew, might come at any moment. It was now or never.

"This Professor Cummings," I began, "he must be twice as old as you are."

Babs grinned at Ed. "It's the age I attract."

"I don't doubt it. I don't want you driving back with him tonight, however."

Babs turned and stared at me. As the import of my words sank in, ripples of anger ran across her brown eyes.

"But, Mother, Arthur is a *wonderful* man. *Everybody* at college is simply ga-ga about him. Why, he could be a friend of Daddy's—"

"You must think of his side of it, too." I tried appeasement.

"But he likes having me along. He brought me with only just a *little* shoving."

"Suppose you had an accident, or broke down. If Professor Cummings were towed into town at two A.M. with a girl from one of his classes—well, it might cost him his job."

Ed put down his pipe. "Your mother is right."

"Now, Moms," Babs's voice rose in despair, "you don't know how *hard* it is to get to see a professor alone. I—I lie awake nights worrying how to fix it so I can. And he'd never understand your not letting me go. He'd be terribly hurt."

"Does that matter—terribly?" I asked.

Babs turned away a little. Then she said in an almost angry tone, "Yes, it does."

I thought fast. "How about taking me back with you for the week end?"

Babs sighed. She looked at her daddy for a moment, hoping for help. "Well, okay," she said, when none came. "I suppose it's better than nothing."

While I was packing my bag, getting out galoshes—a college campus in winter is all wet and not in the slang sense either—and so on, my mind went back to George. After the great decision at the end of last summer to get educated instead of married, George had thrown himself into the hard grind of preparing for medical school before going into the Service. Having settled the marriage question for the time being, he apparently felt no need of a formal engagement. Yet having seen him so much with Babs, I was sure he thought of her as his very own girl. Babs was pretty bitter about the way he took her for granted.

"He's just throwing me to the wolves." And now here was a wolf in professor's clothing. In spite of trying to reassure Ed, I was troubled. I put on my hat so firmly it felt like a blow.

I should have known that if Babs fell for him the professor would be neither nearsighted nor bald nor undersized. The man who came to our door an hour later stood six feet one or two. His eyes, which were blue, had a half-tender, half-mocking expression, which was not without considerable appeal. He was a bit gaunt, and the excellent brown tweed coat he wore swung from his shoulders as from a frame.

As we walked out to the car Babs gave my arm a delighted squeeze. "Wait till you hear him talk," she said.

I didn't have to wait long. He was still basking in the afterglow from an appreciative audience and he launched at once into telling us what he had said. From time to time Babs commented in slow, measured tones that were absolutely new to me. Each of her words was thoughtfully considered. He considered them, too, with respect. I sat in some amazement. *Babs?* I felt left out, yet amused and proud. Once I started to break in on the subject of the small factory; I knew about that because of Ed's plant.

"My husband says . . . " I began.

"Now, Mother," Babs cut me off, "you're not going to quote Daddy. Much as we all love him, he's *only* a businessman. You see"—she turned a serious face toward me in the semi-dark—"Arthur *knows.*"

I relapsed into thoughtful silence. It was almost twelve when we turned in under the maple trees that in summer shade the campus. Because it was so late, I was to sleep in the little room that Babs and Patty, her roommate, used as a study.

I woke next morning to find Babs already gone. Patty was bringing me some coffee. The room was desperately untidy, yet it was gay, too, with a litter of bright pillows and magazines and books and colored articles of clothing. The sunshine poured in. Somehow, suddenly, the disorder didn't matter.

"It's so wonderful to have you here," Patty said delightedly. She is small and yellow-haired, with enormous gray eyes. "Babs has an eight o'clock class. Professor Cummings. I thought of joining the rush and taking it, too, only I'm against anything that happens that early in the morning."

I smiled. I was sure it was so. Patty is the only girl in a family where nothing is really required, neither education nor

ffort, of women. She has a beloved and protected air, but in
ne thing, at least, I knew her to be fierce and that was in her
evotion to George, her only brother.

"Patty," I said as I sugared my coffee, "I'd like to know
what *you* think about this Arthur business. I don't know any-
hing about the man situation with you," I went on tentatively,
"but somehow, I think you'll agree with me George ought
o be able to leave Babs for five minutes without her falling
or another man."

Patty looked up at me from the floor. The white cotton
laisies in her hair gave her a childish air, but looking into her
eyes I saw a deep and mature shadow across them.

"My guy's a flier," she said. "Sometimes I try to work
up an outside interest just to get my mind off things, but I
can't do it."

I sipped my coffee. "That's the way she should be about
George."

Patty got up on her knees to reach for a cigarette. "I rather
thought you were against their getting married."

"Right now—but not in a few years. And it troubles me
that she can be dying to marry George one minute and the
very next, so to speak, be—well—off her head about somebody
else." Patty started to speak, but something, perhaps loyalty
to her own age, stopped her. I went on to explain why I felt
so strongly. "You see, character is one of the things we've got
to put into this war. And being dependable and well—reliable,
emotionally, is something women can do for men. I mean,
this isn't the moment to insist on attention, like spoiled children." When Patty continued to smoke without comment, I
brought the conversation back to George. "He's taking that
very hard short course. He ought to be free to do his work—

he must have peace of mind." I flushed and reached for an unaccustomed cigarette.

Patty glanced at me curiously for a moment. Then she got up. "Well, I'll try to look out for George's interests," she said.

The day passed. I scored a hit by taking the girls to an off-campus tea house for a dinner of burnt lamb chops and hard peas. Then we went back to the hall so that they could dress. It was the night of a sophomore dance to which the girls invited the men. Babs was taking Arthur and Patty had asked her man's younger brother, a freshman from somewhere, named Ronny. We turned on the light. Atop the mound of books and rackets on the desk was a squat florist's box.

"Flowers, for me?" Babs bent over the tag. "No, they're for you, Patty. I didn't think *Cummings* would go all to pieces like that." She disappeared into the bedroom. Patty lifted the gardenias from the box. At this moment a face peered in at the door. It was dotted with cold cream and topped with curlers.

"Company? Oh, 'scuse me." The face disappeared, but the voice persisted apologetically, "Long distance wants Room 202. Somebody here put in a call?"

"I did. I'll take it."

The tissue and gardenias fell onto the armchair as Patty ran out.

Presently Babs reappeared with her dress. It was a tight fitting bodice of green faille with an ample non-priority skirt of green and white stripes. She had made it herself in the summer. With it she wore the ubiquitous white sheepskin. Patty came casually back and slipped expertly into a pastel gown, and threw over it a trench coat of pale gold leather. She looked delicate and expensive beside Babs with her peasant-like gaiety of color. In contrasting ways, each seemed irresistible. I lay down, after they had gone, hoping for the first time that it was not so.

Hours later I woke to feel Babs's hand on my hair. "Listen, Moms, wake up." Her voice was insistent. "We all want to go out to the Brass Bowl. It's not on the approved list, but it's okay if your family takes you." I got sleepily up and went to a mirror.

"Was it a good party?"

"I'll say. Everybody nearly *died* when I walked in with Arthur."

I touched my hair. "How's his dancing?"

"Gorgeous. Very remote control, but very, very smooth. And I snaked him away quite a lot so we could talk." She put a bobby pin in a rear curl for me. "Mother, he's so interesting. He was telling me all about vertical and horizontal unions." She gave me a quick glance in the mirror. "He certainly makes those Princeton stooges look young and dumb. There, your hair's perfect. Come on."

The boy named Ronny put me in the front seat of the little roadster next to Patty, while Arthur and Babs climbed into the rumble. There was a slight drizzle, but I knew enough not to mention it. I was not going to be the one to worry, and if I did, I was determined not to show it. As we left the town behind us, the real rain began. It came with a clash of wind against the car. The water sluiced across the windshield as if thrown from a bucket. It was impossible even to see the road. This boy is a good driver, I thought. He'll turn in or at least draw up at the side of the road. Other than concentrating his gaze ahead; however, Ronny gave no sign of even noticing the weather. The speedometer registered an even forty. I wanted to be casual but I knew that Babs and the professor must be drenched. I shifted a little and peered through the back window into the rain.

And suddenly I saw there was no one there. There was no sign of anyone in the back seat. Nobody. Nothing.

"Ronny!" I could not keep the alarm out of my voice. "Where's Babs? Babs and Professor Cummings are gone!"

Ronny spoke without turning his head. "I shut the top down over them," he said. "There's no seat in back. So while they were getting settled, I just shut 'em in. Don't worry. The air gets in around the edges."

I tried to think what to do. They must be battered and frightened if not actually smothered. There might be an exhaust—monoxide gas! At this moment Ronny leaned forward and peered toward a light at the left. We had driven beyond the storm. We swung in the driveway and drew up before a cabin-like building. This was the Brass Bowl. He got out. I slipped under the wheel after him and simply ran to the rear and lifted the cover. Babs popped up like a large toy.

"Some rumble seat," she said.

Professor Cummings clambered out. As he came up the porch I saw that his face above the white of his evening shirt was gray and lined.

"That could have been very serious," he told Ronny sternly.

"I think so, too," I added. "It's very dangerous, no air in a car . . ."

"We could have died and nobody would have noticed," Babs said cheerfully, "but we didn't. Come on, stop complaining, you two." She linked arms with Arthur and me, "Let's get a nice, cozy corner."

In the semi-darkness of the low-ceilinged room, a juke box ground out "Everything I've Got Belongs to You." We gathered around a small bare table, Babs on a bench against the wall.

"Isn't there some way of shutting off that scratchy thing?" Arthur glanced toward the music box.

"Oh, don't stop it!" Babs's voice was alarmed. "That's what we come for!"

Arthur tried almost visibly to pull himself into the mood of the party.

"I suppose that's boogie-woogie." His eyes smiled into Babs's eager face.

"That? No! But there'll be some soon. You like solid piano?" Ronny was interested in the professor for the first time.

"Well, I can wait." Arthur sat back, his long legs sprawling under the table. He exchanged an amused glance with me. Instinctively, I wanted to help; it seemed unfair that he should appear at a disadvantage.

"Professor Cummings spoke on Manpower and the War in our town Friday night," I told Ronny.

"Is that a fact?" Ronny's nice young face lit up politely while remaining a perfect blank.

"Tell them that incident you told me, driving up," I urged.

"Well, you see," Arthur leaned forward, tapping the metal table with his finger. Babs smiled absent-mindedly. She had brought this human marvel; she did not have to listen. Her eyes roved the room. Suddenly she bounced up.

"George! There's George. Hi! Here we are! We're over here!"

I turned. The inverted shade in the middle of the room

threw the light down on George's honey-colored hair and tanned skin set off by a coat of Bermuda tweed. It brought out sharply his resolute mouth and eyes alive with friendliness and intelligence. I found myself waving, too. He signaled Babs and came straight to me.

"Well, this *is* a party." He looked around the circle while holding my hand. "Hi, kid. Hi, Ron." I introduced him to Arthur. He went and stood over Babs. "Hello, you! Patty phoned me I'd better come over and join the doings." He studied Ronny curiously for a moment. It was evident that he thought Ronny, though an old friend, was the new menace. Babs looked up at him, her eyes alight but a little puzzled. "How about moving over?" he asked. He took his place beside her and laying his arm casually along the back of the seat, he let his hand fall firmly on her shoulder and remain there. Having thus declared himself in, he looked alertly about the table. "Don't let me interrupt you."

Professor Cummings hesitated as if checked by a counter current. Then he lifted his shoulders a little. He began to talk again.

"It's all a question what counts most," George said when the other paused. "Take my case. I'm preparing for medical school right now instead of volunteering for the Army or Navy." He turned his earnest eyes on Professor Cummings' face. "The way I figure it we're in for a long war and they're going to need doctors more than anything. Don't you think so, sir?" When Arthur did not answer, George drew Babs toward him. "Well," he said, "that's the way *we* see it."

There was no mistaking the familiarity of habit in the gesture, no mistaking, either, this boy's assurance that they two were together against the world. And there could be no doubt, least of all to a sensitive man, that with that arm around her, sure and firm, and that husky voice befriending her, Babs was completely at home. For a moment Professor Cummings' gaze rested on Babs's face. It was glowing. His own fell into thin downward lines. Something in his eyes went slowly out. He pushed back his chair.

"If you'll excuse me, I think I'll take the next bus to town. I've—I've got some papers to correct. An old chap like me has to get his sleep."

Babs freed her arm with a friendly but vicious dig of the elbow that brought a grimace of pain to George's face, and put out her hand.

"I'm sorry you have to go."

"Thanks for including me." Arthur stood for a moment looking at the two of them with desolate eyes. "Good night, everybody."

"Good night." George watched the receding back. "I'd liked to have talked to him some more. Nice old geezer, isn't he? And now," he tucked his arm under Babs's, "how about dancing this one?"

"I guess Arthur got pretty fed," Babs said, as we undressed later that night. "Oh, well, he was kind of a strain on me, anyway. You know, all the time intellectual!" She sat down and hugged her knees. "Now with George I can just be my dumb self. He likes me the way I am." Suddenly she looked straight up into my eyes and I saw that her brown ones were full of shining tears. "I *was* crazy about Arthur, really, but, Mother, when that boy came in tonight and sat down beside me, I could have died of pure, unadulterated happiness. I guess I'm just the loyal kind," she said.

Chapter 24

EILEEN," I SAID, "DON'T YOU THINK IT'S ABOUT TIME WE had the baby christened?"

Eileen and I were sitting up in my bedroom with a tray of toast and tea between us. It was late afternoon, the time of day when wherever I am, home begins to pull like a magnet, and never more so than now, with a new baby in the house. Eileen, sitting in the small armchair by the window, uncurled a trousered leg and stared. (Daffodil-yellow slacks and shirt were her working costume as the mother of Ed's and my grandchild.) She tried to keep the look of surprise out of her blue-gray eyes as she's apt to do when she feels she should probably have known something herself.

"Christened?" she asked. "You mean baptized? In church and all?"

"It can be done at home," I said. "But, yes, I mean a religious ceremony."

She turned this over in her mind. Her eyes were shining. "What a wonderful idea! I would *never* have thought of it."

In spite of myself, I smiled. I suppose it was the way Eileen had had to live, with no real home since her parents died, but the most unexpected things astonished her, trivial things like the fact that windows have to be washed and electric light bulbs dusted, big things like the fact that people over forty can still be in love, facts that Babs was aware of just from having grown up in a household.

"Do we know anybody who could do it?" she asked.

"Dr. Howard, from the church," I said. "He's the minister who married you. Remember?"

"Vaguely. The whole thing's kind of a haze in my mind— all those people that you knew and I didn't—and all that worry as to whether the Army would really let Dick off. Oh, Mother Breton," she said, "if I only knew where he was this minute . . . "

I did not speak. Ed's address during the last war, "Somewhere in France," seemed pretty definite beside Dick's. This war is shot through with the element of surprise—learning our troops were in Iceland, that they'd arrived in Australia, that they were in the Solomons, and suddenly, just a few nights before this, by radio direct from the White House, that our forces had landed in Morocco. True, we knew Dick had been in Northern Ireland, but the last letter—it came only a little while after the baby—told us he had been issued clothing for an Arctic climate. After that, silence. It was hard on us all, but most of all on Eileen. And I was hoping that the pleasure of the christening, the arrangements and the event itself, might keep her from thinking so constantly about a letter that just didn't come.

"Isn't that the baby?" A diminutive meowing sound issued from across the hall. Eileen went out and came back, her blond curls, still limp, falling about her face as she leaned over a blanketed bundle. A tiny hand reached into the air, without aim, but not without force. She was very strong, this modern infant stuffed with vitamins. I switched off the lights, leaving only a softly shaded one on the dressing table. Eileen put her down on the bed and loosened the blanket. The baby moved her feet contentedly in the warm air, making a slow, prolonged, almost guttural sound exactly as a hen does when ruminating over a bit of grain on the ground.

"She's such a good baby," Eileen smiled at her. "I'm glad she doesn't know about the war and Dick being in it."

I watched the tiny round face, with tightly shut eyes. "That's why small children are so restful to be with," I said. "They don't know about the fears that eat us up. They're completely unaware of the troubles and tragedies around them. They live in a little world all their own."

Eileen sat on the edge of the bed, looking almost absentmindedly down at her small daughter. "If she's going to be christened, she has to have a godmother. If anything should go wrong . . . " I knew she was thinking of Dick but didn't want to say so, and thinking, too, of what had happened to her as a youngster. I started to say that Ed and I were always here, but suddenly I saw us in the clear grayness of Eileen's mind, an older generation. She was looking for someone from her own. At last she went on, "I know. I'll have Babs."

"Babs?" I was almost as startled as if she had nominated Freddie for godfather.

"Yes. Of all the people I know, I think I'd most like to have my baby be brought up by her. At least she'd be sure of plenty of love around her."

"Babs will be—she'll be overcome," I said.

"And I'm going to ask Dr. Beard to be godfather. He brought her, so in a way she's his, too, and I adore that man. How about you, cherub?" She leaned forward and laid a forefinger gently on the baby's cheek.

The cherub opened her eyes and looked at nothing. Then, like a good little trouper, she smiled obligingly. It was plain that if we thought so, she did, too.

Most of the arrangements for the event were deferred by mutual consent until the arrival of the godmother on her vacation from college. But in the meantime I did go over to the church to see Dr. Howard. I wandered across the barn-like Sunday school room with its red-flowered carpet and along a corridor smelling of rubbers to his office. I found him, however, standing at the side of the church. He was gazing across rows of empty pews to the arches and colored windows. He loves this place, I thought. I felt rather mean about the fact that we always turned to him for great events and went to church so seldom. I told him so. But he only said, "Let's see, your great events have all been happy ones, haven't they? You're very fortunate," and agreed to come.

When Babs arrived she was pushing her roommate, Patty, ahead of her in at the door. "See what I brought to the party. Isn't that nice?"

"Are you sure you really want me? My family's still in the country, so I was just going to New York with some friends. But Babs insisted on my coming here." Patty stood, all golden curls and soft fur, looking anxiously at Ed and me as if even now we might say no and she would have to go away. She gave me a hug. "Hi, Charles. Hi there, Freddie." She wrung their hands. "Hello, Eileen. Here, this is for the baby." She held out a gaily wrapped parcel.

In the living room we crowded around to unwrap a large white lamb with delectable curls, silver bell, blue bow, and a pink nosegay. When you squeezed him, he played a tune. It was only after he had been passed from person to person that we settled down to talk.

"I've arranged with the minister," I told them. "And you know," I added, "I'm going to give this baby a better religious training than you children had."

"Are you?" Ed smiled. "Whose baby is this, anyway?"

"Just the same," I answered, "when you've brought up a family you can see the mistakes you've made . . . "

"Oh, so you don't think much of the way we turned out?" Babs asked. "I like that."

"I like it so much," Eileen said, "that I want you to be the baby's godmother."

Babs was completely taken by surprise. "Who, *me?* Shouldn't you get somebody old and rich?"

Eileen laughed. "No, I want you."

"Gee, I'd love to do it. Have you thought of a name for her yet? George still calls her the Bundle for Breton."

"Sounds like my brother," Patty said.

"She's to be called Barbara for her godmother, goopie," Eileen said.

But anxiety pulled at Babs's face. "What'll Dick say? I bet he'd try to argue you out of it."

"Dick isn't here," Ed put in, "so Eileen must decide."

The mention of Dick's name brought a little silence after it. Suddenly, I had one of those rare moments when I felt as if I was able to see something from a man's angle. Unconsciously, a woman always feels when a man goes somewhere he's having a good time without her. I can't help it myself. Now I was having a vision of army life as one part adventure and nine parts homesickness. "I'm so lonely," he'd written in one of his rare letters to me. "There are plenty of good guys, but now I'm with a new outfit again and, well, it takes time to make friends." I saw him turning this way and that through the misty streets of an Irish town, hunting for someone who would listen, companionably, while he talked about his wife back home ("She's really *sump'n,*" he'd say), and the baby whom he hadn't seen . . .

"Who's coming to the christening?" Ed asked. I produced the list. Freddie looked up from the hall floor where he and

Charles were patiently rolling a rubber ball for Blimp to retrieve.

"*And* Harold Morrison *and* Bingo," he said. "I guess Charlie's and my friends can come, too."

I was about to protest when Charles said, "Bingo's mother never has a party and when Harold's mother gives one, Harold isn't let come," so I wrote down the boys' names. This might as well be an enjoyable day for everybody.

Freddie went on, "What are you goin' to have to eat?"

This was the week no coffee was to be sold, prior to rationing. "I hope I have enough coffee.... Oh!" I moved my feet as Blimp slid by, paws braced.

Babs broke in, "We went to a party at some friends of Patty's and they had the most wonderful tasting stuff. There was beer, but I knew you wouldn't want me to touch it, so I just stuck to this. It's called mince juleps."

"So you stuck to that?" Ed asked. Babs looked from one to the other of us as she saw us smile.

"I didn't know it had anything in it," she said. "That shows you what a nice girl *I* am." Suddenly she looked ruefully around. "This lovely party and nobody's even *thought* to suggest having George here," she said.

"Oh, of course I want him." Eileen was eager.

"Well, I don't think he can possibly come," Babs answered, satisfied now, "but I'd like him to be *asked*. He could sort of stand in for Dick. What's the news from good old Dick, anyway?"

Tears filled Eileen's eyes. "That's just it," she said. "There isn't any."

Patty, with her sure touch, came to the rescue. "When are we going to see the wonder-child?" She got up. "If I'll be very quiet can't I just *look* at her now?" Patty tucked her arm through Eileen's and smiled. Somehow, she conveyed a bit of her own gay spirit. "Come on!" They went out with Babs after them.

The day of the christening was cold and clear. Under government orders we had reconverted our converted furnace back from oil to coal again. With oil the process of keeping the house warm, like the process of digestion, went on unconsciously, its perfection detectable only by the fact that one didn't have to think about it at all. Now the furnace had to be tended, and that was Ed's job. It soon became evident that this was going to be his contribution to the preparations. Patty had volunteered to take charge of the flowers with Babs's help, even paying for them, I found out later, out of her own allowance, fortunately a very liberal one. At first Freddie and Charles and Bingo and Harold Morrison were terribly in the way, but Patty put them to work hauling the stepladder from place to place and handing her strings, thumb tacks, and scissors as she put laurel leaves and yellow and white chrysanthemums about the room. The endearing thing about Patty was the way she acted as if you were *her* family. You knew she must come from a warm and affectionate home. I found myself thinking, "I hope Babs *does* marry George eventually." The centerpiece for the dining room table was her especial pride, a great mound of green and white with a delicious bouquet of sweetheart roses in the center. "It's like having the baby right there," she said. Freddie eyed her disgustedly. He adored her and it was plain he wished the object of his adoration wouldn't be quite so wet in her talk. Norah came in to admire the effect.

"Oh, it's beautiful," she said, "just beautiful. But there, I must get back to my kitchen. I'm not ready yet at all, oh, no, not anywhere near."

At last it was almost time—almost four o'clock. I came down in the violet-colored dress that the children liked and took a last look around.

"Relax, darling," Ed said. "Everything's going to be all right."

The doorbell rang and Norah came in from the hall with an immense box. "Flowers for the baby," I called to Eileen. "Shall I open them?" But the girls ran in together. They took off the long cover. The box was filled with pink and yellow roses and some strange lovely daisies. There were tiny white flowers on top. Eileen opened the card.

"From George. How darling of him! Baby's breath." She picked up a spray of gardenias that lay at one end, across the stems of the roses. " 'For the baby's godmother.' " She pinned them on the shoulder of Babs's scarlet dress. Babs removed them, however, her face serious.

"The pin might stick the baby," she explained. "I carry her, don't I?"

Dr. Howard arrived just then and we asked him about this. "I usually have the father take the baby," he said. "Since he isn't here"—he smiled at Eileen, a direct and kindly smile —"I think you should hold her. She's your baby, isn't she?"

After that friends began to come. Patty, Babs had told us, played divinely, if only we could get her to do it. Together they had pushed the grand piano around so that the keyboard was in a corner, and now Patty sat there thoughtful and composed, her head a blot of light beyond the black of the case. She was no longer looking at anyone; she gazed ahead of her at nothing as she slid from a slow familiar prelude into the brilliant strains of Rimsky-Korsakov. So our baby was to be baptized to the music of the Coq d'Or! Suddenly there was a little commotion at the hall and Dr. Beard hurried into the room.

"Too many sick people," he said. "Hello, Elizabeth. Hello, Ed. Where do you want me?" He went over smiling and nodding (half the people there had been his patients at one time or another) and took his place beside Babs, standing perfectly still, like a dynamo at rest. My eyes searched the room. Where were the boys? It came to me that Bingo had come out point-blank against attending the ceremony. Then I saw them. The windows behind the minister opened on the sun porch, and at one of them the faces of Bingo and Harold Morrison peered in. I suppose, I thought, nothing momentous will ever happen in this family without Bingo's blank button eyes and Harold's pale ones staring at us as if we were caged animals. Even as I watched them, however, they were pushed aside and Charles and Freddie wriggled up from below into front places for a close-up of the ceremony.

At this moment everyone turned to look into the hall. Eileen was coming down the stairs, a slim figure in a dark dress, holding her baby carefully in her arms. I hadn't noticed before how drawn her face was. The music ceased. She crossed the room to the minister. All of us were around her—the family, perhaps twenty-five or thirty friends—but she stood alone. Nothing now could fill that place beside her where Dick ought to have been.

"*Grant, O Lord, to these Thy servants grace to perform . . .* " The minister's voice was full and firm.

The angles of her cheekbones are very sharp, I thought. She looks so white. Perhaps this is too hard on her.

"*What is the given name of this child?*"

Eileen's voice was very low but perfectly clear. "Barbara Elizabeth."

Elizabeth. My name. The baby was named for me, too.

"Barbara Elizabeth, thus acknowledged—is commended to your love and care."

"She shall have it, dear." I was promising it to Dick.

And then it was all over. This swift act of love was done. Still I stood holding on to Ed—

"Weren't you *pleased?* Weren't you simply bowled over? She's going to be called Betty, short for Elizabeth." Babs was bubbling over at me. "And I knew it. I knew it all along!"

"I thought it was what Dick would like." Eileen turned gravely toward me.

Friends were crowding around. "Barbara Elizabeth, eh?" Fred Beard took her in his arms, holding her firmly and professionally. It's funny the way a doctor can hold a child as if it were all of a piece, like a stick of wood. The women were making little clucking noises and the men tried to attract her attention, while her unfocused baby eyes saw light and movement and nothing more.

Eileen turned to Dr. Howard again. "Thank you," she said. "And now I think it's time she went back to her bassinet." She took the baby in her arms and left us.

For a time I did not notice that she didn't come back. I went around the room enjoying our friends—friends with whom we had shared troubles and pleasures over many years. You don't make friends like that overnight. I thought of what Dick had said, "It takes time." He'll make them quickly, though, I told myself. They'll go through so much in a short time. I busied myself seeing that everyone had something to eat and drink. Still Eileen had not come down. It wasn't feeding time—was she worn out? There had been kind of a desperate look about her— I left the crowded dining room, the chatter, the high, feminine notes, the slow, lower voices of the men, and went upstairs. On the landing I stopped and slipped off my pumps. Perhaps she had cried herself to sleep by now. I tiptoed to her door.

It stood ajar. The only light was a shaded one over the head of the bed. Directly below it Barbara Elizabeth was propped against one of the big white pillows. Eileen was lying beside her, her head only a little above the tiny one of the baby. She was reading something aloud—a letter.

" *'My darling,'* " she read, " *'I'm sorry that I couldn't write before. I was one of a few men picked for a special duty. I can't tell you about it now, but I guess the fact that they took me shows they don't think too badly of me.'* That means your daddy's done something very important, Barbara Elizabeth. Do you hear?" The hands holding the letter fell in her lap. She twisted her head and looked down into the baby's face. Then she lifted the bit of paper again. " *'We've been moved, to where it's warm and sunny—the Arctic equipment was just a gag to fool the enemy—but by now you must have read about it all in the papers at home; and here we are. How is our wartime baby?'* That's you, Barbara Elizabeth. Your daddy's talking about you now. *'Taking a pretty cheerful view of things, I'll bet. Tell her I'll be home before long to see her, burned as an Arab.*

" *'My dearest darling, if only—'* " Eileen's face was warm and shining as she turned the page. "That's me, cherub." She slipped down until her cheek was resting against the baby's head. " *'If only I—'* "

I drew back into the darkness of the hall, away from the words that were not meant for me. I saw them now, Dick, Eileen, the baby. They were a little family. It didn't matter that an ocean was between them; that didn't change anything. They had no need of me, no need of anyone. They were complete in themselves.

I turned and went **thoughtfully** down the stairs.